SPECIAL MESSAGE TO READERS

THE ULVERSCROFT FOUNDATION
(registered UK charity number 264873)
was established in 1972 to provide funds for
research, diagnosis and treatment of eye diseases.
Examples of major projects funded by
the Ulverscroft Foundation are:-

- The Children's Eye Unit at Moorfields Eye Hospital, London
- The Ulverscroft Children's Eye Unit at Great Ormond Street Hospital for Sick Children
- Funding research into eye diseases and treatment at the Department of Ophthalmology, University of Leicester
- The Ulverscroft Vision Research Group, Institute of Child Health
- Twin operating theatres at the Western Ophthalmic Hospital, London
- The Chair of Ophthalmology at the Royal Australian College of Ophthalmologists

You can help further the work of the Foundation
by making a donation or leaving a legacy.
Every contribution is gratefully received. If you
would like to help support the Foundation or
require further information, please contact:

THE ULVERSCROFT FOUNDATION
The Green, Bradgate Road, Anstey
Leicester LE7 7FU, England
Tel: (0116) 236 4325

website: www.foundation.ulverscroft.com

D0736241

A LITTLE OF WHAT YOU FANCY

'Teetotal! He'll never live it down. He'll never be able to hold his head up again. Whatever will people think? You'll have to strap him down,' Ma said. *'You'll have to put the handcuffs on.'* After a mild heart attack (caused by rather too much of what you fancy), Pop Larkin finds himself off the booze, off the fine food, and off the good life generally — much to his own and everyone else's horror and upset. And while Ma tries to find ways around the doctor's orders, young Primrose is finding her own way around a rather flustered Reverend Candy . . .

H. E. BATES

---◆---

A LITTLE
OF WHAT
YOU FANCY
The Pop Larkin Chronicles

Complete and Unabridged

ULVERSCROFT
Leicester

First published in Great Britain in 1970
by Michael Joseph
London

This Ulverscroft Edition
published 2018
by arrangement with
Paper Lion Literary Agency
Surrey

A catalogue record for this book is available
from the British Library.

ISBN 978–1–4448–3909–8

Published by
F. A. Thorpe (Publishing)
Anstey, Leicestershire

Set by Words & Graphics Ltd.
Anstey, Leicestershire
Printed and bound in Great Britain by
T. J. International Ltd., Padstow, Cornwall

This book is printed on acid-free paper

1

Most mornings, especially in spring and summer, when the liquid chorus of dawn bird song often roused him as early as four o'clock, Pop Larkin was awake some time before Ma, a circumstance that afforded him the silent pleasure of drinking in the sight of her warm dark head cradled in tranquillity on the pillow and even, sometimes, if the night had been exceptionally warm, of gazing on the olive amplitude of her expansive bust, its naked slumbering curves swelling and slipping from the lace fringe of her flowery chiffon nightgown.

While Ma still slept Pop almost invariably went downstairs in his pyjamas and brewed a pot of strong fresh tea. The exceptions to this occurred on the very warmest of summer mornings, when Pop was inspired to think that Ma, perhaps, would prefer champagne. Ma was exceptionally fond of champagne, more especially before breakfast.

On some occasions Pop was moved to go even further than mere champagne and concoct a cool but potent mixture of about equal parts of brandy and champagne, preferably pink, with a dash of angostura bitters and a slice of orange. This was the perfick stiffener to start the day on. In particular the pinkness seemed always to have a highly stimulating effect on Ma and as he came back upstairs with bottles, glasses and orange, the glasses already frostily sugared, Pop always hoped that Ma, perhaps, would be in the mood.

Very often Ma was.

'Drop o' champagne, Ma?' On a humid morning in early July the voices of wood pigeons liquidly calling to each other across the meadows had, in Pop's ears, a sultry, sensual sound. 'Plain or cocktail?'

'Better make it a cocktail while you're about it.'

'Cocktail it is then. Have it now or afterwards?'

Ma, well-knowing what afterwards implied, responded by a great voluptuous upheaval of laughter, huge sleep-soft breasts half-escaping from her nightgown.

'Better make it a sandwich, hadn't we?'

'Perfick.' Pop liked the idea of the sandwich. 'Which part in the middle?'

'I think,' Ma said serenely, already drawing her nightgown over the dark mass of her handsome ruffled hair, 'we'd better see how we get on.'

Pop now laughed too and said he didn't see why they shouldn't get on pretty well as usual, though it was thirsty work. Was she sure she wouldn't have a drop first, as a sort of pipe-opener?

Ma, responding with a dreamy sigh, her body now stretched out in full nakedness, the bed-clothes thrown back, said well, no, she didn't think so. He'd got her too excited about the other now. She was nicely in the mood.

Pop, declaring with typical gusto that he was very glad to hear it, prepared to enfold himself in the warm, olive continent of Ma when she suddenly interrupted him and asked if he hadn't better lock the door?

'Else we'll have those two monkeys in. Oscar's got eyes all over the back of his head and Phyllida isn't much better.'

Phyllida, Ma's eighth, who had already been christened in perfectly orthodox fashion Phyllida Cleopatra Boadicea Nightingale had turned out, greatly to Pop's surprise, to be blessed with singularly bright red hair, a fact that Pop was utterly unable to square with the fact that both he and Ma were very dark, until Mr Charlton, his son-in-law, knowledgeable in so many matters, explained that it was all to do with the laws of genetics.

'Good Gawd Almighty,' Pop said, 'what next? What the pipe is genetics? Summat to do with the National Elf lark I'll bet.'

Not at all, Mr Charlton assured him. It was just that dark-haired parents quite frequently produced red-haired children.

'Just fancy that,' Ma said. 'We'll soon be having blackbirds with red breasts I shouldn't wonder. Or else donkeys giving milk.'

Donkeys, Mr Charlton assured her in his most knowledgeable fashion, did give milk; and even Ma was silenced.

Anyway, as she was frequently fond of saying, there was no doubt that Phyllida was the pick of the entire Larkin bunch, not at all unlike a perky bright-eyed robin herself, her soft smooth hair rich as purest copper. Quick as lightning too.

Pop having locked the bedroom door, he now paused to listen once again for a moment to the

3

voices of pigeons exchanging sultry greetings across the meadows and then slipped back into bed with Ma, who received him with a deep soundless embrace, her half-opened lips pressed against his. Such was the powerful effect of this union that Pop, conferring the tenderest of caresses on the brown-pink crests of Ma's ample bosom, had no word to say either for the next half hour or so.

It was Ma who spoke first. 'Nice and satisfactory,' she said.

This brief understatement in fact concealed the most affectionate of compliments. That was the nice thing about Pop, she always told herself. He knew his technique all right; very good technique.

'Now for the champers,' Pop said.

'Won't say you didn't earn it,' Ma said and presently sat up in bed, still naked, ready to receive the further blessing of the first cocktail of the day.

'Goes down a treat,' Pop said with a fruity smack of his lips. 'Perfick start.'

'Anything particular on today?'

'Nothing much. Army surplus job. About five hundred walkie-talkie sets. Should show about three hundred per cent.'

'Ought to keep the wolf from the door.'

Pop said it certainly ought and, observing that Ma's glass was already almost empty, reached for the champagne bottle in readiness to top her up. This he did with such typical generosity that he filled the glass to overflowing, the champagne spilling down on Ma's left bosom. Instantly

4

recognizing this as an interesting opportunity for further drinking Pop bent down and proceeded to taste the twin delights of wine and breast, causing Ma to struggle with playful delight, thus spilling more champagne.

'Whatever will you think of next?' Ma said, as if Pop hadn't never thought of it before. 'You must be in your hot-blood or something.'

Pop said he shouldn't wonder if he wasn't and proceeded yet again to taste the twin pleasures of Ma and champagne, so that Ma shook all over with rich gusts of laughter, finally remarking:

'You'd better get it out of your system, hadn't you? Else we'll be here all day.'

'Why not? Perfick idea.'

Ma said she could think of worse.

Pop suddenly felt a great new rush of ardour, his heart racing. This sudden rapidity of its beating seemed for a moment to echo the trilling sweetness of wren song from the garden outside. Then the rippling of it became, for a moment, shot with pain. Pop found himself pausing, then actually gasping, for breath.

Ma, now filled with fresh ardour herself, watched the pause without misgiving, concerned only to ask what was holding him up? She'd had an idea he was going to give her an encore.

The pain having passed as rapidly as it had shot through him, Pop replied in his habitually warm and robust tones that he certainly was. He was all for encores. It was rather like drinking champagne. The first glass, though always nice, was only a sort of pipe-opener. It was the second glass that really got you going.

5

Voluptuously, at this moment, Ma rolled over in bed, her wide and splendid figure half-smothering Pop, who received her breasts in his two hands rather like a hungry man receiving the gift of two round, warm, fresh-baked loaves of bread. From this new and unexpected point of vantage Ma, he thought, looked more inviting and sumptuous than ever.

Ma, at the same time, found herself wondering about Pop's technique. There was, she told herself, no question of it standing the strain. She merely wondered what form it would take. The slow, quick, slow? or what she sometimes called the old-fashioned waltz time? You never knew with Pop. He wasn't merely a man of technical excellence. He went in for a lot of variation.

A moment later Pop, instead of proceeding to demonstrate some fresh variation of technique by physical means, actually started a brief discourse. This was inspired by something he had read somewhere in a magazine. It was all about these two people, he explained to Ma, who didn't get on very well — in bed, that was. They'd sort of kept to the orthodox form of service, Pop explained, laughing richly, for years. Didn't work, though.

How did he mean? Ma said, utterly confounded that such a condition could befall any mortal man and woman. It didn't *work*?

'Well, *he* worked,' Pop said. 'But she was sort of unemployed.'

Ma let out a rich shriek, quivering all over like a vast jelly. 'You mean she was on the dole?' Ma said, 'or on strike?'

Oh! no, Pop explained, nothing like that. She wanted work. Eager for it. But somehow —

'Technique wrong.'

Bit like that, Pop said. How did Ma know?

'Been in the business long enough, haven't I?' Ma said and again gave a shriek of laughter, causing the most disturbing of tremulous movements from her breasts down to the very soles of her feet, which she suddenly began to rub caressingly against Pop's calves. 'I ought to by now.'

'What made you do that?' Pop suddenly said.

'Do what?'

'With your feet. Smoothing me up and down like that.'

Ma said she didn't know. She hadn't the vaguest. She supposed it was some sort of instinct. Why?

Telepathic was the word that sprang instantly to Pop's mind, telepathic being one of those words he had picked up from the informative Mr Charlton, his son-in-law. Ma, in other words, he suddenly realized, was reading his mind.

It was what this woman did, he explained.

'Did what?' Ma said. She didn't get it.

Pop went on to explain that it was about the discovery of a new technique. Well, very old technique really. It was all to do with the time when we were apes and all that and feet were as important as hands and suddenly this woman had discovered it. It was to do with foot-worship or summat. Mr Charlton had told him all about it. He'd discussed it with him.

'Never?' Ma said, amazed.

7

'Fact,' Pop said. 'After years of being on the dole, sort of, this woman had suddenly discovered that by using her feet she'd struck it rich. Two minutes with the soles of her feet and she'd got herself into a tizz like hot rum and brandy. No stopping her. She was on the boil all night long.'

'The things they get hold of in these magazines,' Ma said. 'It makes you wonder.'

'Ended in divorce.'

'Never?' Ma said. That beat the band.

'Beat Fred, that's what it was.'

'Fred? Who's Fred?'

Fred was the husband, Pop explained. Had to drop out. Couldn't stand the pace.

'Well, the fast so-and-so,' Ma said. 'Don't they have a name for that sort? Lesbians? — no, not Lesbians. That's having butter no side of the bread. Well, it doesn't matter, anyway. The things some women do to get hold of what they were after — really I don't know.'

'Lovely grub, though.'

'I should say so. I'd better keep my feet to myself in future.'

Another peal of laughter, rich and healthy, shook both Ma and the bed. All this time Ma had been allowing the warm continent of her body further and further to envelop Pop, whose only evident sign of resistance was an occasional languid attempt to push Ma's breasts away — merely, in fact, so that he could see them better. All this, gentle and modified as it was, was thirsty work nevertheless, and he was on the point of suggesting that Ma, being in the better

8

position, should pour another glass of champagne, when he abruptly realized that Ma was caressing him slowly up and down with the naked soles of her feet.

An instant and totally unheralded nervous spasm shot through him, both exquisite and excruciating. It was a sensation he had never remotedly experienced before, even in the long fruitful years of union with Ma. It was at once a pain and a joy. It ravaged his heart, his chest, his stomach and then ran rapidly and hotly down to the soles of his own feet. He was soon nervously hot all over, his heart painfully racing.

'Here, steady Ma, you'll have me on the boil next.'

And what else, Ma said, did he think she was up to?

Ma, murmuring in dreamy tones something about it was always nicest, second time round, was now in a state of total ecstacy herself. Her compulsive possession of Pop was so absolute that Pop, straining with every nerve and pulse of blood to meet her demands, was suddenly assailed by the idea, at once both joyful and slightly alarming, that if they didn't put the brakes on they might well be in for another pair of twins.

Less than a minute later Ma did, fact, put the brakes on.

'Lovely,' was her next word. 'Lovely. You remember that drink you made once? Peaches and champagne and a bit of maraschino. Like that. Just like that. Lovely.'

Pop, to his slight concern and dismay,

suddenly discovered himself to be unusually tired. He lay back on the pillows, panting. Ma was still spread across him, eyes dreamily half-closed, still locked in the ravishing peace of utter satisfaction.

Now and then she also gave a great sigh of pleasure in recollection, rather as if drinking a draught of one of Pop's more memorable liquid confections. These expressions of ecstacy, far from arousing any sort of response in Pop, seemed to leave him cool, so that presently Ma was prompted to remove one bosom some inches aways from its resting place on Pop's neck and remark.

'Don't want me now, do you? I know.'

Pop murmured that he didn't know about that. They'd had two innings already, he reminded her, and it still wasn't seven o'clock.

'What's time got to do with it?' Ma said. There was a note in her voice of the very slightest injury. 'You feeling weak all of a sudden or something?'

Oh! nothing like that, Pop declared. He felt sort of languid like, that's all. After all, you'd got to re-charge the batteries.

'Better re-charge them with a drop o' champers then,' Ma said and proceeded to reach out of bed for bottle and glasses. 'Don't want you losing grip.'

At this suggestion, faint thought it was, that he was losing grip, Pop felt a little affronted. Him losing grip? That was a bit off, he told Ma.

Ma, not speaking, serenely poured champagne. As she sipped at it there was a glint in her eye that was like a distilled reflection of the bubbles sparkling at the glass's brim. It was more than evident, Pop told himself, that she was in one of her primrose-and-bluebell moods.

Then, as he made the first movement to lift his head from the pillow in order to drink from his own champagne, he became aware again of a curious lassitude. At the same time his chest seemed to ache again. He heaved himself slowly upright, panting a little, and sipped with such slow relief at the champagne that Ma was actually moved to tease him gently, telling him she hoped he wasn't getting past it?

'You won't get very far with your girl friend at this rate,' she said.

Which girl friend? Pop wanted to know. He had so many.

'Angela Snow,' Ma said, blandly. 'I heard you fixing it up with her on the phone the other night. Something about a four-poster bed you'd found for her or something.'

'She asked me if I ever saw one to nab it for her. She wants it for her new flat.'

'Very good excuse. New flat, eh? I wonder what it's like in a four-poster? Four times as good, I expect.'

Ma's joke fell on unresponsive ears. Normally the thought of Angela Snow, that willowy, languid and highly persuasive creature, excited him more than considerably but now the thought of her evoked no response in him either. He merely released a great sigh, totally unlike Ma's deep purr of pleasure in recollection, and in doing so let champagne dribble over the rim of

11

his glass and then down his chin and chest. Ma laughingly reproved him for this, saying he'd need his bib on next if he didn't watch it.

'That'll be the day,' she said, laughing in great jelly-like heaves, in her best primrose-and-bluebell fashion, 'making love with your bib on.'

Again the joke fell on an unresponsive Pop. He merely felt weak, he told himself, and yet was too weak to say so.

'I'll have to give you over to Edith Pilchester for a rest cure,' Ma said, again in teasing fashion. 'I saw her collecting a big bag of lambs' wool the other day. That'll be nice and soft to lay your head on.'

The thought of laying his head down side by side with the spinsterish Miss Pilchester would normally have had Pop in a fit, but now this joke too merely produced in him a vague solemnity.

'Champagne's a bit weak this morning, isn't it?' Ma said, taking a deep draught of it as a sort of test. 'Didn't put too much brandy in, I'd say.'

'Drained the bottle.'

'Nice thing. Only half rations now. We're getting down to something now, I must say. Starvation level.'

Pop managed to say there was another bottle downstairs. He'd go and get it. Heavily he tried, without success, to rise.

With gentle mockery Ma invited him not to strain himself, then promptly got out of bed herself and stood for a moment or two by the window, stark naked, looking out at the garden below, remarking that it was really the week for roses. All the roses were in bloom. Whether viewed from back or front Ma looked not at all unlike an enormous full-blown rose herself, creamy and summery, her bosoms full to bursting.

'Shan't be a tick,' she said. 'Don't overdo it while I'm gone,' and then left the room without benefit either of wrap or nightgown.

It was not uncustomary for Ma to nip downstairs in the early morning without a stitch to cover her vast form and the circumstances held no surprise for Pop. When once reminded that the children might see her Ma had merely remarked with her customary serenity that they'd got to know sometime hadn't they? When further reminded that she might run into the postman she merely retorted blandly:

'Well, I shall have to shut my eyes then, shan't I?'

During Ma's absence, brief as she had promised it would be, Pop became aware that his unnatural spell of lassitude had become an ache, and the ache, every twenty seconds or so, a pain. He was actually lying back on the pillows, holding his chest in the region of his heart, when Ma came back into the bedroom, bearing a bottle of her favourite brandy, Remy Martin.

Something about the incongruous sight of her completely naked and carrying the full bottle of cognac abruptly induced in Pop a notion that Ma was on the verge of being ready for a third innings. Normally on warm early summer mornings this would have been perfick. Now he could only view the prospect with a faint and uncharacteristic dismay.

'Still there then?' Ma said. 'You want to take more brandy with it, that's your trouble.'

Laughing fleshily, Ma proceeded to pour generous measures of Remy Martin into both Pop's champagne and her own. That ought to pep up his ego, as Mr Charlton often said. Ma rather liked the word ego. When she had first heard it she'd thought it was something rather rude. But now she understood, though it really meant the same thing as she'd thought it referred to in the first place.

'Oh! by the way the papers have come and I looked up your stars.'

Ma was a great believer in the stars and what they had to say. Very important, the stars. Pop had been born under Taurus, the bull, which was good. It was strong and lucky. According to the signs it made for a potency well expressed by *Red Bull*, an explosive cocktail of Pop's own invention. It was what made Pop what he was.

Today, however, he told himself that he couldn't care less, either about Taurus, the bull, or the stars.

'Know what they say?' Ma said, meaning the stars. ''A personal relationship will bear fruit early but discretion may have to be exercised as the day goes on. A business project may cast a shadow.'' Ma drank deeply at her brandy and champagne, at the same time slightly raising her glass, as if actually toasting the stars' prophecies.

Pop merely smiled, wanly.

'I like that bit about bearing fruit,' Ma said. 'I think I've borne enough fruit already. Still, while the tree's there it might just as well bear another crop now and then.'

In a sidling, languorous movement Ma started to approach the bed, a brandy-deep glow in her dark brown eyes, her big breasts swinging with lazy invitation. This, Pop suddenly told himself, wasn't merely one of those primrose-and-bluebell moods. It was one of those blinders she went in for now and then. He was in for the third innings any moment now.

'Think I'll get dressed now, Ma,' he said. 'Got a fairish way to go. Got to be there by half past ten.'

What was his hurry? Ma wanted to know. It was summer. It was beautiful. It was warm. All the roses were in bloom. It was there to enjoy, wasn't it? Well then, why not enjoy it? This morning she felt like roaming round all day with nothing on, ripening like a fruit herself in the sun. Tomorrow — you never knew — she might be glad of her lamb's-wool knickers.

All this was so much a reflection and echo of Pop's own philosophy — *carpe diem*, Mr Charlton called it in the infinite wisdom for which he was noted — that normally Pop would have laughed in boisterous agreement and clasped himself to Ma's ample bosom in simmering response.

But now he felt himself locked again in that curious, half painful languor that he couldn't explain and said:

'Think I'll have the papers up in bed for a few minutes, Ma. Look at the race-card. There's a filly up at Pontefract I fancy. Thought I'd put a tenner on its nose. I'll put one on for you too if you like.'

Ma, however, was not to be bought off. Nor was she to be foxed by talk of race-cards. She knew perfectly well what it was behind it all. He wanted to lounge there like some Eastern potentate and watch her dressing.

It was idle, on Pop's part, to pretend that he didn't like to see Ma dressing. On the contrary it was a source of unfailing interest. It was a process of infinite, indeed passionate delight.

Ma had devised two methods of getting dressed. The first consisted of her getting out of bed in her nightgown, which she then proceeded to use as a sort of protective tent. Under this tent she then executed a series of movements, some strenuous, some serpentine, some agitated, a few of positive anguish. Having finished them at last — a performance never either easy or brief — Ma at last emerged completely encased in shining purple corset, knickers of much amplitude and a bra of the expanse and depth of a pair of barrage balloons. That she was still not fully dressed merely added acutely to Pop's enjoyment. The fact that fringes of certain of the more interesting areas of her body were still not totally hidden served to fill him with a curiosity as great as if he had never seen them before. It was a moment of intense frustration when Ma finally covered it all with her slip.

Ma's second method was to emerge from bed as she was now, stark naked, and proceed to go into conflict with her most serious adversary, the corset. This was a process not unlike that of trying to press a melon into an eggcup. In Ma's case there were, however, four melons: two in front, and two, rather larger, though not all that much, behind.

The chief of Ma's early difficulties was not merely to get the rear melons inside the corset, but both of them in, if possible, at the same time. As if counterbalanced by some delicate principle, however, one melon would invariably insist on going in before the other, leaving its fellow exposed. When finally the second melon was induced to slip in the first instantly slipped out. The balance having been partially restored by Ma fighting with all her strength at the purple corset there arrived a moment, miraculous and stupendously fascinating to Pop's eyes, when Ma seemed suddenly to have developed a second bosom at the back of herself, but lower down and even more expansive than the front one provided by nature. At last, under the impulse of a great sigh rising through a slow crescendo to a positive groan, this phenomenon finally disappeared, silkily and firmly encased in shining purple, itself a balloon inflated to bursting point.

This more serious part of the struggle over, there remained only the comparatively minor excursion with the bosom. Even here, however, the principle of counterbalance came again into play, so that as fast as one bosom slipped into its cup one side the other slipped out of the other. Whenever this happened Pop was reminded of one of those little weather houses in which a male figure pops out to forecast rain and a female to forecast fine, a thought that often caused him to call out from the bed, much to Ma's pretended disgust:

17

'Left titty out first this morning, Ma. Going to rain before the day's gone.'

This morning, however, Pop watched Ma proceed through her dressing battle with neither excitement nor comment. The pain across his chest now and then seemed to harden. Each time this happened it grew more stubborn, lasted longer and was more difficult to move.

Ma having at last finished battle with the purple corset, the melons safely encased, both back and front, she now stood in her slip, gazing at Pop from the foot of the bed, inquiring if something wasn't the matter with him this morning? Pop, not daring to confess that there was, replied that he didn't think so and why?

'Must be something wrong with my figure,' Ma said in a tone of slight affront, her figure being, even when firmly corseted, all of two yards wide. 'Don't seem to get much response this morning anyway.'

Pop said No? He'd been taking it all in all right. Not to worry.

Taking it all in all right, her foot, Ma told him. He hadn't even noticed the right boosie had popped out first this morning, meaning it was going to be a fine day. She didn't know what he was coming to. Next thing she knew he'd be asking for his breakfast in bed.

Breakfast? He wasn't all that hungry, Pop said, his voice distant, even a little feeble. At the same time a new ache shot through his chest, causing him sharply to catch and then hold his breath.

Ma, slightly concerned now, told herself that it was bad enough Pop not noticing which boosie had popped out first this morning, even allowing for a natural slackening of interest after passion had been spent, but the confession that he wasn't hungry was a truly alarming one.

'Have some more champers,' she said and was about to proceed to fill Pop's glass when she discovered that he had hardly touched it since she had filled it last. 'Here, drink up. Can't think what's got into you.'

Another sharp attack of pain caused Pop to confess that he didn't feel all that great, to which Ma replied blandly that she expected it was wind, most likely. Or lack of food.

Lack of food, in the Larkin household at any rate, was a highly serious matter. It might lead to all sorts of things. Now what would Pop have? she said, her voice richly cheerful. The usual? Porridge, bacon and eggs, sausage, fried bread, potatoes, tomatoes, the lot? She wasn't sure, but she thought she even had a few kidneys too.

The mere mention of kidneys afflicted Pop with a curious nausea in his throat. He suddenly wanted to be sick, but at the same time knew he couldn't be. The nausea slipped from his throat to his chest, to be joined there by a new stab of pain. Involuntarily he clutched his chest, gasping, and for the first time Ma was visibly alarmed. Even so she couldn't for the life of her think what could possibly be the matter with him and in solution to the problem could only offer the thought that perhaps they'd overdone it a bit that second time. It has been a bit hot and strong, perhaps, after all.

Pop, for once unable to find comment on the

unthinkable and astonishing suggestion that making love to Ma might have serious after-effects, sought comfort in champagne. A slow sip or two of it presently caused him to belch mildly. Ma, relieved to hear it, commented that that was better and urged him to have another good burp or two.

A second rising wave of wind stuck in the lower part of Pop's throat, then receded and became part of his general pain. He could suddenly neither belch nor swallow. He found himself fighting for breath. Involuntarily he clutched at his chest, a gesture that made Ma perfectly sure that the cause of all was undoubtedly going it a bit too strong on an empty stomach. No doubt about it.

'Ma,' Pop tried to say and for the first time in his life discovered that he was utterly unable to say the word. His mouth was suddenly dry and rigid. It seemed to him too that somebody was ramming a crowbar through the upper part of his chest. It was being driven, iron and relentless, clean through his heart.

In his moment of agony he sank back on the pillows, face suddenly white, vision clouded, forehead coldly drenched with sweat. Desperately his eyes searched to focus Ma at the foot of the bed and discovered for an awful moment or two that she wasn't there. A white blank wall had replaced her: a terrible nothingness.

The thought of a world without Ma suddenly brought Pop to the verge of the ghastly conviction that he was dying. He was fighting not merely for breath but for life. Through the insistent pain of all this there shot through him the even more agonizing thought that his last two acts on earth might have been to drink champagne and make love to Ma. He had a sudden desire to cry.

Then he abruptly realized that the blank wall at the foot of the bed was a sheet. Ma was behind it. She was holding it. He could just see the tips of her fingers. She was drawing the sheet over him, gently. A second awful thought that this was death, this was what they did to you, covering you with a sheet, drove him down into a dark silent well of despair.

His pain was now so excruciating that he had lost all capacity and will to fight it. The sheet enveloped him, his face for a moment covered. Then he was vaguely aware of it being lifted from his face. Ma's own face appeared beyond it, faintly smiling but somehow pained too. She spoke; but what it was she said he never knew.

Then Ma wasn't there again. Vaguely he heard voices. They seemed to reach him from the end of a long, echoing corridor. They were the voices of children. Then Ma's voice was among them too, proclaiming silence, breathlessly. The house, suddenly tomb-like, merely served for some moments as a sounding board for the voices of birds in the garden outside, the shrill sweetness of a wren, the rising broken moan of a pigeon. He listened to them too as if they might have been the last sounds he would hear on earth. Then the singing of wrens and the liquid moan of pigeons stopped completely. They too might have been dead.

He lay for a long time alone. His fight with pain had now reversed itself. The pain was fighting him. The bar of iron had driven so far into his heart that he was transfixed immovably to the bed. Everything about him was darkness. Everything beyond the darkness was silent.

After what seemed hours he was dimly aware of not being alone any more. Ma was with him again. Her solitary but amazingly diminished figure stood vaguely at the bottom of the bed. Then it multiplied into three and he realized that his beloved Mariette and Mr Charlton, both in dressing-gowns, were also with her. A searing conviction that he was seeing them too for the last time overcame him so greatly that tears ran bitterly into his eyes a second time. Quite strengthless, he let them flow, so that Ma and Mariette and Mr Charlton dissolved away.

Ma, with a damp towel, gently wiped both his sweat and tears away. The effect of this act was momentarily to clear his vision. He then became aware that it was Mr Charlton, Charley boy, who had, as so often in the past, provided the unexpected. Once so dim and impracticable, Mr Charlton now had a way, a positive genius, for rising to crises with realism. Now he appeared suddenly as a figure possessed with coolness, much resource and calm.

'I'm going to take your temperature, Pop,' Mr Charlton said. 'Dr O'Connor will be here in a quarter of an hour. Lie flat. I'm going to take away one pillow.'

The cool practical nature of Mr Charlton's words did something to restore Pop's faith in living. He was aware of desperately wanting to live. He told himself he had to live, not merely for his own sake but for Ma's sake especially and all the rest of them.

The thermometer seemed to be stuck for hours under his tongue. Mr Charlton, with an air almost professional, was also taking his pulse. Pop, still in insufferable pain, felt him take the thermometer away.

Now he became aware of the smell of eau-de-cologne. Mariette was bending over him, gently assuaging his forehead. He was at once assailed by an inconsolable conviction that he was seeing her, always so like a younger, more shapely edition of Ma, for the last time. He tried to touch her hands, only to discover that they had no response to his. And then, to complete his inconsolable depression, he was aware that Ma was no longer in the room.

'Where's Ma?' he managed to say. 'I need Ma.'

'She's downstairs, waiting for Dr O'Connor.'

And then Dr O'Connor was in the room. Dr O'Connor was thinnish, young, his hair inclined to sandiness, his long hands freckled. His Irish voice seemed to express a certain sardonic amusement at the situation in which Pop found himself.

'Now what's all this, Mr Larkin? Been overdoing it a bit, eh?'

Pop, facing death, fighting with hopelessly diminishing strength the pain that drove deeper and deeper across his heart, actually managed the faintest of smiles.

It was marvellous how the news got round, he

23

started to say and then saw the brief flash of a hypodermic syringe in the air and felt the prick of its needle in his upper arm.

Then he was there no longer.

2

Long, long later — he never knew how long it was — Pop came back to consciousness: to a strange, confused, familiar yet unfamiliar world of living. It seemed to him that he had died and had somehow come back, mysteriously, from death.

His first key to this world was vision. At first he merely saw shapes. After some time the shapes became people. He saw Ma, Mariette, Mr Charlton, another of his daughters, Primrose, and Dr O'Connor. Then he saw another, elderly figure, with a stethoscope hung about his neck. This, he slowly realized, was a second doctor. This doctor surveyed him with eyes of grey calm, from behind gold-rimmed spectacles, with a gaze slightly professional, though also vaguely cheerful.

Pop felt not at all uncheerful himself. He felt rested, calm, relieved of pain.

'This,' Dr O'Connor said, 'is Mr Millington. Mr Millington is a consultant.'

Mr Millington, now advancing closer to the bed, smiled with further cheerfulness.

'We are going to do,' he said, 'a small job of work on you, Mr Larkin. Lie absolutely still. No talking.'

Between them Dr O'Connor and Mr Millington produced a piece of apparatus sprouting many antennae. These antennae were presently attached to various parts of Pop's body, so that he looked very like a prostrate spider with many legs. He became aware of much pressing of buttons and repeated clickings. A long sheet of graph paper then ran from the apparatus: recording, as Mr Millington remarked, what the body had to say.

To Pop there suddenly seemed something curiously comic about this length of paper. It was a great joke to think that, having come back from the dead, he had been reincarnated, as it were, as a printing machine. Irrepressible as ever, he was prompted to remark on this, asking how the racing results were coming through and if he'd won anything on that filly at Pontefract in the two-thirty?

The joke caused, unfortunately, intense dismay.

'I am afraid you have now ruined,' Mr Millington said, 'the whole middle portion of the record.'

Pop made a low apology, which received from Dr O'Connor, in turn, a rather severe injunction for him to keep absolutely quiet. No talking. Absolutely still.

For a second time Pop became aware of much pressing of buttons and many clickings. The sheet of graph paper ran off at great length until at last removed and stopped by Mr Millington, who gave one end of it to Dr O'Connor while holding the other himself.

'We are now going,' Mr Millington said, 'to have a little natter about you. Take it easy. Relax completely until we come back again.'

Dr O'Connor and Mr Millington disappeared. For a few moments Pop lay in suspense, his senses pierced by a single sound of whose intense sweetness he realized he had never been wholly aware before: the trilling voice of a wren in the garden outside. For so tiny and frail a creature its voice seemed suddenly to have an amazing power and Pop listened to it in wonder and fascination. It was his first experience of illness magnifying trivialities.

'Cardiograph.' It was the voice of Mr Charlton, explaining the apparatus. 'Recording what the heart does.' Truly, Pop thought, Charley boy was a wonder. Cardiograph — that unfailing mine of Charley's information had done it again.

Pop, feeling rather like a recalcitrant schoolboy who had already ruined one experiment and was afraid of spoiling another, said nothing, merely permitting himself the faintest of smiles. From far across the room came an answering one from Ma, so subdued and unlike her that it might have come from some old static photograph.

'The heart has suffered some damage.' Mr Millington and Dr O'Connor were back in the room. Mr Millington was speaking. 'It will mean complete rest for several weeks. Lying completely flat. No pillows at first. Perhaps one after a week or two. Then another. Goodbye now, I'll come back and see you in a week. Take care of yourself. Good men are scarce.'

Mr Millington waved a cheerful farewell hand and was gone. Dr O'Connor meanwhile was busy writing what appeared to be various prescriptions. Then he came to the bedside in order to take Pop's pulse. He too looked not uncheerful.

It was perhaps this slight air of cheerfulness, whether forced or not, that now caused Ma to come out with what Pop thought was an excellent and timely suggestion.

'Don't you think it would do him good to have a nice large brandy now. Doctor?'

'Not on any account.'

'I always thought brandy was good for the heart?'

'Not on any account, Mrs Larkin.'

Ma, stunned by the severity of the denial of her proposal to give Pop the very thing that would do him most good, quite apart from the fact that it was the thing he most wanted, let out a very severe pronouncement of her own.

'Whatever next? He loves brandy. He thrives on brandy. It peps him up no end.'

'Pepping him up, Mrs Larkin, is exactly what we do not want to do.'

Well, she would go to the bone-house, Ma said, using one of those expressions that had become part of the family vocabulary ever since she and Pop had taken the family to France for a holiday and had visited an ossuary. Whatever were things coming to? No brandy, her foot.

At the mention of the word bone-house Dr O'Connor gave Mr Charlton a silently significant look as though suggesting — as Mr Charlton afterwards confessed he actually had — that that was exactly where Pop was on his way to if they weren't all very careful.

'Very well, then' Ma said, 'a small brandy.'

'Not even a small brandy. Not on any account.'

'Good God.' Ma looked highly affronted, if not actually insulted, as if her idea of what was best for Pop was being doubted. 'Whoever heard of a drop of brandy hurting anybody? Besides he must be famished. He hasn't had a morsel of anything inside him for twelve hours. We don't want him starving, do we?'

Lack of food was, in Ma's opinion, a very serious matter. The mere thought of starvation was a catastrophe.

'He needs a good square meal,' she said, 'that's all. A beefsteak-and-kidney pud and a bottle of Beaujolais'll put him right in no time.'

Dr O'Connor, appearing to wave aside the suggestion of beefsteak-and-kidney pud and Beaujolais as if it were something subversive, was in fact signalling to Mr Charlton, Mariette and Primrose to leave the room.

When they had done so he turned to Pop and Ma less in the manner of a doctor than a person about to intone, Ma thought, a final benediction. They hadn't quite come to that yet, she thought, and Dr O'Connor needn't start thinking they had. She felt highly aggrieved. The restorative powers of her steak-and-kidney pud had, it seemed to her, been called into question and she didn't like it. It was as bad as doubting her virtue.

Dr O'Connor now proceeded to repeat the injunction that for the next week or two Pop must lie on his back, pillowless, with as little excitement as possible: and then said:

'Now, as to diet.'

'I'll feed him up well,' Ma said, 'don't you worry about that.'

'As to diet. And I mean diet.'

'I know what he likes and what he doesn't like. Good solid rich food and plenty of it. Where d'ye think he'd be today if I hadn't seen he got it all these years?'

'He might not be here.'

'Well,' Ma said, again very affronted, 'there's two ways of looking at that.'

Dr O'Connor said indeed there was and again assumed his benedictory attitude.

'I'm talking about diet, Mrs Larkin. About *not* eating. I am giving you advice as your doctor. Mr Larkin must have no sugar, no butter, no animal fats, very few carbohydrates, no stimulants — '

Good God, Ma said, did he mind? Life wouldn't be worth living.

'No alcohol — '

At the mention of the word alcohol Pop made an involuntary movement to lift his head sharply from the bed in protest, found himself too weak to manage it and fell back, pale as if cudgelled.

'No alcohol?' Ma said. 'No *drink*, you mean?'

'No drink.'

'What's it poison then, now?'

'Tantamount to that.'

Tantamount — another of those big words again, Pop thought. He certainly needed Mr Charlton here.

'I don't know about tantamount,' Ma said. 'The point is how much can he have?'

'None. None at all. Nothing. None whatever.'

30

'*You mean he's got to be T.T.?*'

'Precisely.'

'Good God, you must be joking.'

'I am not joking.'

'You're having me on, then. Been at it all his life and it's never done him no harm yet.'

Gravely Dr O'Connor assured Ma that he was neither having her on nor joking.

'No alcohol,' he repeated. 'Absolutely no alcohol.'

'But how long *for?*'

'The foreseeable future.'

'And how long might that be for God Almighty's sake?'

'For ever. Perhaps for ever.'

If Pop had felt faint and strengthless before these words, he now felt utterly crushed and condemned. He had a feeling of being dragged to the scaffold.

'Teetotal!' Ma said. 'It's a libel. He'll never live it down.'

He never would at that, Pop thought. There was never a truer word.

'He'll never be able to hold his head up again,' Ma said. 'Whatever will people think? What's he going to say when anybody asks him to have one?'

''No.''

'You'll have to strap him down,' Ma said. 'You'll have to put the handcuffs on.'

There was now a sudden silence. In the course of it Pop grew very tired. The rims of his eyes started to quiver. The figures of Ma and Dr O'Connor danced, became glazed and finally, in

31

a renewed wave of semi-consciousness, drifted away, taking with them the ever fainter and fainter trilling sweetness of the voice of the wren in the garden beyond.

Downstairs, in the kitchen, Dr O'Connor held a short conference at which Ma, Mariette, Primrose, Mr Charlton, little Oscar and bright redheaded Phyllida Cleopatra Boadicea Nightingale were the listeners. Its tone was so ominous that towards the end of it Phyllida Cleopatra Boadicea Nightingale burst into tears. Little Oscar burst into tears immediately afterwards and then Ma cried too.

It was left once again to the incalculable Mr Charlton to provide comfort by being practical, resourceful and calm.

'I'll take the children off and go and get the prescriptions,' he said. 'There seems to be one here for you, Ma, too.'

3

Down in the village, in her gimcrack little cottage, Bonny Banks, a converted cow-byre that always looked like a crumbling piece of fairy-tale stage scenery that was about to fall apart at any moment, Edith Pilchester had just finished a late breakfast of oatmeal bread, margarine, sardines, cocoa, rose-hip jelly and a cold fried egg left over from her previous night's supper, when she heard the church clock strike eleven.

She had in fact been up since five o'clock, but it was a morning in which everything, more even than usually, had gone wrong. She had not only lost time but all count of it. She seemed to have done a thousand things and yet done nothing. She still had a thousand more to do and it was absolutely ghastly.

The great trouble was that this month, July, was undoubtedly the busiest, maddest of the whole year. During the six hours since waking she had already spun large quantities of sheep wool, made a dozen pots of lemon curd for the Church bazaar, pulled half a hundredweight of rhubarb and gathered a skip of elderberry flowers, both to make into wine, and had done half an hour of *gros-point* on the cushion she was making for a sale of work being held in aid of some society for unmarried mothers, of whom, in Miss Pilchester's view, there had recently been, in spite of all you read and heard in papers and on radio, a distressing increase. She sometimes wondered how girls found time for these things; she never did.

She had also written several letters and now, having finished her breakfast without clearing the kitchen table, which was still littered with the remains of last night's supper things, the pots of lemon curd and piles of elderflower and rhubarb, realized that she had run out of stamps and would have to walk as far as the village post office to get some.

It was noon before she was finally ready to go. The day, though warm, had a certain promise of thunder about it. The air was drenched with that moist, intoxicating summer richness that was a pleasant though enervating compound of hay, roses, elderflower, pinks, meadowsweet and even a touch of the odour of the first Spanish chestnut bloom. It was what her dear friend Mr Larkin might well have called 'perfick'. In consequence she had not only put on a thin cotton summer dress, an affair of washed-out pink design which looked as if run up hastily out of old curtains, but she was also prudently armed with an umbrella in case it came on to rain and a tattered oatmeal sweater of her own spinning and knitting in case it turned cold. With the English weather you never knew.

As she went out of the garden, closing the gate behind her, she was surprised to see her next-door neighbour, Professor Fane, clipping his privet hedge along the road. She at once said a polite though distant and frigid 'good morning', to which the Professor promptly

34

replied 'good afternoon'. This however in no way surprised her, since the Professor was, in her opinion, quite batty. As Miss Pilchester was equally batty in the eyes of the Professor little was lost on either side.

Apart from his obvious madness the Professor was also, in Miss Pilchester's view, one of those people, a foreigner, who used the country as a mere convenience. He did not belong. His cottage was a mere weekend bolt-hole for escape from London and the exhausting routine of teaching physics to long-haired and unwashed students who apparently spent more time marching with banners of protest than at lectures. The Professor was undoubtedly, as Miss Pilchester had long suspected, a Communist. He was also a sort of blue-bottle fly. He buzzed in and out of the countryside as and when it suited him, a nuisance, impermanent, contributing nothing. Such people didn't, in her view, belong to the countryside. They were nothing more than fleeting parasites.

Not surprisingly, therefore, she looked on the Professor with both suspicion and contempt. It had not always been so. At his first arrival she had been civil enough to send him, as a gift of welcome, a small basket of red currants and a pot of blackberry jelly. These had been returned with a note of acid brevity, explaining that the Professor was on a diet, which appeared mainly to consist, Miss Pilchester discovered, of yoghurt, rye bread and Vichy water. Such poisons as red currants and blackberry jelly were not for him.

Thereafter the Professor and Miss Pilchester scarcely exchanged a word. The Professor regarded Miss Pilchester as a lamentable case of inverted nymphomania, a phrase of his own, whereas Miss Pilchester thought the Professor not only as being a Communist, itself bad enough in all conscience, but also a bilious bladder of lard. Apart from occasionally passing the time of day with her, and then always sarcastically, his only other communication with her was to write impersonal letters of complaint about her bonfires, which he called 'your incautious but calculated conflagrations', a phrase Miss Pilchester thought highly contradictory even if it meant anything at all, which she doubted.

On one occasion, fired by a double whisky followed by parsnip wine, she had thrown over the fence, like a verbal hand grenade, the phrase 'red egghead!' to which the Professor responded by setting his garden water sprinkler in such a way that the west wind blew spray all over her washing. This made her so angry that she seriously considered whether it would be possible to mix strychnine — you could get it legitimately for killing moles, she discovered — with lemon curd without detection, and send him a pot, but in time her fury calmed and she merely accepted the Professor as one of those evils that, in the mysterious dispensation of the Almighty, were sent to try ordinary decent people like her.

Slightly tired, perhaps, on that moist and thundery morning that was presently to become catastrophic, though she did not at that moment know it, Miss Pilchester felt her feathers decidedly ruffle up as the Professor replied to her 'good morning' with his 'good afternoon'.

'Morning,' she informed him.

'Afternoon. If I'm not mistaken.'

'As you habitually are.'

'Indeed? Unless my hearing is defective the church clock has struck twelve. Afternoon it therefore is.'

'I never go by the church clock. It's always fast.'

The Professor, giving a sharp snip with his hedge-clippers, murmured something about *tempus fugit*. The bandying about of Latin tags was always, to Miss Pilchester, a source of annoyance and she instantly surprised herself, in a moment of temper, by tartly retorting:

'All right. Have it your own way. *Chacun à son goût.*'

The Professor laughed, low and despicably as Miss Pilchester thought, and said something about the marvels that women's emancipation had wrought. He had no idea that French had penetrated so deep into the countryside.

This remark brought their conversation, the longest so far between them, to such a point of imminent conflict that it seemed suddenly likely to develop into a combat between hedge-clippers and umbrella. Miss Pilchester in fact actually lifted the umbrella and was only saved from bringing it down on the Professor's head by the wail of an ambulance siren coming up the road.

As the melancholy wail increased and the ambulance finally tore past them, travelling very fast, Miss Pilchester remarked:

'Another accident, I expect. Another poor innocent laid low, I shouldn't wonder.'

'There are few innocents left,' the Professor said. 'And no poor.'

Miss Pilchester, able to stand it no longer, gave a positive snort, together with a savage swirl of the umbrella, and stalked away. As she swept into the road the Professor delivered what he himself would undoubtedly have called his Parthian shot and called:

'French you may speak. But in this country we still drive on the left of the road.'

To her dismay Miss Pilchester abruptly realized that she was wandering, half-blind with anger, somewhere to the right-centre of the road. She wasn't looking where she was going at all. It was truly awful. It was absolutely ghastly.

It was all the fault of that wretched foreigner, that Communist, that cynic, she told herself over and over again as she tramped her way up to the post office, half-exhausted by anger, so that now and then she felt compelled to pause and draw in savage breath. The countryside could well do without such people, it really could. Suddenly the delicious, sweet, intoxicating air of summer felt tainted.

What a contrast, she told herself, with her friend Mr Larkin. Mr Larkin was himself like summer: eternally intoxicating, always sweet, always perfickly delicious. The only thing was that, like the precious days of summer themselves, he appeared so rarely. It seemed weeks since she had seen him last. Now and then she had seen him float serenely past her cottage in the splendour of his shining monogrammic Rolls, once with a brief wave of his hand, once with a few symphonic chords, both high and low, on the horn, and once with a gesture of such meaningful airiness that she was unable to sleep that night and kept telling herself that unless she was grievously mistaken the gesture was, in fact, a blown kiss.

The precious nature of such rare displays of distant affection from Mr Larkin couldn't lightly be dismissed, still less forgotten. She still treasured beyond all expression the original palpitating rapture of the first kiss he had ever given her in the cottage and still more of that other time, after the gymkhana, when Pop had seized her like a sheaf of corn and had passionately urged her with that luscious compulsion of his to give everything she'd got and she had tried so hard to do so, even though knowing it wouldn't possibly be half enough.

Ever since that time she had longed, over and over again, to give all she'd got. She'd give it any time. Sometimes, in fact, she gave it in the last moments before sleep, metaphorically wrapped in Pop's arms, murmuring to herself, as in an intoxicated lullaby, that it was perfick, absolutely perfick, and urging Pop, if possible, to do it again.

As she went into the post office, which was also the village shop, Miss Pilchester found herself as usual in a state of tart wonder at the revolution that had, over the past few years, taken place there.

Where once the counter had held little but a block of margarine, a red wedge of mouse-trap

39

cheese, a few pock-marked apples and a cube of sweet, cheap dates, it was now bright with tempting delicacies, French, Italian, Spanish and even Indian and Chinese, from Bisque d'Homard to canneloni and chop suey. In another corner of the shop stood a vast deep freeze cabinet stuffed with smoked salmon, *escargots de Bourgogne*, scampi, smoked trout, petit pois, smoked cod's roe, smoked eel, salami and sausage of every kind, palm hearts and ice creams great and small, bright-coloured as the flags of the United Nations. On the shelves above stood regiments of tins containing mangoes, paw-paws, lychees, *fraises des bois* and exotics of every kind.

In front of her a fat young woman further rotund in pregnancy, with four children sucking green-and-pink ice-lollies of such magnitude that they were actually washing in them, as in frothy soap, was filling baskets with mangoes, fresh Italian peaches, Bisque d'Homard, scampi, Emmenthaler, Brie and Stilton cheese, packets of spaghetti Bolognese and smoked salmon, at the same time complaining in rough, loud country accents hadn't they got no Rocquefort this week then? It was coming to summat now when you couldn't get no Rocquefort. She didn't know what her husband would say. There wouldn't half be a carry-on. Last week he very nearly hit her with the poker because they never had no *escargots*. She didn't know what things were coming to.

Miss Pilchester, silently and tartly wondering why on earth it wasn't caviare that had caused the incident of the poker — after all the Russians, the Communists, practically regarded

40

it as a staple diet — then had to wait nearly five minutes at the post office counter while the woman drew a vast sum in children's allowances and complained again, as she counted up a fat wad of notes, about the absence of a particular brand of cigars her husband was more than partial to.

'He don't 'alf raise 'ell if he don't 'ave 'is cigars, I tell you. Raises bloody 'ell, 'e does an' all. Ain't you got no chianti again this week then? That'll make 'is blood boil I tell you.'

Finally Miss Pilchester was able to buy six fourpenny stamps, a quarter of tea, a small tin of baked beans, a quarter of mouse-trap cheese and a packet of potato crisps: the limit she could afford. At the mention of potato crisps one of the children started shouting that he wanted potato crisps too, at which the mother promptly belted him across the ear, demanding to know if he thought she was bleedin' made of money?

Trying hard to look the other way, Miss Pilchester then asked the girl behind the counter how much that would be and got the astonishing reply:

'One pound sixteen and fourpence, Miss Pilchester, please.'

Miss Pilchester stood aghast. She knew that prices had risen pretty steeply these last few years; she was fully aware of the social revolution in which, among the working classes, so-called, smoked salmon and Rocquefort had replaced margarine and mouse-trap, but this was, she thought, altogether a bit too much.

'Haven't you,' she said, 'made some slight mistake?'

'Oh! my goodness, Oh! dear, Oh! Miss Pilchester, I'm terribly sorry.'

She should think so, Miss Pilchester told herself. It was yet another example of the futilities of modern education. Nowadays people couldn't even add up.

'I make it, unless I'm much mistaken, nine-and-three.'

'So it is, Miss Pilchester. I'm sorry. I'm terribly sorry. I'm all of a tizzy this morning. I'm all of a heap.'

Some of these words were drowned by the howling of the small boy who, having been belted about the ear once, was now being belted twice, this time with a packet of crisps. Either as an act of appeasement or example his brother and sisters were being belted too and were responding by tearing open the packets of crisps like ravenous wolves who had had nothing to eat for several days.

'Now bleedin' be quiet or else I'll give you summat to remember next time. If you don't shut your gob you won't have no scampi.'

In the confusion of din caused by belting, howling and the crackling of crisps Miss Pilchester started to ask the girl behind the counter why she could possibly be all of a heap when the girl promptly burst into tears.

What on earth was the matter? Miss Pilchester wanted to know. All of a sudden the place was Bedlam.

'Haven't you heard?' the girl said. With painful difficulty she sucked back her sobs. 'I mean — it's so awful.'

'So awful about what?'

'Mr Larkin.'

'Mr Larkin? What about Mr Larkin?'

The girl now broke into louder weeping, causing the children who had been belted to bawl even louder still.

'They say Mr Larkin's dead. Mr Larkin's dead.'

In the confusion of weeping, gossip and crackling of crisps over the next few indeterminable minutes Miss Pilchester stood like a pillar of salt. Vaguely she heard the young woman far gone in pregnancy say Oh! yes, it was right: knocked down by a bus, to which an elderly man drawing his weekly pension promptly corrected her by saying No, a stroke. It was gospel. A stroke. About eight or nine o'clock that morning, he understood. Very sudden. Out like a light.

In a slight pause among all the confusion the voice of the eldest child, having finished bawling, suddenly piped up with the irrefutable truth that 'Ah! well, we all have to go some time,' a remark which caused Miss Pilchester to recover her own voice. A moment later the pillar of salt melted and her voice with it. In that moment too Miss Pilchester remembered the ambulance going past her door.

'Oh! no, it can't be. Oh! no — God wouldn't do it. God would never do a thing like that — '

In the act of frantically clutching her head with both hands she dropped tea, beans, crisps and mouse-trap on the floor and then blindly rushed from the shop.

Totally unaware for the next few minutes of where she was or where she was going, her only really conscious impression was being alone. The village street was utterly deserted. The whole place was like something stricken, itself dead, with not a soul in sight.

Too stunned to cry, she desperately longed for someone, even a stranger, to talk to. The emptiness of the street seemed to mock her. She then observed, coming out of the shade of a big chestnut tree overhanging a wheelwright's yard just beyond the church, a horse.

It was a big, handsome chestnut, coat gleaming in the midday sun, and something about it seemed suddenly of great comfort. One could talk to a horse. One could even confide in a horse. One could even, failing all else, weep with a horse. She knew. Long ago, when times had been better, she had had a horse, a mere hack it was true, but in both body and spirit she and the horse had been one. But those days were far off — now she had no horse. The dividends on her gilt-edged — mocking term — pitiful enough as they were, kept constantly falling, and horses were no longer a possible part of her world.

She then saw that the horse was being ridden by a woman. Horse and woman were, she then saw, well married, the big shining flanks of the animal being handsomely repeated in the round thighs, round buttocks and even rounder bosom of Freda O'Connor, who was dressed in jodhpurs, bright yellow sweater and a crimson scarf on her head.

Freda O'Connor, breasts protruding over the neck of the horse, as Pop Larkin had once observed, like headlamps, was notorious as a woman of shifting affections. During the week she lived with a retired naval commander; at weekends she had matters of great interest to discuss with a horse-dealer two villages away. Out hunting, she had a propensity to disappear into coppices after invisible foxes, closely followed by a former guards officer who was using his gratuity to grow mushrooms that nobody apparently wanted to buy. When new foxes appeared in the village, preferably in the shape of sporting or other military men, she was out hunting for them. The lines of the marriage service, 'to have and to hold', had not, as Pop's friend the Brigadier had once caustically observed, been precisely written for her. A lot of men had had her. Few had held her for long.

'Morning. Damn nice morning.'

Freda O'Connor's voice, as if she had long modelled it on her regiments of men, was loud and brassy.

A bitter thought in the mind of Miss Pilchester, who liked neither Freda O'Connor nor the men with whom she consorted, reminded her that nice though the morning might be it was also damned.

'Corn looks well. Early harvest I shouldn't wonder. See the show-jumping on TV last night?'

No, Miss Pilchester had seen no show-jumping on TV, purely because, as she put it, she

45

had no machine. Nor could there be any harvest, she thought, now that Pop was dead.

'You've heard the awful news, I expect?'

No, Freda O'Connor hadn't heard the awful news. What awful news?

'Pop — Mr Larkin — is dead.'

'God. Holy catfish. You don't say.'

Miss Pilchester was silent, merely staring at the bright eyes of the horse, soft and oily as it seemed to her with comfort, at the same time ignoring the big yellow figure of Freda O'Connor swelling like a brassy statue above it.

'What happened? Accident?'

There appeared to be, Miss Pilchester said, conflicting reports. Some said a car. Some said a stroke.

'And some say elbow-lifting, I shouldn't wonder.'

Miss Pilchester icily begged her pardon?

'Bit excessive with the old bottle, I mean. Get me?'

Miss Pilchester said No, she didn't get her and added, in a voice frozen now to flat, level bitterness, that there were, after all, excesses and excesses. Or didn't Freda O'Connor know?

The oblique, insensitive reference to Pop's drinking habits enraged her so much that she was a hundred yards away from Freda O'Connor, striding past the old wheelwright's yard and then the church, before she was fully conscious again. When her mind finally began working once more she could think of only one thing. Like Pop himself, she needed a drink. She needed a long, stiff, powerful whisky.

Somewhere between the church and The Hare and Hounds a sudden pang of conscience arrested her. Perhaps, after all, she ought to go into the church instead: there to pray, if only words could be found, for Pop's departed soul. Thus stricken, she stood for fully a minute in the middle of the road, struggling with her conscience and its problem until she decided after all that whisky, rather than prayer, was perhaps the more appropriate medium with which to send the soul of Pop on its last, long journey.

Inside The Hare and Hounds she found herself still so possessed by the struggle with conscience and mournful thoughts of Pop that in the abysmal agony of trying to grapple with them she actually found herself talking in his language.

'Give me a snifter. God, a big one too. God. Whisky.'

It was of course awful to speak of the Almighty in such terms, in the same breath as whisky, but the occasion, she felt, was hellish enough to demand it. It was hellish enough for anything. It wasn't merely absolutely ghastly. It was sheer absolute, nightmare hell.

Mr Foreman, the landlord, was himself serving at the bar, his only other customers being a farm labourer apparently half-talking to himself over a pint of beer, his jacket covered with sprigs of boughs and leaves from a hedge he had been clipping, and a retired butcher who, himself red and beefy of face, with small jolly blue eyes, looked not at all unlike a prize piece of beef cattle fattened and ready for market.

47

'Don't often see you in here of a morning, Miss Pilchester,' the landlord said. 'What'll it be? Black and White? Johnny Walker?'

'Hell. Anything. The stronger the better. And double please.'

Knocking back a good half of the whisky with a speed not unworthy of Pop himself getting outside one of his special Red Bull cocktails, Miss Pilchester gave a great sorrowful gasp and muttered in a voice slightly incoherent something about she might well be seen there all day and every day from now on — God, how she'd needed that — the snifter, she meant, the stiffener.

This slightly wild demeanour of Miss Pilchester's drew from the landlord, who was used enough to seeing people go out of the pub drunk but not to come into it in the same condition, the question as to whether she was all right? Was something the matter?

Draining the whisky, growing slightly incoherent but not enough to prevent herself ordering another, Miss Pilchester gave the astounding reply that the roof had fallen in and God shouldn't have let it. It was hell. It was absolutely ghastly.

The reference to roof, God, hell and the ghastliness all in one breath left the landlord with a growing suspicion that Miss Pilchester had already been at the bottle somewhere. That was largely the trouble with women in the country. Frustrated and lonely, they got at it in secret and then didn't know when to stop. If he knew the form, which from long experience he did, Miss Pilchester would at any moment start weeping.

Which, at the arrival of her second whisky, Miss Pilchester promptly did.

'Now, now, what's it all about?' the landlord said and thought it a not inappropriate moment to shift the burden of responsibility to his missus and then remembered that she had gone into town, shopping. 'It can't be as bad as all that, surely.'

Bad? Not bad? Not hell, when a great, good man like Pop Larkin had gone? Wrested from them, struck down.

'Larkin? Pop? You don't mean? — '

Yes, she meant, Miss Pilchester said. She was sobbing openly now. Some said it was a stroke, some a car. She had seen an ambulance. The details didn't matter. All that mattered was the going, the fact of it —

'Might be just a rumour.' The landlord made consolatory gestures as he mopped up spots of moisture, that might well have been Miss Pilchester's tears, from the bar. 'You know villages. Rumour fair gallops round.'

No, no. Rumour she was sure it wasn't. Rumour it couldn't be. She felt it in her bones. Her heart. 'The Lord giveth,' she suddenly said, starting in further incoherence to make consolatory gestures herself, 'and the Lord taketh away' — but there were plenty of others he could have taken, she declared with vehement sorrow, other than Pop. She could name them too, she thought, thinking of Freda O'Connor and her horsey, whoring crowd.

49

'I could name them. I know them. They should have been cast out of the Temple long ago.'

This further mystifying excursion into vehemence, accompanied by strange accusations about the Temple, utterly convinced the landlord that Miss Pilchester had undoubtedly been at the bottle all right somewhere, but not in time enough to prevent the butcher from coming up to the bar and ordering her another whisky, at the same time offering the consolatory but sensible suggestion that wouldn't it be a good idea to telephone somebody and find out if it was true? The butcher knew old Pop Larkin wasn't one to give in lightly.

'Give in? You don't give in when somebody knocks you flat with a car. You're in Kingdom Come. The Lord hath taketh.'

'Best to telephone.' The butcher offered her the third consolatory whisky. Miss Pilchester grabbed at it eagerly but vaguely, hardly seeing it through her tears. 'It'll set your mind at rest.'

Miss Pilchester waved her glass about; as if, apparently, ready to strike the butcher with it. At rest? *Rest?* The word was a hollow, absolutely ghastly, mockery.

'I'll ask my Jackie. He'll know.'

The voice of the labouring hedge-clipper had a certain sepulchral quality. It seemed to Miss Pilchester to come from afar off, from some region of outer darkness.

'Jackie? Who's Jackie? How would he know?'

'Jackie allus knows.'

To the mysteries of accusation, expulsion from the Temple and whether or not Miss Pilchester

50

had been at the bottle all morning was now added the mystery of Jackie.

It took Miss Pilchester some moments longer to solve it and when she finally did so it was with a mixture of repugnance and disbelief. The labouring hedge-cutter had been talking not to himself but to a jackdaw, darkly nestling between his jacket and waistcoat as he sat at the end of the bar.

'This is my Jackie. Allus take 'im wimme.'

At once Miss Pilchester was sure that the bird was one of ill omen. Jackdaws — or was it crows? — or ravens perhaps? — she had read about them all somewhere. They were all birds of ill omen. In united blackness, without doubt, they foreshadowed misfortune, catastrophe and death.

At the very thought of it she started to feel physically, positively ill. In an equal spasm of depressive gloom she knocked back the butcher's whisky and in return, hardly knowing what she was doing, invited him to have another with her, an invitation to which the butcher readily and solemnly assented.

'Talk to 'im all day long,' the hedge-cutter said. 'Talks sense too. Talks a damn sight more sense than some I could name.'

In loud agreement Miss Pilchester banged her glass down on the bar.

'That I will second! That I will drink to!'

'This 'ere bird,' the hedge-cutter said, 'talks more sense in three croaks than you'll hear in Parliament in a month o' bloody wet Mondays.'

'That I will second!' Again Miss Pilchester banged her glass, this time a fourth whisky, on to the bar. 'That I will certainly drink to!'

The jackdaw now gave a loud, harsh croak, cocking his head out of the hedge-cutter's waistcoat, saucily making his presence felt.

''e 'eard you, Miss. Wants a drink.'

Drink? Drink? Miss Pilchester again waved her glass about. Did jackdaws, for heaven's sake, drink?

'Gin,' the hedge-cutter said. 'Makes 'im talk more. Drop o' gin and 'e'll talk till the cows come home.'

Then, Miss Pilchester said, give the bird gin! A large gin. Let the bird talk for goodness' sake.

'Says the Lord's Prayer sometimes.'

'Didn't I hear him,' the butcher said, 'say the 23rd Psalm once, too?'

'You did, Bill, that you did.'

'Masterpiece of a bird,' the butcher said, eyeing the jackdaw over the top of his whisky. Miss Pilchester, scarcely able to focus by this time, eyed it too.

'Two gins,' the hedge-cutter said, 'and 'e'll recite the whole of bloody Genesis.'

At these words Miss Pilchester suddenly realized that the jackdaw hadn't even got its gin. Peremptorily she banged the bar again and demanded that gin be brought. A double gin at that.

'Now Miss Pilchester — ' the landlord started to say.

'Bring the poor thing its gin! Great God Almighty, we all need a drink some time, don't we? I'll say we do. You wouldn't deny the bird a drink, would you? You're here to serve drink, aren't you? Then give the bird its drink. The poor wretched ceature may be shot down at any time. Cut down in its prime. Give it its gin for goodness' sake. I'm paying, aren't I?'

There being some show of reluctance on the part of the landlord to give the jackdaw its gin, Miss Pilchester now made further loud noises of remonstration, at the same time fumbling for her purse in her shopping bag. Eventually a double gin was pushed along the bar to the hedge-cutter who, while Miss Pilchester fumbled in her purse, lifted the gin to the beak of the jackdaw, making at the same time moist sucking noises, earnestly trying to beguile the bird into at least the pretence of consuming alcohol, even if it didn't want to.

'Not very dry this morning,' he was moved finally to observe. 'Perhaps don't like this pertickler sort. Very fussy sometimes. Very dainty.'

As if the gin was in fact not of the pertickler brand to suit the jackdaw's palate, the hedge-cutter was moved to taste it for himself, finally pronouncing it to be quite all right, very good in fact, nothing wrong with it at all. A second pretence of offering gin to the bird having had the same result the hedge-cutter took a second swig, pronouncing it to be in fact, rather better than before.'

'What about the Lord's Prayer?' the butcher said.

'Give 'im time. Give 'im time. Got to 'ave 'is tot.'

The hedge-cutter having chosen to take the

jackdaw's tot for him, the next thing Miss Pilchester heard was the first low muttered notes of the Lord's Prayer, croaked out as through a veil of muslin. Unable to see through her watering eyes whether in fact it was the beak of the jackdaw or the lips of the hedge-cutter reciting the familiar, sacred words, Miss Pilchester felt deeply moved, feeling more ill now than ever, cruelly on the verge of new floods of emotion.

After a time she became aware that the recital of the Lord's Prayer had stopped. This moved her still further. The bar, it seemed, was very still and she in turn couldn't see very straight.

'What about the rest?' she said, gropingly.

'Doesn't he know the rest?'

The hedge-cutter, having got as far as 'which art in Heaven', said no, he didn't think he did, he wasn't in much of a Lord's Prayer mood.

'Try the 23rd if you like,' he said.

Miss Pilchester, now past the moment of caring or knowing whether it was the Lord's Prayer or the 23rd Psalm that she wanted the bird to recite, actually heard, a few moments later, the first gentle croaking syllables of 'The Lord is my Shepherd' and had got as far as 'He maketh me to lie down' when she herself proceeded suddenly to lie down, not in green pastures, but on the floor, and very heavily, with a very loud bang, of the saloon bar of The Hare and Hounds.

At the sound of her falling the jackdaw gave a short, funereal croak. The hedge-cutter downed the last of the gin. The landlord went to the back

54

of the bar and shouted down the open hatch of the cellar to the cellarman below:

'You there, Alf? Better bring the wheelbarter.'

Ten minutes later the hedge-cutter and the butcher were wheeling Miss Pilchester home in the barrow, the jackdaw perched on one handle, through a lane summery with the cream of cow-parsley and meadow-sweet, rich with wild rose and honeysuckle, beyond which flocks of sheep were safely grazing in green pastures.

Women were funny, the hedge-cutter said and the jackdaw, with another funereal croak, might have been in agreement. Didn't take much to upset 'em.

4

At regular intervals throughout the rest of the day Pop, as in a spider-web of his own making, emerged for a few vague inches towards the fragile outer threads of full consciousness and then drew darkly back again.

Free of pain, tranquillized, he was only faintly aware of Ma occasionally coming to administer pills and tuck in the bed sheets, of occasional comforting glances from two of his daughters Primrose and Mariette, and for a longer period of some mysterious manoeuvres, at first barely understood, by Mr Charlton.

Remarkable feller, Mr Charlton. He seemed to be weaving a web of his own. With skill and stealth he unwound a complex of wires round, under and behind the bed. These were finally attached to the bed-post, giving the impression that Mr Charlton had himself turned doctor and was about to conduct his own researches into the state of Pop's damaged heart.

'Inter-comm.' Mr Charlton at last explained. 'Press the button and Ma'll hear you in the kitchen. Just press the button — anything you want — '

Miraculous bit of work, Pop told himself. Trust Charley boy to think of a thing like that. He smiled faintly at Charley in gratitude and then withdrew again into his web of unconsciousness.

Downstairs, in the kitchen, Ma was deeply immersed in manoeuvres of her own, in culinary exercises on a gigantic scale. The many pills and tablets Mr Charlton had brought back for Pop, red, white, blue, green and even brightest yellow, were no doubt as necessary as she hoped they would be effective but what Pop clearly needed was, in her own view, nourishment. And plenty of it.

To this end she was making steak-and-kidney pie, apple-and-apricot flan, dough cake, plum cake and caraway cake, the last a special favourite of Pop's, maids-of-honour, curd tarts, strawberry and raspberry mousse, both from fresh fruit, cheese straws, shortcakes and coconut ice. She had pondered for some time on whether or not to cook a turkey and with it a plum pudding left over from Christmas but had finally decided against these as being on the heavy side until Pop gets his strength back.

She was in no possible doubt that Pop would get his strength back, and quickly; you couldn't keep a man like Pop down for long. What chiefly troubled her was the possible cause, or causes, of Pop's sudden and distressing decline in the first place. Once or twice, casting her mind back to the events of the early morning, she told herself that perhaps it might conceivably have been something to do with doing too much on an empty stomach.

It was hardly likely, though. He had, after all, done it often enough before. It had never set him back at all in the past. It was quite unthinkable that it could do him any possible harm. On the contrary Ma thought of it rather as something in the nature of a hobby. Nor, she reasoned, could it possibly have anything to do with the early consumption of champagne, still less of brandy. They were, after all, like making love to Ma, everyday features of Pop's life, the very bone and marrow, as it were, of his entire existence.

If she was troubled at all by these things — and she was troubled by one thing especially — she scarcely showed an outward sign of it. Vast, placid, hands and bosom flowing over the pastry board, Ma characteristically told herself that it was no use moaning about these things. Moaning would get her nowhere; nor weeping. She had had her little weep; it had done her good; and that was that.

What really troubled her, and very often, were those words of Dr O'Connor, ominous and incredible, about 'the foreseeable future — for ever, perhaps for ever'. The mere suggestion that Pop might have to forgo the pleasures of alcohol for some brief period was in itself outrageous enough; but the notion that it might be for the foreseeable future, perhaps for ever, was plain purgatory.

Pop would never endure. If anything was calculated to set him back at all that was it. A good stiff brandy, of which she and Mariette had already had several during the course of the day, would in her opinion work wonders in no time. There was nothing like spirits, as she often remarked, to keep your spirits up; nothing like a little of what you fancied to do you good. She would have to have a serious word with Dr

O'Connor about the matter.

The house was very quiet. Scarcely a sound came from the warm, flower-drenched garden outside. Heat quivered in shimmering pulses across the meadows where hay lay about both in frothy rows and pale green bales ready for carting. On the kitchen table, among all the paraphernalia of cooking, stood a vase of honeysuckle, freshly gathered and waiting to be taken up to Pop's room, and the heavy fragrance of it, exquisitely intoxicating, was strong enough to rise above the smell of cooking.

Mariette, a tower of wonderful strength all morning, had now gone home, taking the youngest children, Oscar and Phyllida, with her. Mr Charlton and Montgomery had gone off in an attempt to complete the deal in walkie-talkies that Pop had missed. The twins, Zinnia and Petunia, were now away at boarding school, an exclusive and expensive establishment at which they consorted with at least one princess of the realm, together with another half dozen from foreign parts. Victoria was at a finishing school at Château d'Oeux, in Switzerland. All costing a shilling or two, Pop was the first to admit, but wurf while, very wurf while. His children deserved the best. You had only to consider Mr Charlton to see what education would do.

All this left Ma alone with Primrose. The development of Primrose into a creature both physically celestial and alluring, even more devastatingly so than Mariette, was something to astonish even the habitual tranquil attitude of Ma towards matters of sex, a word she herself never used, preferring to call it 'letting Nature take its course'. Nature had in fact several times so taken its course with Primrose, so aptly named, that Ma had been mildly disturbed by several false alarms, until Primrose had told Ma not to worry, the Pill was taking care of that.

When Ma told Pop about Primrose and the Pill he wasn't sure that he was exactly overjoyed. He was all for letting Nature take its course too. When Ma pointed out blandly that consumption of the Pill allowed Nature to take its course even more freely and enjoyably than before Pop was forced to admit that this was so. He only hoped Ma wasn't taking the Pill too.

'Do you mind?' Ma said. 'I haven't come to that. I've got on very well without it so far.'

Pop said he should think so too. His motto being the more the merrier, he wasn't at all sure he approved of this Pill lark. There was something a bit immoral about it, sort of. Very thing for girls like Edith Pilchester though, he said, in his customary rousing jocular fashion, to which Ma offered a slightly stern reproof:

'Have a heart. Poor Edith. She drew the curtains a long time ago.'

In the warm July afternoon Primrose was dressed — if the word was not inappropriate — in an almost transparent yellow blouse with small red spots on it and the briefest of mini-skirts in delicate green. The blouse was remarkable for being less of a blouse than a piece of loose material tied across her breasts, revealing six or seven inches of bare midriff and navel below and an even wider expanse of naked

60

flesh above. The mini-skirt contained hardly less material and from under it her legs swept in brown, ravishing curves. Ma guessed that she was wearing neither stockings nor tights and also rather suspected she was not wearing panties either. You could hardly blame her though, Ma told herself as she glanced at the rich curves of Primrose's firm high breasts protruding over the open blouse: the afternoon was hot enough for anything.

Ma, having now finished making the last of her curd tarts and maids-of-honour, was on the point of taking the vase of honeysuckle up to Pop in case he was awake and would like a cup of tea, when she suddenly heard the front door bell ring. The front door bell was in fact a whole concerto of rings, rather like a combination of a Venetian carillon, 'The Bluebells of Scotland' and the chimes of an ice-cream van.

'That'll be the doctor back again,' she said. 'I'll go.'

'Sit still. You've been rushing about enough as it is. I'll get it.'

Primrose sidled sinuously rather than walked from the kitchen to the front door and then came back, some moments later, with a visitor.

It was the Reverend Candy.

Mr Candy appeared, at first sight, to have suffered the grievous blow of some recent catastrophe. He was pale. There was even a certain trembling clutching of his hands about his neck, rather like that of a nervous hen scratching at its feathers. It at once occurred to Ma that all this was the probable natural reaction to the news of Pop's illness and she promptly got up from the table to make a cup of tea.

The catastrophe that had overtaken Mr Candy was, in fact, Primrose. He hadn't seen Primrose for some considerable time. Nor had he actually gone out of his way to do so. There was no need. The vision of her, ripe in prematurely rich development, honeyed, seductive, even exotic, with the beautiful dark stare that always had him swooningly trapped in a vice, was almost always in his mind. It scarcely ever left him. Nor did all the other moments of being with her, including that moment of near-disaster when he had christened her Narcissus instead of Narcissa, had sprinkled holy water on that most luscious and yet disturbingly innocent of foreheads and had received her half-seductive, half-forgiving smile in return.

Now the sight of her in the miniest of mini-skirts, blouse unbuttoned, the upper rims of her breasts white as washed seashells against the sun-brown of her neck and legs and face, was too much. It turned him cold and flaky.

'I must apologize for not having — that is, I only just heard — just after lunch. Then there were all sorts of rumours — I trust that — '

'Heart,' Ma said. 'Sit you down. I'm just going to make a cup of tea.'

'I'll make it,' Primrose said. 'You haven't been still all afternoon.'

'No, I can do it,' Ma said. 'You sit down and amuse Mr Candy.'

The words, Mr Candy told himself, were scarcely well chosen. Amuse! — he could have thought of better. Mesmerize would have been one of them. Who could be anything else, faced with those melting, honeyed black eyes, the shell-like breasts and that most compulsively seductive, miniest of skirts.

'Yes, do sit down, Mr Candy,' Primrose said in the creamiest of voices. 'Hot, isn't it? You look a bit tired.'

Mr Candy was indeed tired. Far from being hot, however, he felt himself turn colder, flakier than ever.

In confusion he began to say that he was relieved to hear that it was only heart, then realized that relieved was hardly the right word either. It was in fact hard, even impossible, to think straight. What he actually meant was that he had heard of an accident — a car — of Mr Larkin — well, gravely injured. He trusted all was not too serious?

'Sleeping like a lamb,' Ma said. 'They knocked him out after it happened. Very good thing.'

'I'm so relieved. So relieved.'

Ma, after buttering a heap of fresh scones, began to pour tea.

'Sugar? One lump or two?' Primrose said to Mr Candy. 'Cream? You like it in first or last?'

Dear God, Mr Candy thought. Heaven help me. Really the use of words like cream ought not to be allowed. Ever. Not from those lips, anyway. Cream: the word was torture.

'Apricot jam, lemon curd or quince jelly?' Ma said.

'I adore quince jelly,' Mr Candy said, relieved beyond measure to be able to concern himself with the comparatively innocent virtues of quince jelly, a pot of which Ma now passed to him, at the same time apologizing:

'Excuse the pot. We're a bit bottom-uppards today, what with Pop and all that.'

'Oh! please don't apologize. Quince jelly is splendid at any time. I adore it. Pot or no pot.'

Something about this remark made Primrose laugh, her voice low and deep with what seemed deliberate allurement, so that Mr Candy sought desperately to escape from it by delivering a totally unexpected sentence:

'Not that one can't have too much of it, like anything else. Someone once said — I rather think it was Coleridge — that one can't live for ever on quince jelly.'

'I don't see why not,' Ma said. 'Mine's always pretty good.'

'Oh! I didn't mean that,' Mr Candy said. 'Don't misinterpret me. It's excellent. More than excellent.'

It was now Primrose's turn, to Mr Candy's intense embarrassment, to produce an unexpected question of her own.

'Didn't the Greeks — or was it the Romans — use it as an aphrodisiac?'

Dear God, Mr Candy thought again and could find no word to say.

'What's aphrodisiac?' Ma said. 'Sounds like an insecticide or something,' and laughed in her customary ripe, bouncing fleshy fashion. 'Or else a rude word.'

'You never needed it,' Primrose said, giving Mr Candy one of those long, sideways, serpentine glances that seemed to coil about him, enthralling his very flesh. 'Some people never do.'

Desperately Mr Candy sought to extricate himself from the torture of this moment by saying:

'There was, in fact, a curious rumour going about — oh! I don't mean about Mr Larkin — quite apart from that. I had to verify it three times before I found it was true.'

'Never believe rumours,' Ma said. 'They got it about once that Pop had run off with Angela Snow. Piffle.'

'Well this, though I say it as shouldn't, as they say, is gospel. It concerns — '

'Come on,' Primrose said, 'I love scandal.'

'Scandal I suppose you could call it, too.'

'Come on, let's have a bite then,' Ma said.

'Well it seems — and I've got three unimpeachable sources of information — that Edith Pilchester went into The Hare and Hounds and got tiddly. Helplessly, hopelessly tiddly. Sozzled. Stoned, as I believe they call it nowadays.'

Ma started laughing again like a jelly, unable to draw breath through her great wobbling frame except in a series of loud gigantic wheezes.

'And had to be taken home in a wheelbarrow.'

Ma fell about, helpless. She couldn't contain herself. She half-wept into her tea.

'Whatever did Edith want to go and do a thing like that for?'

Mr Candy paused, glad of the momentary chance of being distracted from Primrose, who was laughing too but in a very different way from Ma. Her laughter had a liquid, seductive, dangerous sound.

'Well, it appears — it would seem that she'd been very upset by — she heard a rumour — just a rumour of course — about — ' Here Mr Candy paused again, searching for the appropriate, least embarrassing word — 'about Mr Larkin's demise.'

'Oh! really? Do you mind?' Ma said. 'He's certainly not suffering from that.'

Desisting suddenly from laughter, she gave Mr Candy a stern, reproving sort of look, at the same time handing him the choice of a plate of shortcake or lemon curd tarts. Mr Candy accepted shortcake, of which he was very fond, and in politeness offered the plate to Primrose. She thanked him with one of those smouldering, bewitching looks of hers that always turned him cold and flaky and said no, she'd rather have a slice of the caraway.

Demise, Primrose now explained, meant that Miss Pilchester had heard that Pop was dead.

Ma said Really? Whatever next? The things people got about. If some of them didn't keep their traps shut she'd have to iron them out. Gossipy lot — she expected some of them would like to see him dead.

These unchristian remarks, so unlike Ma, briefly shocked Mr Candy, who hastily sucked at crumbs of sugar from the shortcake and didn't know what to say. Perhaps one could excuse such outbursts at such a time of tension.

Then Ma, never one to be put out of her stride

for long, started laughing uncontrollably again, the great wheezes for breath once more turning to tears.

'In a wheelbarrow. For crying out loud. In a wheelbarrow — Oh! my lord. I remember once they brought my old Dad home in a wheelbarrow, but I thought that sort of thing had gone out of fashion.'

The laughter having at last calmed down through a series of hilarious sobs until her body merely heaved in huge ponderous breaths, so that she looked not unlike a porpoise about to give birth, Ma finally got up from the table and said she would really have to go up and tell Pop all about Edith and the wheelbarrow. She really would. That would set him up all right. It would do him more good than all the pills in the world.

Taking the little vase of honeysuckle with her — it was Pop's favourite flower, one that always gave him ideas, as he put it, and would make the bedroom smell nice — she left the kitchen and went upstairs, pausing only to remark from the door:

'If the colour television set arrives tell them to wait while I give the all clear.' One of Ma's first acts after the trouble with Pop's heart was to ring up a radio dealer for a colour television set. It was the least she could do. Pop could have it in the bedroom and it would cheer him up. 'Help yourself to anything you want, Mr Candy.'

Mr Candy, far from helping himself to anything he wanted, sat in a sort of trance, left all alone with Primrose, a circumstance that never failed to cause him the acutest embarrassment.

This hot afternoon the embarrassment seemed to have properties almost lethal. He hardly knew which way to look. He positively snatched at a second piece of shortcake, biting into it desperately.

By contrast Primrose was eating her slice of caraway cake very slowly, with an absent air. Both sunburnt arms crooked on the table, she held the caraway gently against her lips and now and then took soft exploratory bites at it, rather like a drowsy butterfly at the petals of a flower. From Mr Candy's point of view this looked like a deliberate essay in seduction, in every way devised to torture and beguile and defeat all sensible resistance on his part.

But to Primrose the situation was in fact entirely the opposite. It was Mr Candy who was seductive. It was that shyness of his, that sort of she didn't quite know what. It was the paleness and the quiet. There were times when it really sent her. She would have to do something about it, seriously, one day.

From one of these dreamy, absent bites at the slice of caraway cake a crumb fell. Like a stone lightly dislodged from a cliff-top it fell gently down the slope of Primrose's chest, at last coming to rest midway at the exposed curves of bosom. It lay there like a magnet, transfixing Mr Candy's gaze with utter torture. He had always been commanded, as a child, not to drop crumbs down himself. He had been severely scolded if he did so, and now the sight of the caraway crumb lodged in the ivory cleft of Primrose's bosom filled him with guilt remembered — so painfully remembered that he felt an intense compulsion to tell her about the crumb or pick it off with his own fingers.

He was saved from the necessity of doing either of these things by Primrose suddenly and sharply leaning back in the chair, again reduced to some moments of laughter by a remembrance of her own — the picture of Edith Pilchester taken home in the wheelbarrow.

This new recumbent attitude of Primrose's was worse than anything that had gone before. It served to bring her naked midriff, and its navel, into fullest view. Magnetized to a degree hitherto unconceived. Mr Candy now dropped crumbs down himself too and gave unsteady gulps at his tea. The sight of this fresh display of nervousness or whatever it was, that sort of she didn't know what, set Primrose gently laughing again and her midriff quivered sinuously and softly, all pulsating fleshy tenderness.

At the same time her mini-skirt was drawn up almost to its fullest extent, so that Mr Candy was suddenly assailed by the same convictions that had occurred to Ma, only in her case by no means seriously: namely that Primrose was wearing nothing whatever underneath. Primrose was in fact wearing something underneath, brief though it was, and a sudden sight of it, a mere pink triangle, had a more palpitating effect on Mr Candy than if she had been wearing nothing at all.

Before he had recovered from this shattering moment a second crumb fell, this time in the form of a caraway seed. In one of the ripples of

Primrose's laughter it was shaken free from the slice of cake and fell downwards towards her navel. This unnerving sight drove Mr Candy to a point of silent excruciation. He was momentarily paralysed. Torn between an almost frantic desire to remove the caraway seed or to do something about the mini-skirt he did neither. He merely sat transfixed, hopelessly mesmerized, instead, by the navel and the caraway seed.

His silent stare at the bare midriff for fully half a minute finally drew a remark from Primrose.

'Penny for your thoughts.'

A millionaire couldn't have bought Mr Candy's thoughts at that moment. In silent, wild surmise he had just found, he thought, the exact simile for the navel. It was exactly, he told himself, like a soft young raspberry. That was exactly it; and in another moment he was aware of the taste of raspberries on his lips, and his mouth watered.

He was distractedly wondering what might possibly happen next, and had almost decided that nothing more devastating possibly could, when Ma came back into the room.

'Another cup, you two?' Ma said. 'You haven't been sitting there letting it get cold, have you?'

Mr Candy told himself they certainly hadn't been sitting there letting it get cold, far from it; and there was little doubt that his cup was full, almost, to overflowing. Nevertheless he thanked Ma, then said he would have another cup of tea.

'I'll pour it,' Primrose said. 'Mr Candy likes the cream in first.'

Cream! — This household, Mr Candy

thought, dear God, this household; and was on the verge of doubting if he would ever have the courage to visit it again when his practical self reminded him that he hadn't asked after Mr Larkin. How was Mr Larkin?

'Well, I know what Pop would say,' Ma said. 'Bad a-bed and wuss up. But there's an improvement. He's had a good long sleep. I don't think he still quite knows where he is but he loved the honeysuckle.'

'Is there something I could do? Could I possibly go up?'

'No visitors today,' Ma said. 'Got to be kept absolutely quiet today. He's doped anyway. He'd hardly know you.'

Feeling slightly doped himself, Mr Candy watched Ma pick up the teapot and then, after urging Mr Candy to have a slice of caraway cake, he'd hardly eaten a thing, said she thought she'd make a fresh pot for Pop and take up a cup to the bedroom.

Mr Candy replied with thanks that he'd really had quite enough. The word crumb, he told himself, was a meal in itself. He would never forget that crumb, or that caraway seed.

'Did you tell Pop about Edith?' Primrose finally wanted to know.

Ma confessed she hadn't. On second thoughts she'd decided it might be too much for him. It might, she said, laughing again but no longer so boisterously, give him another turn. It would keep, the bit about Edith, it would keep.

'Yes, indeed. Might act as a sort of therapy in good time,' Mr Candy said and Ma gave him another stern sort of look, half as if he had suggested something rude.

'How is he really, Ma?' Primrose said. Primrose, perhaps of all the children, with the possible exception of Mariette, was closest to Pop. There was much of Pop in her, Ma often thought. There was that something — you couldn't say what it was but it was sort of rich and warm and it got at you. It was like something catching. The sudden shocking business of Pop's heart had very much upset her. 'When does the doctor come again?'

'Before surgery. About half past five.'

It now suddenly and instinctively occurred to Ma that Primrose's question was one of real anxiety. Rapidly she changed the subject by running a hand over Primrose's smooth brown bare shoulder and with disarming innocence asking Mr Candy a question:

'Getting nice an' brown, isn't she, Mr Candy? Pretty well the same all over.'

Mr Candy, having seen pretty well all over by now, was unable to think of a word to say in answer.

'I tell you what,' Ma said. 'I was going to get some flowers for Pop's bedroom but by the time I've taken him a cup of tea and shaken his bed a bit the doctor'll be here and I won't get time. Why don't you two go?'

'Oh! let's do that. Shall we, Mr Candy?' Primrose spoke with that warm allure that was part of her inheritance from Pop and that always sent Mr Candy cold and flaky. 'Shall we?'

Hesitating, trying hard to think of some valid

excuse for refusal but able to recall nothing but a meeting of the Parochial Church Council, more than three hours away — Great Heavens, Miss Pilchester was supposed to be on it too, and what on earth would people say? — he was saved from further trial by Ma, now back to her usual, outwardly buoyant self, saying:

'That's it, you two go along. Get some nice things with plenty of scent. You know how Pop loves perfume. Carnations and lilies and roses and all that sort of thing. Plenty of scent.'

'Come on, Mr Candy,' Primrose said. 'I'll cut and you hold.'

Cut and hold — Oh! the profundity of simple words, Mr Candy thought and prepared to follow the glorious, brown mini-skirted legs of Primrose into the garden, shining in shimmering July sunlight.

The heat of the sun had scarcely touched his face, however, before he was arrested by the voice of Ma, calling from the kitchen door.

'Here, take a basket. You can get some raspberries too while you're at it,' she was saying, and Mr Candy could have fainted.

5

Three mornings later Pop woke to see a clear limpid blue sky shining beyond the windows. Somebody, he could only suppose Ma, had already drawn back the curtains and now brilliant early sunlight was streaming strongly into the bedroom. Lying flat on his back, without pillows, he had a slightly upward view of the summer sky and against it, at the edge of the open window, a single rose-leaf, new, pink-copper in colour and slightly curled, not unlike a curved sea-shell half-transparent in the sun.

He watched this single leaf for some long time. Soon he saw it not as a shell but a map, a small leaf-island crossed by a central river, with many little tributaries and a host of even tinier streams. At the edges of it the brightness of sun, clear gold, created an illusion of delicate little waves breaking on the leaf-shore; and the sky the further illusion that the sea itself was spread far beyond it, an expanse blue as chicory flower, and marvellously calm. This leaf-island and its surrounding summer sea he saw as something not merely wonderful; it was a miracle. It was yet another experience that illness incredibly magnifies the most trivial of things.

His long preoccupation with the marvel and loveliness of this single simple rose-leaf also created in him the strongest feeling of suspense. He might have been poised in space, a leaf himself, breathlessly held in air. He took several long, deep breaths: he felt unbearably glad to be alive.

All this was rather like a man savouring the marvels of a dry crust at a table laden with a bountiful and luscious feast. His bedroom seemed to be a combination of green house, wine-shop and fruit stall. Flowers — carnations, roses, gladioli, even nosegays of meadowsweet, wild grasses and willowherb — stood fragrantly about in vases everywhere; the sun gleamed on the necks of champagne bottles as on crusty golden candles; a pyramid of fruit, a glowing cornucopia of pineapple, peaches, pears, white and black grapes and apples stood on top of his new colour television set, a note on it from Angela Snow saying in words as languid and liquid as her own voice: 'Wanted to send you something madly in character: mangoes, persimmons, paw-paw, passion fruit and all that — but those scabs in London wouldn't play. Get well soon, dearest man. Fondest thoughts, Thirsting to see you soon. P.S. Your pining Jasmine joins me in profoundest embrace and all that.'

The cheering comfort of those words, together with the mental vision of the willowy and honeyed Angela and the magnificent sculptured flesh of her friend Jasmine Brown, of whom Pop had memories that didn't now bear dwelling upon, had served to raise his spirits, though not in the manner that Ma sometimes referred to as 'the old pepper and mustard'. He still felt fragile; the recollection of moments of velvet flirtation with both girls didn't merely seem impossible: it made him continually wonder how he'd stood up to it at all. You needed a bit of strength for that sort of thing; and strength, he often felt as he lay there pillowless and prostrate, was something that seemed to have left him for ever.

And not merely strength; but gaiety too. It was a very solemn Pop who lay there finding solace of amazingly restorative depth in a mere rose-leaf. He hadn't even been able to raise much of a smile at Ma's story, jubilantly told, of Edith Pilchester being taken home, 'laying-down drunk', as Ma said, in a wheelbarrow. It didn't somehow seem very funny; on the contrary it struck him as rather sad. It belonged to the ghastly fact, as Edith herself would have put it, that he was never going to be able to drink again, perhaps never to taste the twin delights of Ma and champagne in bed, still less the surreptitious delights of girls like Jasmine Brown in the boat-house. His heart would clearly never stand the strain. It was, in Edith's words again, 'absolutely ghastly'.

It was, in fact, far worse; it was funereal. There were even depressive moments when he thought it was the death knell — no more champers, no more brandy, no more cigars, no more stiffeners in the shape of his favourite cocktails, Rolls-Royce and Red Bull, no more Ma and all that, no more nothing. You might just as well get ready, he told himself, to tuck down under the daisies. It was the bone-house. It was as good as all over.

He was suddenly shocked out of these melancholy reflections by a staggering vision entering the room, accompanied by an equally shattering sound. The vision was that of a pure white, starchy, over-blown administering angel. The sound was like that of the crackling of a vast packet of potato crisps.

'Good morning, Mr Larkin, good morning. And how do we find ourselves this morning?'

Pop was about to reply automatically that he was fit as a flea, then realized that he wasn't and furthermore that the words wouldn't have been very well received even if he was.

'I am Nurse Soper. I have come to relieve your wife for a few days. The strain was proving rather much for her.'

Pop lay speechless. This was less because he could think of nothing reasonable to say than because he was trying to drink in the magisterial figure of Nurse Soper, now shaking a thermometer and preparing to plunge it into his mouth. The presence of the thermometer having finally removed all idea of speech completely, Pop merely gazed at the vast starchiness of his nurse with wonder, awe and disbelief.

Nurse Soper appeared to be a figure composed on the one hand of one of those marble attendant angels you saw in churchyards and on the other of a heavyweight boxer who had forgotten to shave for a day or two. A thickish area of dark moustache on her upper lip seemed to have sown fresh progeny, in the shape of a ring of little tufty beards, on her chin. Her nose, like that of a boxer, was broad and slightly flattened. A further area of dark moustache had sprouted from that too. Her hair, or as much of it as Pop could see from under the stiff-starched helmet of her nurse's cap, was naturally grey in colour but had recently been dyed an unpleasant shade of yellow, so that it looked rather like the coat of a moulting vixen.

As if these things were not hard enough to bear her voice sounded like the engine of a car that had run out of oil and was about to seize up. Pop was briefly disposed to think that her big end had gone.

Having taken Pop's temperature, Nurse Soper grunted, though whether in approval or disapproval of the reading Pop found it impossible to tell, then lit a cigarette. The fact that smoking was yet another of the pleasures of life Pop was having to forgo, perhaps for ever, the cloud of cigarette smoke she now blew into the summer morning air served to irritate him even more than the *words* which followed.

'And now, Mr Larkin, do we wish the bottle?'

Something about the offensive commanding nature of this sentence served not merely to irritate Pop still further; it suddenly and unexpectedly inspired him to a breath of mischief.

'Yes, good egg. I'll try the champers.'

'No champagne, Mr Larkin. As you well know. No alcohol.'

'Brandy then.'

'No alcohol. Nor was it that kind of bottle to which I was referring.'

Nurse Soper glared. Her eyes were like ice-grey screwdrivers. They were, Pop was beginning to think, not quite human. It was clearly obvious, too, he decided, that she and him were already off hooks.

'Well, Mr Larkin, do we wish the bottle or not?'

Pop was now amazingly inspired to a second flicker of mischief and said:

'I always use the Throne.'

'You mean you have been getting out of bed? That is very, very naughty. Who authorized *that*? That is extremely naughty.'

'Very comfortable, the Throne.'

The Throne, which stood by his bedside, was in fact most comfortable. It had been sent for Pop's use from the village by the two Miss Barnwells, the genteel freckled little ladies, daughters of a retired Indian Civil Servant, who found times under the all-sheltering roof of the Welfare State more than a little hard and were now classed, sadly, as Distressed Gentlefolk. The commode, Victorian, with cabriole legs, in smoothest walnut and covered with ruby velvet, had seen much service East of Suez, and inside was inscribed with the words 'The Royal Universal'.

'There will be no more using the Throne, as you call it, while I'm here. Let's get that quite clear. Now do we wish the bottle or not?'

'Very nearly breaking my neck,' Pop said.

'Then we'd better have it quick, hadn't we? Before a mistake is made.'

With the bottle under the sheets, Pop proceeded to spend a few quiet contemplative minutes while Nurse Soper went along to the bathroom.

Pop was still urgently concerned with the business in hand when to his great relief Ma appeared. She looked tired, apologetic and generally not quite up to the mark, he thought.

'What the pipe, Ma?' he said. 'What did we have to have her for? Old Soapy?'

Ma proceeded to explain, in tones unaccountably subdued for her, that she was sorry but the whole thing had begun to get her down. It was fifty yards from the kitchen to the bedroom, up and down, which Mr Charlton had worked out was as something like two miles upstairs and downstairs a day. It was like training for the Olympics.

Clever fellow, Charley boy. Very strong on mathematics. But why her? Why the Soapy?

'Had to get somebody quick,' Ma said. 'Dr O'Connor insisted. She was the best we could get.'

Pop silently reflected that if this was the best what in the name of all that was holy could the worst be like? It had already been at the back of his mind that, in a day or two, if all went well, Ma and he could be having a quiet, secretive snifter up in the bedroom and nobody the wiser. Now clearly, that was out. The bedroom was more than ever a prison. With the Soapy in charge, the wardress, he was chained hand and foot. There was no escape. He was sunk in gloom.

'The doctor said we had to do it,' Ma said. 'If we didn't I might crack up and then where would we be?'

Where indeed? Pop thought and had no

answer to this depressing question except 'up the ruddy creek' when Nurse Soper was back, carrying wash-bowl, sponge, soap, towels and a bottle of eau-de-cologne.

'I understand that Mr Larkin has been getting out of bed, Mrs Larkin. That is strictly forbidden. Is it understood? Strictly and absolutely taboo.'

'He said he felt well enough, so I let him.'

'There could be nothing more dangerous. This business is very much an affair of snakes-and-ladders. You are up one day and down the next. One minute you are at the top of the ladder, the next you are at the tail of the snake.'

Pop, not being very fond in any case of snakes-and-ladders, took the whole comparison of himself with that game as yet further proof that things were getting very dicy. With gloom he surrendered the bottle to Nurse Soper, who promptly held it up to the light for critical scrutiny, as if perhaps it were a light Hock or some special vintage. The vintage having been finally passed as apparently satisfactory she then stalked out of the room with it, to return some moments later with the bottle empty.

'Now we must have our bath. Thank you, Mrs Larkin.'

This signal for Ma's dismissal depressed Pop yet further. He was only partially restored by hearing Ma ask from the door:

'Like a cup o' tea? I've got the kettle on.'

'In half an hour,' Nurse Soper said. 'Not before.'

'And put a drop o' cream in, Ma,' Pop said

and for the first time Ma could have sworn he actually gave the minutest of winks at her. 'You know, from that Scotch cow.'

'Now, shall I shave you before we bath or afterwards?' Nurse Soper said, standing above Pop rather like an eager executioner.

'Might as well get my throat cut first,' Pop said and stared, his brief moment of mischief destroyed, at the rose-leaf by the window. Even that, in his gloom seemed to fascinate him no longer.

The last vestige of shaving soap having been wiped by Nurse Soper from his chin, Pop just managed to resist an impulse, rising from his old self, to say that it might not now be a bad idea if *he* shaved *her*, when she started to take his pyjama jacket off, then cover the sponge with soap and then begin to wash him down.

As she leaned closer over him, stern and stony-faced, Pop felt he now knew what it was like to be face to face with one of those distorted gargoyles that you saw glaring and pouting down from above the buttresses of churches. He told himself that he'd never given Edith Pilchester better than a 300–1 chance in a beauty contest, but the Soapy was far down already, in his estimation, among the also-rans. The strenuous diligence of her scrubbing gave him the painful impression that his chest was being scoured by sandpaper: and on purpose at that.

Having washed and dried him, as Pop put it, upstairs, she put back his pyjama jacket and then proceeded to take off his pyjama trousers in readiness to wash him downstairs. The possible direction of the rest of the programme began to fascinate Pop no end. He awaited it with much expectation, even eagerness. It would be a bit of a lark, he couldn't help thinking, when she reached the point of no return, sort of.

Point of no return: he must tell Ma that. He betted she'd heard it called a lot of things but never that. The idea made him, for a brief moment or two, feel quite his old self again. Perhaps a bit of the old buck would work on Soapy if he tried? After all, he reasoned, she must be human underneath, even if it was a long way under.

Anyway, he'd see what the point of no return did for her. According to which way the cat jumped he might get a thick ear or perhaps, on the other hand, persuade her to share a mid-morning snifter or something of that sort. Who knew?

Meanwhile Nurse Soper was busy as a bee in Pop's downstairs field. With diligent energy she scrubbed his calves and feet, minutely ferreting between his toes, and then worked upwards to his thighs. All this time she never spoke a word and it couldn't help crossing Pop's mind that the silence might be one of anticipation. Was it a possible idea that the point of no return might get her in a tizz? You couldn't tell. Interesting thought, though.

At last, after she had scrupulously dried him from feet to thighs, it suddenly seemed to Pop that some sort of skirmish was about to start in the middle. Was the point of no return about to be reached? He found himself not at all unfascinated by the prospect. Might as well be at the ready in case of attack, he told himself, and was on the point of considering a few tactics when he found himself with a wet sponge in his hands.

'Perhaps,' Nurse Soper said, 'you would care to finish off the rest yourself?'

Finish what off? Pop thought and then wondered briefly what might happen if he said no, he wouldn't. She could hardly disregard the call of duty. Perhaps a bit of what Mr Charlton would have called shrewd compromise might be a good tactic after all, he decided, and was prompted, with a slight sign to confess that now he felt a bit tired.

'Surely not too tired to deal with a little thing like that?'

Little thing like what? Pop thought. Did she mind? There were two ways of looking at that. Another bit he'd have to tell Ma, he thought. That would cheer her up.

'Come along, Mr Larkin. We haven't got all day. I've work to do.'

So, apparently, had he, Pop thought, and said:

'Do-it-yourself lark, now, is it? I thought that was your job?'

'Now come along, Mr Larkin. Don't tell me you're incapable — '

Incapable? Pop thought. That was coming the old acid a bit, wasn't it? For crying out gently — incapable, eh? Well not yet, he hoped.

'I'm afraid I can't stand here all day, Mr Larkin. Are you going to do the rest yourself or are you going to leave it as it is?'

84

Going to leave it as it was, Pop said. After all it had been there a good long time.

'I don't *think* I care,' Nurse Soper said, 'for innuendo.'

Nor did he, Pop said with a remarkable flash of his old sharpness. It always gave him wind.

At this point Nurse Soper stalked from the room. The battle was won and lost, whichever way you cared to look at it, and Pop was left to deal with the point of no return alone.

The rest of the day passed miserably. It was a day, largely, of refusal and denial. No, Mr Larkin could not have sugar in his tea; nor butter on his bread. Sugar and animal fats were utterly and absolutely out. No, Mr Larkin could not have a slice of pineapple; the fruit was too acid. As lunch-time drew near Pop detected in himself the return of a slight peckishness and said he rather fancied one of Ma's cheese-puddings and a slice of treacle tart. The result was two dry cream cracker biscuits, three lettuce leaves and a plate of orange jelly.

At each bestowal of these munificent offerings Nurse Soper grew more than ever like a stony gargoyle: ruling not merely with a rod of iron but with one of sharpened steel and a whip too. Even the already infrequent visits of Ma were now much constricted and timed, as it seemed, by stop watch.

'Time we went, Mrs Larkin, time we went.'

During one of these brief and precious conclaves together Pop confessed to Ma that he was going downhill fast. He couldn't stand it much longer. With unaccustomed asperity Ma agreed, then declared she had no doubt where the trouble lay.

'Never had the pleasure, that's what. Never had the pleasure. It makes all that difference.'

You bet your life it did, Pop said and wretchedly wondered if he would ever again have the pleasure himself either.

Down in the kitchen, at last, towards early evening, the crisis between Ma and Nurse Soper became precisely that of two wrestlers standing face to face, ready for a final deciding bout. Ma's temper, which she had tried to keep down all day, was now truly up, so that she viewed Nurse Soper with a certain robust and radiant scorn, ready to put a half-Nelson on her.

Periodically, throughout the day, Nurse Soper had recited, as from Holy Writ, the text not merely for the day but, it appeared, for all and every day.

'Mr Larkin is my patient and as long as he is my patient he will do as and what I say and how and when I say it.'

Ma, fortified by a second large brandy and half in a mind to take one up to Pop and chance the consequences, was at last able to bear the sanctimonious creed no longer.

'And I'll have you know he's my husband and if he's going to die I'll see he dies happy.'

'Your husband is not going to die.'

'No? I'm glad you think so. From where I stand he's gone downhill since morning.'

'Your husband is in no danger.'

'Not while you're about. That's for certain.'

Which, Nurse Soper said with level acidity,

was a most uncalled-for remark.

'Well, you call for it any time and you can have it. Wrapped up. With pink ribbon.'

Nurse Soper snorted. There was a certain vulgarity in the house, she told herself, that was hardly describable in civilized terms. She had already noted the three television sets, including the colour one; the Rolls-Royce and the Jaguar; a vast new cocktail cabinet in the shape of a Venetian gondola, complete with gondolier holding a long champagne swizzle-stick and lamps that actually lit up when you lifted the ice-box lid; the incredible suits of armour, also illuminated, now accompanied by two figures of black boy slaves holding torches; an electric organ which apparently nobody ever played — it hadn't at first occurred to Ma that it could be a possible joke when she had first declared her intention of giving Pop an electric organ for Christmas — and an entirely new bar set up in the style of a French *bistro*, with gay French posters on the walls and sawdust on the floor, just to remind the family of the time, both happy and otherwise, they had once spent across the channel, seeking a breath of French air.

It was all, in Nurse Soper's eyes, of an incredible, stupefying vulgarity. She had in her time worked for the nobility, the diplomatic service, the racing set, even the theatre: but never once, never, for anything quite like this. She supposed it was true that money would buy anything — with one exception: manners.

Hereabouts, in order to preserve sanity if not calm, Ma proceeded to pour herself a third, very

87

handsome brandy. This, with that churchy, gargoyle look of hers, Nurse Soper viewed with stone-cold eye. That was clearly another thing about this house: alcohol had taken charge.

The thought moved her to reflect, aloud, that she wondered if half a bottle of brandy by half past five in the evening was exactly wise?

'I never consider the wise,' Ma said, 'only the why-for. Perhaps if you'd seen your husband as good as dying before your own eyes you'd take a nip or two yourself.'

'Nip? I only hope you know what it's doing to your liver.'

'I haven't been in to see,' Ma said. 'But it hasn't complained yet.'

'Complain it undoubtedly will. One day. With cirrhosis.'

'Who's he when he's at home? It's nothing to what I'll complain with if — '

At this moment, before Ma could finish what was clearly about to be, in wrestling terms, a fall, the outraged Nurse Soper looked sharply at her watch, muttered 'Pills', actually seemed to take wings, and departed.

Ma sat at the table alone, partly in fury, partly near to tears, and swigged hard at her brandy. She was half a mind, she told herself, to phone everybody up and have a party. Everybody: Angela Snow, Jasmine, the Brigadier, even the Miss Barnwells and Edith Pilchester. She'd rope the whole family in too. They'd have a real old beat-up. It was the only thing to save her from going completely stark, staring crackers.

She was about to telephone Mariette and Mr

Charlton to see if they too thought it a good idea when there was a loud and repeated buzzing at the receiving end of Pop's inter-comm.

Ma rushed swiftly upstairs. Pop, it was clear, was in sudden need of her. On the landing outside his bedroom she almost crashed into Nurse Soper — the two vast figures once again meeting as in the opening hold of a bout of wrestling — carrying a large vase of scarlet gladioli. On the floor of the landing other vases stood about: roses, carnations, even the jug of wild flowers gathered by Phyllida and little Oscar.

From the bedroom the voice of a strangely rejuvenated Pop was shouting:

'You meddling virgin old tit, what the ruddy blue hell are you doing with my flowers? Bring 'em back for Christ's sake — quick, afore I bend your arse across the bed. Can you hear me, you old vinegar tits? Bring 'em back!'

Dashing into the bedroom, Ma was astounded to see Pop actually sitting bolt upright in bed, shaking with such righteous fury that she was actually pleased rather than alarmed, as she knew she ought to have been. The fortification by brandy had done its work on her and she was glad.

'Don't let her take my flowers, Ma. Don't let her take 'em. For Gawd's sake.'

Once again, now in the bedroom, Ma and Nurse Soper stood facing each other braced in the very act of physical sparring.

'Bring his flowers back,' Ma said. 'He wants 'em. He needs 'em.'

'I shall do no such thing. It is customary in nursing to remove flowers from bedrooms and wards at night.'

Customary, her foot, Ma said.

'Bum!' Pop said very loudly from the bed.

'Why?' Ma said. 'Why?'

Nurse Soper proceeded to explain that it was all to do with oxygen being taken up by the plants and carbon dioxide being given off at night and so on when Pop shouted 'Bum!' again from his bed, louder than ever.

Icily, a vase of orchids poised archly in her hand, Nurse Soper inquired if that offensive remark was intended for her?

'Yes!' Pop shouted. 'You old fat arse.'

'His flowers are his life,' Ma said. 'He loves 'em under the electric. That's when he has all the pleasure — '

'Very well,' Nurse Soper said, 'it is entirely up to you whether you wish to defer Mr Larkin's progress or not.'

'He'll progress!' Ma said, 'as soon as we get some stale air cleared out!'

Nurse Soper banged down the vase of orchids on the table by the colour television set with such force that the screen actually shook and the delicate pink and cream lips of the orchids trembled.

'In that case,' she said, 'my services are clearly no longer required.'

With totally unexpected vehemence Pop declared that they never were and never had been; and then further informed her, with a flash of the old jocularity that if it didn't quite have

Ma in a fit at least woke her to the refreshing fact that he must be on the mend, that she ought to have been a nun.

'Never want none, never give none and never had none!'

Nurse Soper, with immense cold dignity, swept from the room.

A moment later Ma found herself in Pop's arms. Apart from the pure physical sublimity of the moment Pop was acutely aware of another pleasure. With his sharp, hypersensitive gift of smell he suddenly detected that Ma, languished in his arms, smelled unusually nice.

Ma agreed. 'Want some?'

Pop said he thought he could do it a little justice.

'Double?' Ma said.

'Treble,' Pop said and Ma, unbalanced, began laughing so much that she finally fell off the bed with an elephantine crash and for a long time couldn't get up again.

6

By next morning Nurse Soper had departed, though not without leaving behind her a warning ghost: namely that the business of the heart was like snakes-and-ladders. One day you were up; before you knew it you were down.

That morning Pop was very down.

Even Ma was forced to admit that the set-to with the Soapy had set him back a peg or two. He was down at the tail of the snake. It was very serious. For this she partly blamed herself, partly the brandy. She was used enough to the brandy, but she didn't often lose her temper. Her extreme affability led her to take people much as they were; her motto was live and let live.

'He will *have* to have a nurse,' Dr O'Connor informed her. 'There's no questioning that. It's absolutely essential.'

'Not another Soapy,' Ma begged. 'Not another old bag. That'd finish him off good and proper.'

'Well, we must see what can be done.'

Dr O'Connor had appeared at eight o'clock, in response to Ma's agitated call that Pop was in a state, as she put it, of God-awful pain. The searing crow-bar had again driven its torturing stab through his chest. He lay grey, gasping, fighting a deeper, vaster agony than the first that had struck him a week before. As he lay there, struggling, open-mouthed, eyes dilated, it struck

Ma that he looked exactly like a mouse caught, still alive, in a trap.

While Dr O'Connor was giving him a pain injection the telephone rang. Ma went to answer it and heard the voice of Angela Snow.

Angela had rung up every day, regularly, with fondest felicitations, to inquire of Pop. In those sinuous tones of hers from which it was difficult to keep a certain seductiveness even when inquiring about the sick she always wanted to know how that sweetest pet of a man was? Had they taken the handcuffs off the dear thing yet? — a reference to the fact that Pop had been compulsively driven out, rather like a John the Baptist, into a teetotal wilderness. She simply couldn't bear the wretched thought of it. It was hideous. It had her on her knees.

Ma, in a state of totally uncharacteristic agitation as she answered the telephone, mumbled in answer to Angela's usual seductive inquiry about her dear lamb that Pop was all right, well no he wasn't really, he was a bit down this morning, and finished by murmuring confusedly something about that woman, that old bag.

Angela at once pricked up her ears and said what was that she heard? Woman? Some floosie tampering with his hormones she shouldn't wonder.

Ma didn't comment on this. She knew all about hormones. They were the things that interfered with sex.

Not that she and Pop ever discussed things like that. They never in fact ever used the word sex. They enjoyed a bit of indulgence and all that now and then but that was what it was for, wasn't it? Not to talk about. As a result they tended instinctively to turn away from the word and its all too frequent use in newsprint, on television and on radio. After all there was sex and sex. It was one thing to hear and read about it, and even see it, on television; it was quite another matter what you did in your own home. She and Pop knew that it was all right without bandying a lot of words about it in public. There was an awful lot of bare bosoms and people in bed together naked and a lot of squirming about and biting and all that and there were times, watching television, when she didn't think it was very nice. It struck her as being sort of immoral.

Calming a little, Ma proceeded to explain to Angela Snow that it wasn't some floosie but a nurse she was referring to. The old bag had gone but not before the damage had been done. Now they had got to get another and God knew where.

'*The Angela Snow Distressed Chaps Aid Service Speaking,*' Angela promptly informed Ma, much to Ma's astonishment, in tones both dulcet and dryly mocking. '*You have the worst crises, we solve 'em.*'

'Come again?' Ma said.

'Leave all with me. I know a virginity graduate with First Class Honours who runs a sort of Sainted Aunt thing — gets your smoked salmon for you and your Pill and sees grannie across London and knows where all the nicest tarts live and acts as general dogsbody for anything from trial marriage to baby-sitting for a crocodile. Fabulous gal. What you haven't got she'll see you soon have.'

Ma, being in her present state of distress not quite able to grasp all this, merely murmured did that mean she could get a nurse for Pop and if so how soon?

'*Toute suite*, darling. She'd even get you a dirty-weekend with the Foreign Secretary if that's what you wanted.'

'That'll be the day,' Ma said, knowing who the Foreign Secretary was and added, rather ambiguously: 'How soon can you let me know?'

'I'm practically on the hot line to the dear gal now. I'll get her out of bed if necessary and if I can find the bed. She has a slight propensity towards nocturnal wander-lust at times.'

Ma was slightly stupefied by such language; but by and large, thought she got what it meant.

'I'll buzz you back,' Angela said. 'Not to fret. Meantime give the dear man my fondest and tell him yes. I couldn't come and hold the frail hand for a time I suppose? I long to see him, the pet. It's been an age. I'm an-hungered and a-thirst.'

Ma thanked Angela very much but said she was sorry: the doctor still said no visitors.

'No? Not even the dear Edith?'

The conversation with Angela was such that Ma now actually laughed. Edith? — she must remember to tell her about Edith some day. Not now though. There wasn't time. That was a laugh all right. That would bring her on.

Angela now laughed too, so that it was as if a whole carillon were in full peal at the other end of the line. She didn't want bringing on, however, she informed Ma. She wanted holding back.

'Bye,' she said at last. '*The Distressed Chaps Service* will be back. Meanwhile fondest salutations and all that. *Avec* knobs. Bless.'

Pop, deeply drugged again, slept through the morning. The day was one of those wrapped in soft, mizzling humidity, when minutest myriad drops of night rain still clung glistening to every leaf and blade and branch, undispersed by sun. Mistily, like pearled head-dresses, spiders' webs had been woven everywhere, so that Ma, rather as Pop had done, felt herself enmeshed in a strange sort of muslin drowsiness as she again engaged in a heavy session of cooking in the kitchen, always listening for a buzz on Pop's inter-comm., never quite sure whether silence from it was bad news or not.

It was just after ten o'clock when the telephone rang. Again it was Angela Snow.

'Hullo, darling. *Distressed Chaps* again. Sorry to have been an age. I always thought Fridays was her Cypriot night, but she's switched, it seems. Found her with a Korean eventually. In Windsor of all places. However, all is well. All fixed.'

Ma felt so relieved that for one desperate moment she thought of brandy again and then swiftly rejected it and told herself to be sensible.

'I only hope she's not like the last. Can't do with another like her.'

'Sweet child, I'm told. Level-headed, strong sensible shoes type, unfussy and competent. How's that?'

Ma indicated that she heard it with relief. She

was glad and grateful.

'Trust my girl friend. She may go in for sport but she's got the business head all right. You want it, she'll get it. Anything more I can do for you, darling? How is the dear lamb anyway?'

Ma, saying that there was nothing more, thanked Angela again and said that Pop was sleeping.

'Splendid. Bless him. Oh! her name's Trevelyan. The nurse, I mean, I think she's colonial or something.'

Colonial? Ma said. She hoped that didn't mean she was black? She didn't mind lending Pop out a bit to most types, even to Angela and the luscious Jasmine Brown, but she wasn't sure about these coloured bits. She well remembered Pop watching some African tribe on television with all the girls dancing about with bare titties and all that and how the effect on him had been something chronic. No, she was a bit against black bosoms now she thought of it.

'Oh! no. White. Australian, I think. And she'll arrive bang on the dot at twelve o'clock. By train. Can you meet? If not, darling I'll be glad to cope.'

Ma, again thanking Angela, said that she thought Mariette could well meet the train.

'Splendid. Anything more I can send the dear man? I'm still trying to get those mangoes and passion-fruit but those swabs in London still won't play. Disappointing. I thought the passion-fruit would be much in his line.'

Ma confessed she didn't think Pop had much time for passion just now, as things were.

97

'Devastating thought. Jolly unfair. Like a nightingale going off song or something. 'Thou wast not born for — ' Good God, what am I on about? It's jolly unfair, anyway. Shouldn't happen. Well, if you need *The Distressed Chaps* again you know where I am. Farewell for now. Kiss the slumbering forehead for me. Farewell, darling, farewell.'

Behind the smooth, honeyed tongue of Angela Snow there lay something very human, warm and practical. It was much after Ma's own heart. In consequence she was able to go through the rest of the humid, mizzling morning, enmeshed in its bright spider webs, with faith restored.

She was further comforted, about half past eleven, by the unexpected arrival of the Reverend Candy, accompanied by Primrose, still wearing the briefest of mini-skirts, this time in brilliant turquoise. The Reverend Candy had been picking raspberries again. Primrose was carrying two vegetable marrows, young and pale cream, one under each arm, in a position that the Reverend Candy found more than slightly disturbing.

'Oh! hullo,' Ma said. 'I didn't know you two were here. When did you creep in?'

'You were on the phone when Mr Candy arrived.'

Well, it was very nice to see Mr Candy, Ma said. Mr Candy had discarded all clerical gear for the morning and was dressed in a surprisingly ochre-yellow open-necked shirt and pale blue trousers. And how was Mr Candy?

Mr Candy responded with a positively

spring-like enthusiasm that he was well, very well indeed, in the pink. He was only sorry that he understood the same couldn't be said for Mr Larkin.

'Have a cheese-straw,' Ma said. 'Oh! he's having a nice long sleep. It'll do him the world of good. And he's got a new nurse coming.'

Mr Candy helped himself to several of Ma's cheese-straws, still warm from the oven. Primrose said she would get the raspberries ready for lunch. What else were they having?

'Well, I've got a roast leg of pork with stuffing, braised onions, new potatoes and carrots, baked potatoes and broad beans and we can have the marrow with cheese sauce too if you like.'

To Ma's way of thinking there was no sense in going hungry even in times of extreme crisis. You'd got to keep your strength up. You'd got to eat. Didn't Mr Candy agree?

Mr Candy agreed with the utmost cordiality. He already felt in torture. The very smell of roasting pork and stuffing was itself enough to drive one crazy. He could actually hear the pork and its crackling sizzling in the oven and the echo of this most delicious of sounds seemed to go hissing through his insides like some exquisite set of variations played on fragile strings.

By this time the rain, never more than a lightly clinging mist, had cleared, leaving a sky gently breaking into sun.

'Who's this new nurse?' Primrose said. 'I hope she's better than the old bar of soap.'

Ma, now peeling and cutting the two young vegetable marrows into shapes less disturbing to

99

Mr Candy, said that Angela Snow had managed to get hold of her. Ma understood she was a nice, solid, level-headed, sensible sort of girl and no nonsense about her.

'That sounds about right,' Primrose said. 'We can't have Pop boiling over any more. He needs peace and quiet from now on.'

And peace and quiet, Ma said, was what he was going to get.

Presently, tortured still further by the fragrance of roast pork and stuffing, Mr Candy started to say that he thought he really ought to be going. It was the better part of valour, he told himself, or something. Ma, however, cut him very short, and rather severely. Go, her foot. How was all the roast pork going to get eaten up if Mr Candy didn't do his bit? No, no, she said, she wouldn't have Mr Candy going. There was more than enough for everybody, she assured him. Gracious, they'd got to eat, hadn't they? she demanded of him in slightly indignant accents, as if it were some sort of crime not to.

Though protesting diligently, Mr Candy in fact needed no second asking and thanked Ma in terms of generosity that he could only hope matched her own. He secretly confided to himself that he couldn't have borne that torture much longer. It would certainly have had him down.

'Well,' Ma said, 'that settles that. You and Primrose can lay the table. There'll be five of us for lunch. That includes Mariette and the new nurse, Little Oscar and Phyllida have gone off to the seaside with the postman's wife and her two.

How about a snifter all round?'

Mr Candy murmured 'excellent' and, modest as always said he would settle for a glass of sherry. Ma, remembering the near disasters of brandy, thought she possibly ought to draw her horns in a bit and helped herself to a gin-and-tonic very nearly large enough to wash in. Primrose declared she wouldn't have anything; it was alcohol that put the weight on, a statement that made Ma look quite concerned. She didn't believe in losing weight. Very bad thing. It wasn't long since that Pop, watching her dress one morning and observing that the rotundities of her figure didn't seem quite so jolly as usual, inquired with some anxiety if Ma was slimming or something, a remark which made Ma shiningly indignant. Did he mind? Slimming, her foot. She liked her figure as it was and was going to keep it that way. It was all hers, wasn't it? All 55–55–55 of it.

The train evidently being slightly late, it was one o'clock before Mariette's car was heard drawing up outside the house.

'Now for it,' Primrose said.

'She'd better be good,' Ma said, 'else it'll be marching orders.'

Some few moments later Ma, Primrose and the Reverend Candy appeared to have been suddenly shattered by some dire explosion. Mr Candy actually felt the onset of an acute paralysis and even Ma, for fully half a minute, had no word.

'This is Sister Trevelyan,' Mariette said. 'Sorry we're a bit late. The train was held up.'

'Hullo,' Sister Trevelyan said with only the very slightest of Australian accents in her low warm voice.

'Hullo,' Ma said too. Even she, never at a loss for a word, could find no other to say.

Sister Trevelyan was rather less like a girl than a big, smooth, handsome chestnut mare. Her gleaming hair was neither auburn nor blonde. Her eyes were two black olives, glistening with melting brilliance. The sensational curve of her splendid shoulders was only matched by the further splendours of a superlative bust. Her legs were long, brown and athletic. Bronzed, magnificent in carriage, smooth as a deer in movement, she had altogether the look of some prize and lovely animal entered in a show.

Even Ma, who was ever ready to make her daughters odds-on favourites in any beauty contest you cared to name, was fully prepared to admit, even if not aloud, that in Sister Trevelyan you had a right starter and one with a bit of pedigree. Nothing virginal about it either, she told herself, having a quick eye in these matters.

'Like a drink?' she managed to say at last. 'Sherry, gin, whisky, bitter lemon — '

'Brandy,' Sister Trevelyan said, 'if there is.'

There certainly was, Ma said, mightily pleased. Girl after her own heart.

'Cheers,' Sister Trevelyan said, raising a glass containing the largest brandy she had ever been privileged to see. 'Not supposed to drink on duty, but I'm not quite on duty yet, I suppose. How is my patient?'

'Sleeping,' Ma said, 'like a dormouse.'

'Should I take a peep at him?'

No, no, Ma said. Lunch first. They must all have lunch first. She was all ready to dish up.

'Shall we have wine, Ma?' Primrose said. 'And if so, what?'

Of course they were going to have wine, Ma said, with no little indignation. They always did, didn't they? The idea of not having wine was on the verge of shocking. And what sort? Better have a choice, she thought: drop o' red and a drop o' white. She thought the Beaujolais and the Liebfraumilch. Pop always had a choice. It was only good manners.

'Mr Candy'll get the corks out, won't you, Mr Candy?' Primrose said and then, finding him almost sightlessly transfixed by the vision of Sister Trevelyan, gave him a look of a certain critical severity. 'Corks, corks — the wine — draw the corks — '

'Oh! yes, yes, of course,' Mr Candy said and as if to excuse his dilatory lapse added, at once drawn into a state of fresh hypnosis by the incredible figure of Sister Trevelyan, something about a day without wine being like a day without sunshine.

It was now Ma's turn to look at him with some severity. Shrewdly detecting his eye positively dithering over Sister Trevelyan, she wondered if there wasn't something behind that last remark?

As if the stunning surprise of Sister Trevelyan wasn't enough, Ma produced another as they all sat down to lunch.

'Pork or pheasant, Mr Candy? or both? I

popped a couple of pheasants in too just in case,' though in case of what Ma didn't say. 'Remembered I'd got 'em out of the deep-freeze last night. Have both if you like. Or start with pheasant?'

To be caught between the succulent tortures of both pork and pheasant was exactly like being caught between the torturing beauty of Primrose on one hand and the new nurse on the other. Mr Candy, for some moments, simply didn't know where he was.

'Really, honestly I don't know. It's an awfully difficult choice. I really don't mind — both or one — '

Rather tartly Primrose suddenly urged him to keep his mind on his work, which Mr Candy at once proceeded rather guiltily to do.

Ma, who was carving while Mariette poured the wine, chopped a pheasant in two and put a half on Mr Candy's plate, together with a vast slice of pork and crackling, adding that he could come again as soon as he'd got outside of that lot.

'Wine, Ma?' Mariette said. 'Red or white?'

Ma said no thanks, she didn't think she'd have wine. She'd have a Guinness instead. She needed building up.

Having now served Sister Trevelyan with exactly the same portions as Mr Candy, Ma proceeded deftly to carve for herself and the girls, giving herself the knuckle end of the pork, her favourite bit. Her Guinness having now been brought in by Primrose, who suddenly seemed a bit aloof-like, Ma thought, for some reason, if not even toffee-nosed, Ma raised her glass to Sister Trevelyan and said:

'Well, cheers and welcome,' and added that she hoped the pheasants were tender. They ought to be: they were both females.

The explanation behind all this was that Mr Charlton and Montgomery, Ma's eldest son, had now gone into the pheasant lark. This was another of Pop's ideas and a very good lark it had turned out to be. Pop had shrewdly noticed that England was rapidly becoming populated with a new kind of country gent. These invaded the countryside, if they didn't live there already, with one avowed intention: namely that of shooting pheasants. The fact that you could buy a pheasant for twenty-five bob at the poulterer's, and ready plucked, was no sort of deterrent; it was far more fun to shoot them on freezing winter days, in miserable discomfort, at ten quid a time. As all the pheasants were near-tame when let loose in the autumn they constantly flew so low when driven from copse and hedgerow that the shooters not only massacred them without mercy but all too frequently shot each other as well.

As for Pop, he vastly preferred to sit in his own garden in comfort and shoot whatever of his neighbours' stray birds happened to fly over. This sensible habit finally inspired him to reason that because so many birds were shot an even greater number were needed to replace them, since the population of shooters was already increasing every year, in spite of a growing tendency on their part to kill each other off. It was the old law of supply and demand again, Pop told himself. You couldn't go wrong.

So now Montgomery and Mr Charlton were in the pheasant lark: the raising of eggs and poults, a business that to Pop's native wisdom made a great deal of sense. This new passion for having a place in the country had brought so many mugs out of hiding that even Pop, sometimes, thought it wasn't quite fair. It was daylight robbery. It was cruel to take their money.

'And what's your other name?' Ma said to Sister Trevelyan. 'We can't call you Sister all the time, can we?'

'Vanessa.'

'Oh! lovely name,' Ma said. Oh! she liked that. She really genuinely loved Vanessa.

This friendly genuine enthusiasm of Ma's was not reflected in Primrose, who picked up a piece of crackling in her fingers and snapped at it loudly with her teeth.

'Your first visit over here?' Mr Candy said.

Oh! no, she'd been here before, Sister Trevelyan said. Last year she'd been all over the Continent too. France, Spain, Italy, Germany, Switzerland. She'd really been around.

Silently Mariette betted she had, then exchanged a low, calculated glance with Primrose that was not precisely friendly.

Totally unaware of these feminine exchanges Mr Candy ate and drank his delicious, tortured way through lunch. Not only was the food delectable in every way — the choice between the excellence of pork and that of pheasant could only be described as being between manna and the food of the gods — but the Liebfraumilch, with which he had started the meal, had its virtues too. When Ma finally reminded him that 'he hadn't got no Burgundy' Mr Candy agreed with almost apologetic alacrity and at once proceeded to sample several glasses of Beaujolais. That was pretty good stuff too, he told himself. More body, more fire. He could fairly feel it singing through his veins.

Body and fire: the words were, perhaps, not inappropriate. Just as he had been tortured and torn between the succulence of pork and pheasant so he continued to be even more enraptured by the opposing bodies and fire of Primrose and Sister Trevelyan. Under the influence of the two wines, it sometimes seemed, the two bodies actually melted together. They were marvellously, celestially fused.

'Vanessa — at least I hope I may call you Vanessa — I haven't got my dog-collar on but I am the parson here — and I was just wondering what denomination you might be?'

'Oh! no denomination,' Sister Trevelyan said and gave a laugh of such honeyed physical richness that even Angela Snow could scarcely have rivalled it. 'I'm what we call in Australia a 'oncer'. I went once and never again.'

'We must see if we can't convert you.'

And what exactly might that mean? Primrose thought and sharply bit at another piece of crackling like a sniper biting at a bullet.

It finally became clear to Ma that the air was growing more and more electric with tension.

The fire was in Mr Candy's eye; you could see it. And the look in those of Primrose wasn't exactly yesterday's ashes either.

It was time to clear the decks and change the subject, she told herself. She didn't want any more truck with tension. She'd had enough of tension with Soapy yesterday.

As she served raspberries, strawberries, meringues, treacle tart and mixed fruit pie, all with cream, she pointedly remarked that she thought the raspberries would only just go round. Somebody had better pick some more this afternoon.

Ten minutes later Primrose, as if more in response to command rather than suggestion, went upstairs to change into what Mr Candy had come to think of as her 'raspberry blouse' and finally came downstairs wearing a garment that seemed composed of nothing more than two children's handkerchiefs, pink and practically transparent, leaving a greater area of midriff than ever exposed.

At the same time Ma had deemed it tactically wise to suggest that it was time for Nurse Trevelyan to go up and see her patient, leaving Mariette to clear the table. She could only hope that Pop was feeling strong.

The afternoon was turning out to be very warm and muggy. It was one of those dog days of July when you felt you needed to find somewhere cool, silent and in the shade, only to sleep.

This was the very thought in the mind of Primrose as she and Mr Candy reached the avenues of raspberry canes, red and fragrant with fruit in the sun.

Here Mr Candy, groping among the canes, his legs deliciously unstable, stretched out a hand in order to steady himself and instead found it grasping Primrose's smooth naked shoulder.

Great God, he thought, how warm the flesh was.

★   ★   ★

Soon Primrose was inspired to suggest that it was becoming too hot to gather raspberries. It seemed slow work, she thought. It took a long time to fill a basket.

'Ah! well, two for the price of one,' Mr Candy said, *apropos* of nothing much, except possibly the fact that, with benefit of wine, he could now see double. 'Aren't they large too? Marvellous.'

They certainly were, Primrose said, and pressed another huge luscious one to her lips, so that they too seemed to be smeared with the crimson of new-pressed wine.

'That pheasant was pretty marvellous too,' Mr Candy said, by no means for the first time. He would never forget that pheasant: food of the gods. Manna, indeed.

'Talking of pheasants,' Primrose said. 'Have you seen where Montgomery and Charley raise them — I mean the eggs and the chicks? It's in the field beyond the wood.'

'Oh! so that's what they're for, those pens. I often wondered.'

'That's what they're for.'

As he and Primrose started to walk across the meadow the great conflicton in Mr Candy's mind was inspired not only by the memory and effect of pheasant and wine but by a recollection that went much further back in time.

It was of the occasion when he had first been passionately kissed by Primrose as a girl of fourteen and she had quoted to him, with an exhilarating earthiness that amounted to sheer, deliberate seduction, Donne's lines 'I wonder by my troth what thou and I did till we loved'.

Ever since that devastating moment, to be followed not long later by others still more devastating when he had been called upon to christen her and the rest of the Larkin brood in a sort of holy package deal, Ma and Pop having overlooked the fact of having the ceremony performed when they were in infancy, he had tried to avoid Primrose, not because he didn't like her — quite the contrary — but because she frightened him cold stiff. Now the crisis of Pop's heart attack had brought them together again.

The trouble with Primrose was that she was not only the most beautiful and earthy of all the earthy Larkins; she was clever too. She found much of herself reflected and expressed in the poets. This found Mr Candy all too often out of his depth, in more ways than one. Some years of curacy in London's East End dock areas had prepared him for many things but not for rural seductresses who disarmed you not by physical means alone but by quoting Herrick and Donne, two gentlemen who didn't, as Mr Candy had once remarked, cut much ice in Stepney.

'It's getting hotter and hotter,' Primrose said. 'Shall we sit down and rest a minute? Can you smell the honeysuckle?'

Before Mr Candy could give any answer about the honeysuckle Primrose was lying down, not sitting, in the shade of the woodside. Rather like a man not too anxious to sit too close to a roaring fire, in case he got roasted, Mr Candy sat down some two yards apart from her, confronted by a wide expanse of naked sun-brown midriff in the centre of which the navel dwelt darkly, ripely pulsating.

Though trying desperately not to look at it too obviously Mr Candy found that frequent recurrences of his double vision merely had the effect of providing him with two navels, as it were, for the price of one. That the price itself had the prospect of being heavy was reflected in a sudden huge sigh, which caused Primrose to inquire of him, with a slow voluptuous look, if he was tired?

'Oh! no, not tired. Not tired at all. It's merely that it's — after all that — you know, the food, the wine — it's all so — so heavenly.'

'The honeysuckle's heavenly too, isn't it?'

Intoxicating was the word for honeysuckle that crossed Mr Candy's mind like a wave of the sublime fragrance itself but he merely murmured:

'Yes, heavenly.'

'Come and lie down.'

Mr Candy presently found himself stretched full length on the grass, less perhaps in obedience to another slow voluptuous look of invitation than in the sheer relief of being able to look up at the purity of the sky above rather than down at the darkness of the navel below.

In its overpowering sultriness the afternoon was hushed. There was no note of birdsong. Mr Candy wondered once or twice about the young pheasants and where were they? and then let such a mundane thought drift down the stream of the afternoon like a light fallen feather.

'There's a line in Blake that I keep thinking of,' Primrose said at last. 'You know Blake?'

Dozily Mr Candy confessed that his acquaintance with Blake was slight, always supposing he had the right Blake — 'England's Green and Pleasant Land' and all that?

'That's him. It isn't all in the poetry, though. The verse. Did you ever read 'The Marriage of Heaven and Hell'?'

No, Mr Candy said, he feared he hadn't read 'The Marriage of Heaven and Hell'; and with trepidation he wondered what was coming next.

Primrose soon enlightened him.

''As the caterpillar chooses the fairest leaves to lay her eggs on, so the priest lays his curse on the fairest joys.''

Mr Candy was silent. Dreamily spoken though the words were, with an intoxication of sound even more soothing than the smell of honeysuckle, he couldn't quite make up his mind whether he was being educated, teased, or merely got at.

'Isn't that beautiful? And true too — as true now as the day it was written.'

'Oh! no, I can't have that,' Mr Candy was spurred to sudden mild indignation. 'I think that's jolly unfair.'

'And how can it be jolly unfair?'

'Because it is. It just is.'

'But how? Just how?'

'Well, in the first place — '

'In the first place, what? The caterpillar chooses the fairest leaves to lay her eggs on, doesn't she?'

'Not always. Sometimes they lay them on nettles.'

'In which case the priest would have to be careful he didn't get stung.'

Mr Candy found himself utterly at a loss to say anything in answer to this. That was the trouble with Primrose — she was so awfully unpredictable. You never knew quite what form she would appear in next. He wasn't at all sure she wasn't like a caterpillar herself, smooth and golden and sinuous, creeping and entwining herself about him, weaving a sort of cocoon. It was the caterpillar that weaved the cocoon, wasn't it? or was it the chrysallis? He didn't really know. He was getting terribly lost.

'I suppose it was actually the next bit that you thought was jolly unfair, wasn't it?'

'The next bit?'

'"So the priest lays his hands on the fairest joys."'

'Curse, you said the first time. Not hand. Curse.'

'No, hand I think it is. 'Hand on the fairest joys.''

Mr Candy felt desperately confused. He was sure it was curse; he was sure she was making it all up. It was all deliberate. She was deliberately misquoting. It was all jolly unfair. Curse was what she had said, curse.

Then, just as he was trying to express at least some of these protestations into words, he discovered that she had suddenly abandoned her prostrate position and was sitting up, bending over him, closely.

This was bad enough; but worse followed a moment later. He knew suddenly that she was reading his thoughts. He had always said of her that you could fairly hear her thinking with the pores of her skin, but now she was reading his mind. She had this awfully intuitive thing that was all the more terrifying because it wasn't really conscious.

It wasn't only the mind that was intuitive, either; it was the body too. The body was now very close to him. The upper of the only two garments she was wearing was as flimsy as a pair of butterfly wings. They were fully spread and her two big, firm young breasts, now close to his face, seemed about to fall out of them.

'I know what you were thinking,' she said. 'You were thinking I was a caterpillar.'

'No, no, I wasn't. Really. Never. I never thought of you as a caterpillar.'

'Then what did you think of me as?'

'I don't know — really I never thought — '

'A butterfly?'

There she went again: reading his thoughts.

'I hoped you'd think of me as a butterfly. They're so nice, don't you think, butterflies?'

Yes, yes, Mr Candy agreed. He knew that. He knew about butterflies. They were beautiful, very beautiful.

114

'And they lay the eggs.'

'Oh! do they? I thought it was the caterpillar. Isn't that what Blake said? The caterpillar — on the fairest flower — '

'Blake was dotty.'

'I thought you said he was wonderful.'

'All wonderful people are dotty. Don't you think so? Genius and all that. Don't you think so?'

Mr Candy was about to say that he thought he'd need notice of that question when he felt Primrose stroking his nose. Her fingers tickled him softly and he lifted his hands to brush her own away. In doing so he caught his own hands against her breasts and in a moment of stuttering confusion said he was sorry.

'Whatever for?'

Mr Candy didn't know whatever for. It was all the fault of Blake. Perhaps he'd better get back to Blake.

'Now is it the butterfly or the caterpillar which — '

'Don't take your hands away. There's nothing there to bite you.'

Great God, that's where she was wrong, Mr Candy thought, that's where she was wrong.

'After all, who brought all this up, anyway?'

Mr Candy, who wasn't aware of having brought anything up, now felt a surge of excitement run through him like a spear. What on earth was she talking about, bringing things up? Here he was, enmeshed in a cocoon of her own making and all this talk of Blake and caterpillars and flowers and eggs and all that and

115

she was trying to blame him, Mr Candy. Trying to make him the guilty party. Whereas it was she who was to blame; it was all her fault. No, it wasn't. It was the fault of the two of them, she and that fellow Blake. It was all a conspiracy.

Her breasts were warm. His hands trembled as he took them in his own.

In that exquisitely unbearable moment Primrose kissed him, but neither too long nor too lusciously but rather as if letting him take the first delicate bite from the outer flesh of a peach. Mr Candy felt all his senses water; and then she said:

'You know something else Blake wrote?'

At that moment, feeling one of her hands free one of his and take it in a long drifting line of exploration down her body until it came to rest on, so to speak, the equatorial line, Mr Candy couldn't have cared less what Blake had written.

''The road of excess leads to the palace of wisdom.''

Great God, Mr Candy thought, he didn't doubt it. He was, without question, on the road of excess already. Whether it was wise or not he wouldn't know, it was impossible to tell, until later.

'Well,' Primrose said at long last, with a slow sigh, 'that was nice while it lasted.'

Mr Candy, with a great thundering of excess pounding through his blood, fully agreed. He was only sorry it hadn't lasted longer.

'Is there any reason why it couldn't?'

Borne far down on the road of excess Mr Candy found himself overcome by an earthy,

116

delicious sleepiness. He was woken out of it not long later by the near distant voice of a cowman calling his cattle home across a meadow and this earthiest of country sounds woke him at last to a new consciousness of the naked body lying beside him. It seemed to him very, very beautiful.

'From now on,' Primrose at last said, 'for 'curse' read 'hands'.'

'Agreed. Or blessing.'

'Blessing, I think. I'm sorry I fibbed.'

'And is it the caterpillar or the butterfly? — '

Primrose laughed with that deep midsummer laugh of hers.

'Perhaps it's both. Perhaps it's a bit of cross-pollination.'

Mr Candy laughed too. There she went again: thinking through the pores of her skin, going deep to the heart of the matter.

'After all,' she said, laughing again, 'that's what everything's all about, isn't it? Cross-pollination?'

That indeed, as Mr Candy had discovered, was what everything was all about: a sort of sublime, celestial cross-pollination.

Long later, he thought at quite six o'clock, Primrose got up and dressed herself — that is if you could call putting on two garments a process of dressing — and Mr Candy watched her with all the minute and fascinated attention that Pop always gave to Ma on similar if slightly more complicated occasions.

'I'm a bit surprised at you,' Primrose said. 'Where did you learn all that?'

All what? Mr Candy started to say and then,

117

rather airily, as a man recently returned from pleasurable conquest, said he didn't quite know. He could only suppose he'd picked it up as he went along.

At which Primrose laughed her rich midsummer laugh again.

'That's the best way,' she said. 'Next time you'll be able to play it by ear.'

'Certainly not,' Mr Candy said. 'I shall play it the way we played it today.'

7

It was soon after five o'clock that same afternoon when Ma, having provided Sister Trevelyan with what she called 'a rough cup', consisting of tea, buttered scones, shortbread, iced buns, plain and plum cake, four sorts of jam, chocolate biscuits and strawberries-and-cream, together with tomato ketchup, in case she might want a little with the iced buns, as the Larkins often did, remarked that she was sorry she'd had to knock it all up rather quick but Dr O'Connor was coming at a quarter past five, before he began surgery.

'In that case I'll go up and see that my patient's fit and ready,' Sister Trevelyan said, 'and got his clean bib and tucker on.'

'I'll come with you.'

Ma, always quick to sum up people in the shortest possible time, had already decided that Sister Trevelyan came, as Pop might have said, from the right stable. She was without doubt a girl after her own heart. She was also more than good on the eye. If out of uniform she looked very much like some splendid gold-brown mare, in uniform she looked more like a statue of one, the lines of her figure sculptured, smooth and polished, purest snow-white marble. The uniform also gave the impression that she was, both in shape and bearing, even more magnificent. There was something little short of sensational in the carving of the bust, something classical about the brilliant gold-auburn helmet of hair.

Some minutes before this Pop had woken at last from a long drugged slumber with that strange uplifting feeling of resurrection that he had experienced before, the wondering sensation of having come back from the dead. Through the divisions of the drawn curtains of his bedroom he could just discern thin swords of gold brilliance tipped with blue. He lay watching them without daring to move, fearful that pain might come back.

Pain didn't come back and he closed his eyes, seeming to float gently in a vacuum. In this state of light suspense he presently heard voices. He then opened his eyes, only to feel that he was now the victim of a great illusion.

It seemed to him that the ghost of Soapy had incredibly come back, much enlarged, whiter, shining, in readiness to haunt him. He instinctively slipped a little lower under the bed clothes. Then Ma said:

'This is Sister Trevelyan, Pop. Our new nurse.'

There was something immensely reassuring about that one word 'our'. Pop lifted an eye over the edge of the sheets. The passing of one illusion left him with another. Soapy had somehow undergone an astonishing, stunning transformation.

The creature into which Soapy had been transformed quietly moved towards him and then actually stretched out a hand.

'Hullo, Mr Larkin. What on earth have *you* been up to?'

Very personal, those words, Pop thought, very

intimate: as if he and this amazing creature had known each other closely for a long time. They gave Pop not merely the feeling that an old friend had turned up but that the friend was one full of the warmest affection.

Her hand touched him. It too was warm. Then she actually allowed him to hold it for what seemed a long time. His own hypersensitive touch responded to this so sharply that she in turn responded by squeezing his fingers gently, at the same time giving him a slow soft smile.

This so comforted and brightened Pop that he was briefly moved to joke.

'You the new medicine?'

'I'm the new medicine.'

'Perfick. Three times a day in water?'

'Four times if you don't behave yourself.'

Pop gave her one of those quick looks of his in which there was faintly visible a touch of the old self.

'Behave? My blood pressure's up already.'

'Then,' she said, 'we'd better see about getting it down, hadn't we?'

She gave a light laugh. Her fingers moved to his pulse. While she was busy taking his pulse Pop was able to give brief study to her splendid bust, her olive-black eyes and the gold-auburn fringes of hair creeping in burnished curls from under her cap. These having proved excitingly satisfactory, a great thought crossed his mind.

What price the point of no return now? he thought, the do-it-yourself lark? Inspired by possible answers he told himself that he felt a lot better already. Life was getting interesting again.

121

She had cheered him up no end.

'Where have they been keeping you all this long time?' he said.

'Australia.'

'I had an uncle went out there once. Years ago. Good looking feller. Probably chased your mother.'

'Now, now,' Ma said. 'None of that. I told you he'd be cheeky, didn't I, Sister.'

Sister Trevelyan laughed again and astonished Ma by saying she liked cheeky patients. They were inclined to get on. It was the groaners she couldn't do with.

'Well, don't you encourage him too much,' Ma said. 'He'll be running you round like the hens before you know it, trying to make you lay.'

For a few moments Sister Trevelyan lost what little dignity she had and shrieked with laughter. Ma laughed like a drain too and said she really hadn't meant it quite like that, not the laying part anyway.

'I'll bet,' Pop said, looking at Sister Trevelyan's rich sun-brown skin, 'you'd lay nice big brown 'uns if you did.'

'Now, now,' Ma said. 'You've got him cheeky already, Sister. Just you calm down, Sid Larkin. You'll have your blood pressure up a lot more by the time the doctor gets here and then where will you be?'

'Bottom of the snake,' Pop said.

'Perhaps a little wash might be a good thing before the doctor comes,' Sister Trevelyan said. 'Just a freshener.'

Perfick, Pop thought. Just what he was waiting for. He watched the upper half of Sister

Trevelyan glide smoothly from the room, wondering at the same time what the bottom half looked like. If it matched the top half there was no doubt she'd be perfick too. Unfortunately, lying on one pillow, he couldn't yet see the bottom half.

While Sister Trevelyan had gone to the bathroom to fetch soap and towels and warm water Ma deemed it a prudent moment to take the opportunity of giving Pop a brief lecture.

'Now none of your hanky-panky larks with this one, Sid Larkin.' It was always a very serious matter when Ma called him Sid Larkin. Sometimes he knew he even had to watch out when she called him 'young man', but Sid Larkin was serious indeed. 'She's a very nice girl and she comes of a very good family. Her father's a very high-up brain surgeon in Melbourne. Don't you start any of your saucy tricks with her. She's not that type.'

Never crossed his mind, Pop said, never even crossed his mind.

'And it better hadn't, either. Besides, there's the ethics.'

Pop didn't quite know what Ma meant by ethics. He only hoped it wasn't something catching.

'What I mean is don't you try one of your Edith Pilchesters on her. You know what I mean.'

Pop murmured something about it being a different technique altogether with Edith and then asked how Edith was? He'd missed his friends: Edith, the Brigadier, Angela, Jasmine and all the rest. None of them had been allowed to see him yet. It was worse than awful. It was even as bad as not drinking.

'Nobody's seen her much since what I told you about. She's sort of been in *purdah*.'

At this Pop gave the strongest, healthiest laugh that had passed his lips since he had been first laid low.

'And whatever is there so funny about that?' Ma said.

'I thought you said in pod, Ma. I thought you said in pod. That'll be the day.'

'Outrageous,' Ma said and then proceeded to laugh twice as heartily as Pop, shaking all over like a jelly.

There was still a trace of laughter on Pop's face as Sister Trevelyan started to wash him. The first few strokes of the sponge were like balm. It was as different from Soapy as wine from vinegar. The only worrying problem was how to keep his eyes shut so that the soap shouldn't get into them and at the same time keep them open enough to allow him as frequently as possible to look at Sister Trevelyan's face, held just above his own.

He didn't suppose she'd be doing a point of no return job this evening, he told himself. That would be something to look forward to tomorrow. But it was all very pleasant, very soothing, very beautiful. To be back from the dead yet again was marvellous enough in itself. To be back and resurrected by a face like that of Sister Trevelyan was little short of a miracle.

'Now is there anything else you'd like me to do for you?'

Normally such a leading question would have inspired Pop to very interesting replies but now, remembering the severity of Ma's injunctions about his behaviour, he merely shook his head, disregarding all possible jocularity about the bottle and said no, thank you and shook his head.

'I thought I heard a car,' Ma said and went from the room, taking off her pinafore designed in bright orange poppies and purple butterflies as she went. 'I expect it's the doctor now.'

'Good boy,' Sister Trevelyan said. 'You look fine.'

With the smile of a goddess she ran her hands smoothly, gently and warmly across Pop's forehead and Pop could have wept.

During the next week or so the arrival of Sister Trevelyan had two main revolutionary effects. To the resurgence of Pop himself — he was now allowed to lie a little less horizontally, propped by one pillow — was added an astonishing revival among his friends. Where no visitors at all had been allowed, dozens now seemed to spring up from everywhere, like mushrooms appearing overnight.

The very first of his visitors was his old friend the Brigadier. Ill-shod in a pair of old white cricket boots tied with brown laces, a cream shantung jacket of which one pocket was entirely missing and the other patched up with what looked suspiciously like an old face flannel, his much-washed University tie, a brown straw hat that looked like a beehive riddled by buckshot and a pair of cream trousers, once long, that had been cut down to just below knee length for coolness in the summer heat, with the edges left frayed, the Brigadier looked seedier, poorer, shabbier, yet somehow more English and aristocratic, than ever.

'Frightfully sorry to hear of all this, Larkin. Damn bad turn of the wheel. Struck down when I heard it. Plunged in gloom.'

Already restored to a certain quickness of eye, Pop told himself that the Brigadier, far from being plunged in gloom, had about him a certain eager perkiness. After sitting for a mere moment or two by the bedside he was continually nipping up to peer out of the window.

Pop couldn't think why. It couldn't be the garden, which under pressure of recent events Ma had to her sorrow been forced to neglect a good deal; nor could it be the junk-yard, the only new addition of any importance to which was a vast collection of army surplus foot-baths, which Pop with his natural aptitude for a good thing hoped to sell to a firm of landscape gardeners for flower urns. You could never tell what they were going to put flowers info next, nowadays, what with chamber-pots and all that, and he thought the baths were perfick, besides being capable of showing a profit of about 700 per cent.

'Splendid new item of scenic detail, Larkin.'

Scenic detail? Pop couldn't think what the pipe the Brigadier was talking about. He could think of no scenic detail.

The shape, the Brigadier would have him know, the shape.

For some moments Pop could think of no shape either.

'Get her by advertisement, stealth, subterfuge, bribery or what?'

It now became suddenly clear to Pop what had been the cause of the Brigadier's constant nipping and bobbing up and down to the window.

'Oh! my nurse. Sister Trevelyan. Angela got hold of her. Australian.'

'I heard rumours. But by God.'

'Very nice girl. Comes of a very good family.'

'Sensational.'

The Brigadier said the word as if taking a draught of some exquisite drink, a fact that caused Pop to ask him if he wouldn't have one? The Brigadier accepted with a muttering show of reluctance which in fact concealed a positively panting eagerness, so that Pop invited him to help himself: it was all on the table beside the television set.

Addressing himself to the vast array of bottles there, the Brigadier inquired if he couldn't knock up a chota peg for Larkin at the same time? When Pop immediately informed him that he was on the wagon, utterly teetotal, perhaps for ever, the Brigadier turned extremely pale.

'Good God.' The Brigadier was aghast. 'Under whose edict is this? Rome? New encyclical or something?'

'Doctor. Two doctors.'

'Catastrophic. Is this yet another of the legion of sufferings under the National Health Service?'

'No, General, this is private. Private practice.' Pop laughed. 'Probably if I'd been on the National Elf lark I could have got it free, by prescription.'

The Brigadier felt a great compulsion to take a deep earnest swig at a large whisky-and-soda. The world was becoming a damn rum place.

'I rarely ask for special dispensation, Larkin, but this might be an occasion.'

Oh! he was getting used to it, Pop said. There were compensations. Silently he thought of his coming back, twice, from the dead, and the rose-leaf by the window.

'Such as the scenic detail? Don't say that field is taboo as well.'

He hadn't had much chance to exercise his talent lately, Pop said and then remembered the occasion when, contrary to Ma's instructions, he had briefly tried to. It had been the occasion of his first bath, some few days ago, with Sister Trevelyan: the old point of no return.

Pop had decided that when the opportunity of the do-it-yourself lark arose he would respectfully decline. He didn't know what the odds against success were but it was wurf a flutter. In due course Sister Trevelyan washed him upstairs with gentle thoroughness and then downstairs with equal efficiency, leaving the way open to the expected invitation of 'would you like to do the rest yourself?' to which Pop replied with a sort of amiable innocence, No, he didn't think he would.

'No?'

'No.'

'And why ever not?'

Pop had long had his answer ready. He was too tired.

This confession drew from Sister Trevelyan

the sweetest of smiles and then a short sentence that perfectly matched it.

'Little boys who don't do their homework can't expect to have any privileges, can they?'

After which, without another word, Sister Trevelyan glided from the room with all the grace of a ballet dancer, her head uplifted with the very slightest hint of victorious *hauteur*, an exit which left Pop, for once in his hitherto optimistic and exuberant life, both crushed and speechless.

He was just reviving memories of this infinitely depressing occasion when Sister Trevelyan came into the bedroom, carrying Pop's late morning dose of pills and medicine on a tray, looking if anything more elegant and ravishing than ever, so that Pop's heart gave a dangerous somersault or two.

Nor was this supreme entrance lost on the Brigadier, who at once leapt up and bowed slightly from the waist, almost as if to royalty.

'This is my new nurse, General,' Pop said. 'Sister Trevelyan.'

'Madam,' the Brigadier said and bowed a second time, now rather lower than before, extending his hand and shaking hers, half in the act of kissing it. '*Enchanté.* We have already met.'

To all this Sister Trevelyan responded as if the Brigadier had been some sort of ambassador presenting his credentials. She was already charmed by the Brigadier. He was a bit of the real old, vanishing England, a relic of the old imperial. That was what made England and the English so fascinating: on the one hand you had

129

perfect gentlemen dressed rather like absent-minded tramps and on the other girls with micro skirts up to their navels and somehow it all fitted beautifully together in unparalleled eccentric pattern.

'Excuse me while I give Mr Larkin his pills,' she said.

The Brigadier promptly and graciously made way for her, at the same time seizing the opportunity to pour himself another large whisky-and-soda. This he did without benefit of invitation, having long learnt that in the Larkin household you lived according to the Larkin philosophy, which was 'it's there, ain't it? Help yourself then. That's what it's for.'

Pop having been given a dose of his many pills the Brigadier then turned his attention once more to the seductive sculpture of Sister Trevelyan.

'I hear you're from Australia, Sister.'

'That's right. Melbourne.'

'I would never have guessed it,' the Brigadier said with gallantry, 'from your accent.'

'Well, you see, I'm only half Australian. My mother is English.'

'Splendid. From which part?'

'Worcestershire. She was a Bressingham-Coutts.'

The Brigadier gave a large and astonished gasp, drank deep of his whisky and then gasped again. Suddenly, as in the flashback of an ancient film, he was transported some six thousand miles away, over a space of many years.

'By Jove. Good God.' The Brigadier drank deep again. 'Unless I'm vastly mistaken I once knew a relative of yours. Was her name not Cicely?'

'Surely, my grandmother. Cicely Victoria.'

'Great God. Small world. Damn small world.'

The Brigadier positively preened himself. His veins now running warm with the fires of memory he permitted himself the luxury of recalling that not only had he known Cicely Bressingham-Coutts; he had in fact seduced her. In Simla, on several occasions, in the summer time. The fact that he was seducing another young married woman at the same time had never at any time caused him any excess of guilt, but rather the contrary. Seduction, in those days long before mini-skirts, had been both an art and a military exercise. The doors were well guarded, the defences materially impregnable, or apparently so. There had to be a great deal of subterfuge, deployment of forces, flanking manoeuvres and even ambush. A chap could reckon that surrender achieved under such conditions was indeed a feat of arms. He had reason to know; he had won many a distinguished and rewarding campaign.

'Yes, we met in India. I knew her well. Tolerably well at least. Socially, socially. Charming woman, charming.'

'Was she married then?'

The Brigadier thought it prudent to say that he couldn't remember. Nearly all the women he had seduced while a young officer had been married; it was a great deal more fun, the conquest sweeter.

'I just wondered, that's all,' Sister Trevelyan said, 'only there's always been a sort of scandal about her in the family. We always laugh about it. That was in India too.'

'Oh! India teemed with scandal. The gossips fed on it like termites.'

The sensational possibility that he might well be Sister Trevelyan's grandfather suddenly filled the Brigadier with highly conflicting emotions. He had already toyed with the idea of asking her to his little place one evening for a spot of light supper. He was still confident that age had not entirely extinguished his powers of entertainment. A little salmon trout, if he could get it; and a good light Hock might well work the wonders that had once been worked, on a not dissimilar occasion, with the glorious and uninhibited Angela Snow. He flattered himself that he had not entirely failed on that occasion.

Nevertheless he had to admit that the possibility of blood relationship rather spiked his guns in that direction. That was damn serious. He could hardly start committing — well the unmentionable — at his age. You had to draw the line somewhere — with granddaughters anyway.

Compromise in these matters was perhaps, as always, the safest ploy.

'Perhaps you might care to drop in at my little place for a drink one evening?' he said. 'Very modest. I'm afraid. But I'd be delighted. I've still a good few old photographs of India lying about in albums — we might peep through them. Might well be fun.'

'It might. I'd love to,' Sister Trevelyan said and gave the Brigadier the most alluring of anticipatory smiles.

The old dog, Pop thought, and lay plunged in increasing gloom.

Life, he couldn't help telling himself, was getting worse than awful all the time. It was enough to make a saint swear. No drink, no cigars, the old point of no return lark a complete flop and above all, worst of all, Ma sleeping all the time in a separate bedroom. That took some getting over if you like. That was immoral all right. Most things he'd been able to bear, but Ma in a separate bedroom was just plain criminal. There should be a law against it. Not to wake in the middle of the night and feel Ma beside him, like some vast warm sand-dune, was enough to drive him to drink, except that, damn and blast it, there was no drink he could be driven to.

In the depths of these depressing thoughts he looked up in time to see the Brigadier raising his third large whisky full in the direction of Sister Trevelyan's black glistening eyes as if he was either toasting or celebrating something, though in his gloom Pop couldn't think what.

'Well, don't hog the bar to yourself, General,' he said. 'Remember the workers.'

'Ah! deeply sorry. My apologies. Is she allowed — I mean in the course of duty and all that?'

'Always has a nip about this time,' Pop said miserably. 'Her and Ma. Brandy.'

A light of gaiety, almost mischief, lay in the Brigadier's eye as he poured brandy for Sister Trevelyan. 'Well, cheers, Larkin. Here's to the day.'

Pop couldn't think what day, except perhaps some far distant day, deep in the future, when he might be permitted to become human again. 'I must say I admire you. I mean the resistance to temptation and all that. How on earth you do it I simply don't know.'

'Will power,' Pop said, more miserably than ever. 'Will power.'

'Ah! the day will come,' the Brigadier said with revolting cheerfulness, 'the day will come, won't it, Sister?'

'Not for a good while yet,' Sister Trevelyan said. 'Not unless he wants to poison himself.'

Pop shut his eyes, hardly able to bear any more of it. He then opened them to see Sister Trevelyan draining her glass and to hear her telling the Brigadier that she was afraid his time was up. She had to get Mr Larkin's lunch now.

Lunch? Pop knew what lunch was. Dry toast, calves' foot jelly, stewed prunes and water. It was a wonder he lived through the day.

'Well, farewell, Larkin.' The light in the Brigadier's eye shone still more cheerfully. His voice was rich with the plumminess of good cheer. 'Will report at the same hour tomorrow if the medico permits. Press on.'

Pop, never having felt less like pressing on in his life, waved a wretched and feeble hand in farewell.

The next day the Brigadier was back again, prompt as if taking parade.

But now, on him too, a revolution had been worked. No longer was he dressed in seedy habit, in shabby rags left over, as it were, from some distant and dusty Afghan campaign. Instead he wore a pair of cream flannels that had been pressed with knife-edge creases, a red, white and purple college blazer, an almost new panama hat and a certainly new pair of white tennis shoes. His hair and moustache had been sprucely clipped. Fuzz of long growth had been clipped from his nose and ears. He even smelled, with some pungency, of a combination of eau-de-cologne and a hair cream impregnated with what seemed to be a strong essence of clove carnations.

'Hail, Larkin. How fares the patient?'

The abounding cheerfulness of the Brigadier's presence, spruce and spry, plunged Pop still further into gloom. This was by no means improved when the Brigadier said he hoped Pop didn't mind that he'd brought his swimming trunks too? They were all going for a dip in the pool: Sister Trevelyan, Mariette, Primrose, Ma, and he even believed, the Reverend Candy.

'Your dear Mem Sahib suggested it. She also asked me to stay to lunch. Roast duck and green peas I fancy she said.' God, Pop thought, God. He could only urge the Brigadier not to swim on a full stomach. You never knew what might happen.

The Brigadier was undeterred. They were going to swim before lunch. Then they were going to lunch under the big walnut tree in the garden, where it was cool and quiet, so that they shouldn't disturb Larkin while he had his afternoon siesta. Splendid idea all round, the Brigadier thought.

It was purgatory, Pop said.

'Oh! and I believe there's just a chance that Angela may come. She telephoned but wasn't

135

sure. She's ringing back.'

This additional and unexpected news cheered Pop no more than ever so slightly.

'I only hope she hasn't aged a lot,' was all he could think to say, with an echo of gloom. 'It seems like a ten-year stretch since I set eyes on her last.'

Everything, in fact, had begun to seem like a ten-year stretch. The impression that he was a man serving a long prison sentence for a crime he hadn't committed increased considerably during his meagre lunch of toast, cold turtle soup and prunes, none of which he wanted anyway and after which he fell uneasily to sleep.

In the last few minutes before he dozed away he could hear, very faintly, the sound of voices, among them the shrieks of children, coming from the swimming pool through the open bedroom windows. The afternoon was hot. Normally the tinkle of children's voices about the pool on such a day of high summer would have drawn from him the old habitual comment that it was perfick, absolutely perfick. Now he had no feelings about it. Nothing was perfick now. Nothing was perfick any longer.

When he eventually opened his eyes again it seemed already to be twilight. Then he realized that someone had been into the room to draw the curtains. Waking thus, alone, in the shadowy prison of the bedroom, he found it impossible to resist fresh waves of gloom. The dismal conclusion that life wasn't worth a hatful of crabs, which was one of Ma's expressions for how she felt after a particularly miserable hang-over or something of that sort, grew stronger, unrelieved by an uneasy sleep in which he had seemed to grope down long and interminable corridors, like a purblind mole, seeking some way out.

In this funereal state of mind, rapidly approaching one of self-pity, an emotion he had never experienced in his life before, he told himself not only that he was unwanted but that he didn't want to have anything to do with anybody even if they wanted him. Let them all go to hell; he was there already anyway.

A soft tap on the bedroom door fell on ears that he deliberately made deaf. He didn't want visitors. Damn all visitors. A second and rather louder tap caused him to vent snappy irritation on it with the words 'Well, who is it? If you want to come in, come in. Don't just stand there tapping.'

It sounded like some ruddy woodpecker, he told himself, and further that it was probably that old dog the General back again, still hoping to try his military craft on Sister Trevelyan. Pop knew, he reminded himself miserably, what the General and all the rest of them wanted. It wasn't him; it was Sister Trevelyan they were after.

The door opened. The sight of a figure in a cornflower blue two-piece swim-suit of unparalleled brevity failed to arouse him to any more than a grunt in answer to a question that hadn't even been asked.

'No tea, thanks. No tea.'

'Sweetie, I am not the bearer of tea.'

A pair of light warm lips pressed themselves

first on his forehead and then on his lips.

'Darling man. It's me. They tell me you need a night nurse.'

The lips and the voice were those of Angela Snow. He couldn't see her very well in the half gloom of the bedroom and he gazed up at her much as if he were still the purblind mole of his dreams, groping for some way out.

'Shall I draw the curtains? Nice sleep?'

Without waiting for an answer she started to draw the curtains, saying that she'd been up once before to have a peep at him but that he'd been well and truly away. Cruelty to disturb him.

He muttered half to himself that he'd never been asleep. All he had been was a ruddy mole in a dark ruddy tunnel. He'd once known a girl with a mole of a different sort on her right bosom and normally the recurrent memory of it would have caused him to make some nippy joke about it, but now who cared?

'How's my sweet man? Haven't seen you since the Ice Age.'

Ice Age? Pop thought. This was the Ice Age.

Angela came to sit on the edge of the bed. Normally a situation where Angela Snow, covered merely by three cornflower triangles that revealed rather more than concealed the fundamental parts of a figure smoothly brown as an autumn beech leaf, would have had him at the starting gate, like some race-horse steamed up. Now he merely gave her the palest of smiles.

'Ma said to ask if you needed tea or anything. Buzz and she'll bring it up.'

Pop merely shook his head.

'I brought champers. And a box of Havanas. Would you like those instead?'

'Give 'em to the rabbits.'

Angela slightly changed her position on the bed. This smallest of movements so jarred his nerves that he begged her, not with the flippancy that would normally have accompanied the words but with the despondency of a man already half thrown overboard, not to rock the boat.

'We had some of the champers before lunch. It's '59. A girl friend of mine knows a type in Rheims who loads her with the stuff every time she beds down, which is a fair amount of frequency, and not only with him. Amusing creature. When asked if she preferred it sweet, dry or extra dry she simply said demi-sex.'

Pop failed to respond. Angela, granting that the joke might well have been too subtle, went on:

'Ma's duck was marvellous. In fact it all was, as if I didn't know it always is. Besides the champagne — this girl friend gives me a case now and then as a sort of ten per cent for having introduced her to this Rheims joker in the first place — we got outside three bottles of Volnay '53 and ended up happily ever after.'

Pausing for a moment, Angela gave one of those golden provocative laughs of hers that would normally have had Pop more than half way on the boil. This time he merely listened without a simmer.

'By the way, I must say our Mr Candy is a changed man. Of the three bottles I should say he practically killed one on his own. So much so that I asked him if he wasn't giving Unholy Communion, but he didn't seem to think it awfully funny.'

Pop didn't think so either. Mr Candy hadn't been to see him more than once or twice, and then only with formal brevity. He expected it was another one who really came to see Sister Trevelyan. From the General to the Parson they were all at it.

Ignoring, or trying to ignore, the prevailing air of gloom, Angela continued to elaborate and expand her dry jocularity.

'Actually the demi-sex thing isn't so way off the ball it seems. You know the reputation these frogs have got — magnificent bedders and all that — I mean you practically have to take out an injunction every time they look at you — well, it seems with this character it's practically a case of unleavened bread, sort of, most of the time, if you get what I mean? Hence the demi-sex. *Très* disappointing.'

There being no sort of response in Pop to all this Angela now gently took his hand and, as if with casual idleness, held it lightly against her thigh. To hold a hand lightly against the thigh of Angela Snow under any circumstances, let alone in bed, would normally have been a signal to Pop that he was practically in business. Now he could only mournfully tell himself that, like the character in Rheims, he was in the unleavened bread lark. He had a certain sympathy with the feller. If you couldn't make the bread rise it was clearly a pretty poor look-out all round.

'I must say it had no ill-effect,' Angela went on, 'I mean the Volnay and Mr Candy. After lunch he insisted on taking your Primrose out for a ten mile walk or something. Most athletic. When I pulled his leg and asked him if he was training for the Decathlon he looked a bit peeved and said he hadn't started to read it yet. Thought I meant *The Decameron*.'

What with Decathlon and *Decameron*, Volnay and demi-sex, the look on Pop's face was now becoming one of intensive despondency. Normally he would give Angela as good as he got, in more ways than one, but now his light was less than that of a glow-worm against the sun itself. And more worm than glow, it seemed, at that.

In a further attempt to rouse at least a spark of that interest which normally, Angela Snow had to admit, had her swiftly on the boil too, she now leaned over him, one breast actually brushing the sleeve of his pyjama jacket and murmured Sweetie, wasn't there something she could do for him? He'd only to name it and she was ready to play. Though she didn't openly suggest it, it would have been the easiest possible thing in the world to have slipped into bed with him, even if only for five minutes of demi-sex.

'Play?' The word struck Pop, in his gloom, as being one of doleful irony. He couldn't even play dominoes.

Angela, fully aware that Ma's injunction of 'you go up and have half hour's *tatey-tate* with him' had in it that touch of more serious meaning that Ma had once expressed in the words to Pop: 'Why do you think I let you out to

141

have a bit of fun with Edith and Angela now and then? Variety,' now began to have more serious thoughts herself.

The quick and high degree of intelligence that lay under the languid, golden surface of her wit and patter was one of the things that had first drawn and then endeared her to the Larkin philosophy: namely that life was sweeter, fuller and richer if you went with the stream rather than tore your heart out rowing against it. Ma's apparently casual air of allowing Pop licence to seduce others wasn't a sign of levity; it was naturally wise. And Angela was deeply happy and satisfied now and then, to be part of it.

Nevertheless the *tatey-tate*, she realized now, was going badly. She had had other *tête-à-têtes* with Pop, notably on the hot sand-dunes on the Brittany coast, and there had been nothing demi-sex about them. They had filled her with a sense of deep fruition in which there was no hint of guilt, so that she perfectly understood Ma's licence to permit occasional variety, Ma well knowing that her own love was as solid as the Rock of Gibraltar and as deep as the ocean.

In one last attempt to let light into Pop's deep passages of gloom she started to recount yet another anecdote of her friend in Rheims who, rather like Hamlet, had come to the moment when she needed to ask 'The Pill or not the Pill? that was the question' and had decided, wittily, as Angela put it, that it was of no consequence; but the joke, like the others that had preceded it, fell somewhere far away, like a dismal arrow.

It seemed to Angela, in fact, that Pop had now

reached his own special point of no return. He lay enshrouded in a vast frustration. His tunnel had no light at the end of it and none had ever been needed more badly.

'I'm thinking of taking a house or bungalow or something over in Le Touquet for August and September,' she suddenly said. 'You know — gorgeous sun-bathing all day, casino at night, walks in the forest, marvellous picnics on the beach, lovely wine. I thought you and Ma might share. It's big enough for six. I mean as my guests of course. You remember France?'

Pop remembered France: but not, now, with much relish.

'I thought it might be something for you to look forward to.' That, she thought, was the whole core of the matter. Pop must set his sights on something far beyond the confines of the bedroom. 'I might get my chum from Rheims to come and share. She's a great sharer. She's shared more beds than anyone since Catherine the Great. She'll come at the drop of a pillow, so to speak, if I ask.'

Normally such a sketch, brief as it was, suggesting both beauty and licence, would have been enough to prompt Pop to ask, at least, what the girl looked like. But having waited more than a minute for even a hint of inquiry Angela was forced to supply the information herself, doing it with that dry, offhand graphic method of hers that normally had Pop near-mesmerized in admiration.

'She's a sort of super relief map. All curves and contours. A kind of luscious mountain range. Some chaps climb the Alps — a lot prefer exploring her. I'm sure she'd love to lead you over the passes.'

It was all too much for Pop, who silently stared at a bee in one of the bedroom windows, striking its head with senseless futility against the glass. It too was struggling in vain, to get out.

'Would you come?' Angela said. 'I thought about the middle of August. The way you're going you'll be fit for the Decathlon yourself by then.'

The way he was going, Pop thought, he'd be down the drain any day now. Either that or up the ruddy creek.

'Very dark. Almost swarthy, you might say. Of course she's half-French herself and it's probably that that gives her that *je ne sais quoi* touch. I always think she's rather what Cleopatra must have looked like. Serpent in the boosie and all.'

Extravagant though the description of the temptress from Rheims was it failed to produce more than a murmurous grunt from Pop, but whether of approval or indifference Angela didn't stop to think. She made one more try:

'I can have the house from August the fifteenth. If I had a week to get installed, you and Ma could come about the twenty-fifth. How's that? That gives you more than a month to get your sea-legs. Not that you'll need them. We can fly in a quarter of an hour.'

In hollow tones Pop begged her not to make him laugh. Sea-legs? He hadn't even been out of bed yet. Not even to get on the Throne.

'You know, I knew a bomber pilot once,'

Angela suddenly said with that skilled propensity of hers to strike off at an unexpected and dazzling tangent. 'He told me that the only thing that kept him from going stark stinking bats on those ghastly night trips over Bremen and the German wilderness generally was fixing his mind on a pub he knew in some village near his station. The Cat & Custard Pot it was called. Cat, custard, cat, custard: that's all he'd think of all the way home. Cat, custard, cat, custard — it was the only thing that stopped him from going utterly round the twist.'

It was only towards the end of this longish attempt to get Pop to set his sights on something pleasant and not too far ahead that she suddenly realized that she was talking to a man with closed eyes. It occurred to her that she might have lulled him to sleep: and then that she had talked too much.

She had sense enough to sit there for another five minutes without a word. It was a spell of silence that touched her very deeply as she looked at his face, apparently in repose but curiously not restful. She couldn't help telling herself that he looked like a balloon, once gay, high-coloured and irrepressibly buoyant, that had become shrunken and deflated. There was a grey pouchiness about the eyes that was negative. It prompted in her the uneasy thought that a man could easily die of things less tangible than a heart attack and that one of them was, in fact — she scouted for a word and then thought: the heart has many — then couldn't remember the rest of the sentence and at last was frightened.

145

She moved quietly off the bed in readiness to go. The slight movement roused him. The greyish eyes looked up at her half in a daze and half as if begging her not to depart. She decided she must, smiled gently and said:

'Must go. Your nurse'll be up soon. Anything you want?'

'Tell Ma that if anybody else comes visiting today I don't want them.'

'Sorry I stayed so long.'

He gave her the very slightest hint of the old smile. No, it wasn't that; not her. He was thinking of stinking bores like Captain Perigo, who lived a life based on the Gospel According to Hunting and hardly ever said a word except 'I mean t'say — '; or a man named Fanshawe, who had exhausted most if not all of the local mistresses and had merely made a visit to Pop the excuse to see if Sister Trevelyan, of seductive report, would perhaps make up the deficiency; and a dozen others, even Edith Pilchester's hated Freda O'Connor, who had been one of Fanshawe's mistresses in between being somebody else's and had also made a visit to Pop an excuse for seeing what the nurse's profession had produced by way of possible rivalry. He was sick of them all; he wanted only to be left to himself.

Lightly Angela kissed him. Rarely had a body been held so closely to him with so little cover to it without invoking anything more than the briefest of smiles in response. Even then his eyes had little light in them and she said:

'Think of France. August twenty-fifth. That's your date. Think of that.'

'Right.'

'Say I will.'

'I will.'

'Darling man.' Her smile, superficially gay, almost brought tears to his eyes. 'That makes you married to the thought if not to me.'

She was about to kiss him yet again and this time in final farewell when there was a series of bird-like tappings on the door and into the room came Phyllida and little Oscar.

Each was bearing an untidy, bountiful bunch of wild flowers: clover, meadowsweet, rose-bay willow herb, purple loosestrife, honeysuckle, wild roses, marjoram and even ears of gold-green barley. The gift of his favourite flowers from his two youngest was accompanied by a mixed duologue explaining in touching terms that they had also brought him a frog, but Ma wouldn't let them bring it up to him.

'I thought you were going to bring me mushrooms,' Pop said, a fraction more cheerful now.

They were going to, they brightly explained, again in a jingled duologue, but Primrose and Mr Candy had got there first.

'Primrose and Mr Candy mushrooming, eh?'

'That's what they said they were doing.'

'Get many?'

They really didn't know, little Oscar and Phyllida said. Mr Candy and Primrose had told them to go away. They were lying down and having a rest by the wood.

'Alas! dear Yorick, no mushrooms for breakfast,' Angela said and blew Pop a fond and final kiss of farewell.

Somewhere about that same time Mr Candy had begun yet another pleasant excursion down the road of excess. The air was rich with the scent of honeysuckle, wild clover and the thick odours of Spanish chestnut bloom from the great trees in the wood overhead.

The blissful if slightly exhausting nature of Mr Candy's excursion left him in a state approaching swoon. This in itself was so pleasant that he was hardly prepared for the next move from Primrose, who rather to his surprise and dismay again began to talk of her favourite among poets, Donne.

'Do you know what his greatest poem was? The greatest, the absolute greatest?'

Mr Candy drowsily confessed he didn't.

'It was his last. His very last.'

'Quote,' said Mr Candy, who had long since become resigned to poetry being mixed with love.

Primrose, softly caressing Mr Candy's face with fingers like the wings of an amorous moth, quoted:

''When thou hast done, thou hast not done. For I have more.''

8

Ma was sometimes very critical, indeed scornful, of what she called the *status quo* symbol. She didn't altogether hold with it. There was, in her opinion, far too much of it about nowadays.

You never knew what was going to be a *status quo* symbol next. Swimming pools, yachts, electric organs, deep freezes, colour television, washing machines, spin dryers, vintage cars: all these of course had long been in the *status quo* symbol lark. But now people were going in for old steam rollers, old threshing machines, old hansom cabs, brakes and landaus, quite apart from converting old windmills and chapels and warehouses and cow barns into cottages in the country or keeping peacocks, pythons and even crocodiles. The best *status quo* symbol Ma had ever heard about was a swimming pool that had heating and tropical palms all set about it but no water. It made you wonder what was coming next.

And then education and all that: degrees and universities. She wasn't at all sure they weren't *status quo* symbols too. She didn't hold with all this business of students parading and marching about in protest about this, that and the other, carrying banners with slogans, especially when half the slogans were spelt wrong. It just showed you where education could land you if you let it get on top of you.

The fact that Pop hadn't had any education and couldn't even write his name had never worried Ma very much. After all he'd got on very well without it so far. Ma couldn't grumble. She and Pop had three television sets, including the new colour one, a Rolls-Royce, a Jaguar, and an estate car just for running about in, a washing machine, a washing-up machine and a spin drier, a deep freeze that was too big to go into the kitchen and had consequently to stand in one of the out-houses, three ponies for the children to ride, a heated swimming pool, the new French bar, a private cinema which Pop had rigged up in the cellar with nice plush seats and a fridge so that everybody could have ice creams in the intervals while Mr Charlton changed the films, a nice boat and a nice boat-house to put it in, and above all plenty to eat and drink. You couldn't say they lacked for very much and you couldn't say it was the result of education. You really don't need education and writing and all that when you got on with things like Pop did.

Nevertheless she had to admit that there were times when writing helped. For instance she would have liked Pop to write to the Miss Barnwells and thank them for the loan of the Throne. It was only decent and proper, she thought to write to them a little note about it. Unfortunately Pop wouldn't have been up to it anyway at the present time even if he had been able to write and it would therefore have to be Mr Charlton, as usual on these occasions, who'd have to come to the rescue.

This was one of the things that Ma, Mariette,

Mr Charlton and Angela Snow discussed as they sat in the kitchen drinking champagne cocktails later on during the evening when Angela Snow had suggested a course of convalescence in Le Touquet as something for Pop to look forward to and when Mr Candy had taken another course in the pleasures of excess in the mushroom field.

'Well, how did he strike you?' was the first question of importance that Ma put to Angela after Charley had mixed the cocktails. 'Pop, I mean.'

Sipping her champagne cocktail and at the same time recalling how little effect her story of her chum in Rheims and the demi-sex had had on Pop, except if anything to increase his gloom, she said she might as well be frank about it: Pop didn't strike her very favourably at all. In fact she thought he was very low.

'I feel he needs something to look forward to. Like a child looking forward to Christmas,' she said.

Then she went on to tell of the house she was renting across the Channel and how she'd like Ma and Pop and anyone else in the family to come and share it for a month, since it was her belief that another breath of French air would do everybody, Pop especially, a power of good.

Ma said it was very generous of Angela and thanked her very much. They would have to see when the time came.

'That's exactly the point,' Angela said. 'We have to fix a time. A date. If we said the twenty-fifth of August or something definite like that he'd have it fixed in his mind and every day he'd be able to feel it was that much nearer.'

Ma agreed. It was very like the children. Only ten more sleeps to Christmas they would say.

'Yes,' Mr Charlton said, 'there's no doubt that there comes a point where the psychological approach is essential.'

At the mere mention of the word psychological Ma gave Mr Charlton an extremely severe look. She didn't altogether hold with this psychology stuff. She wasn't at all sure it wasn't another of those *status quo* symbols. You saw a lot of it on telly. You had situations, for example, where a child had done something terribly wrong, like hitting its grandmother with a poker and nicking her old age pension, and all you did to punish it was this psychology thing, instead of giving it a good belt and telling it to give over or else. It wasn't right. Or if it was an adult person you got him or her lying on a couch and there was a lot of probing into their past sex life and all that: as if that got you anywhere.

She then proceeded to make a remarkable psychological suggestion of her own.

'It's my belief,' she said, 'that he wants something to make him good and angry.'

The utter astonishment caused by this totally unexpected remedy for Pop's gloom and apathy expressed itself in fully a minute of complete silence, which was finally broken by Mariette getting up to fetch another bottle of champagne and saying:

'Oh! no. I don't think that would work. After all, he's only allowed to sit up with his second pillow for half an hour at a time. Anything that made him angry would be enough to finish him completely. His heart would never stand it.'

A profound, far-off look on Mr Charlton's face presently told Ma that he was thinking; and some moments later this proved to be right. Mr Charlton said he wasn't at all sure Ma hadn't got something there.

'Like hair of the dog,' Mr Charlton said.

Hair of the dog was Pop's favourite remedy when you'd had one or two over the eight and there was no doubt, as Mr Charlton well knew and Ma had to admit, that it worked. You were, as Pop often remarked, back on your feet in no time.

'No, no,' Mariette said. 'I can't see it. Look what happened when he got mad with old Nurse Soper. It set him back weeks.'

Mr Charlton disagreed. He didn't think they should underestimate the curative powers of anger, a remark of such profundity that everyone was again stunned to silence for several minutes until Mr Charlton eventually proceeded to reinforce his point by quoting, of all things, the Scriptures.

'After all, the refiners fire and all that,' Mr Charlton said, to Ma's utter stupefaction. '"And he shall purify.' In other words fire not only burns and kills. It refines and restores. You follow me?'

Ma didn't. She'd never heard anything like it. Either Charley had been drinking more than she thought he had or else it was education again. It just showed you where too much of it got you if you didn't watch it.

Angela Snow on the other hand was impressed. She was in fact about to offer a parallel to the hair of the dog theory by adding something about serum and snake-bites when, by a fortunate chance, Primrose and Mr Candy walked in.

'Oh! Hallo,' Ma said. 'Where are they?'

Where were what? Primrose wanted to know.

'The mushrooms. Oscar and Phyllida said you two were mushrooming.'

Mr Candy, who had been too immersed for the past couple of hours in exploring the pleasures of excess to think about mushrooms, looked so embarrassed that he actually blushed and said:

'Oh! they turned out to be toadstools. They're awfully deceiving from a long way off.'

Ma wondered. She had had her suspicions about Primrose and Mr Candy for some time. Her guess was that the Reverend Candy was turning out to be another Mr Charlton. She wondered if he knew his technique? If not, some way would have to be found in learning him.

'Ah! you're just in time, Mr Candy,' Charley said. 'We were discussing Pop and saying he probably needs some treatment other than medicine to get him going again. Ma suggested a spot of anger and I was inclined to agree. I was trying to quote that bit from the Bible about the refiner's fire and He shall purify when you came in, but I couldn't quite remember chapter and verse.'

Mr Candy couldn't remember chapter and verse either. He was however, saved from

154

eventual embarrassment by Primrose, who promptly came up again with Blake.

''The tigers of wrath,'' she said, ''are wiser than the horses of instruction.''

Good God, Ma thought. Though proved right after all she silently asked herself whatever next? She really didn't know. The things Primrose came out with sometimes. Well, she could only suppose it was education again.

'And which chapter and verse does that come from?' she said.

''The Marriage of Heaven and Hell,'' Primrose said, leaving Ma still further stupefied. 'Blake. Any champers left? It's thirsty work looking for mushrooms that turn out not to be. We're famished too.'

Mr Candy couldn't help agreeing. He was, to quote the scriptures again, an-hungered and a-thirst. The road of excess certainly took it out of you.

'Get another bottle, Charley,' Ma said, 'and I'll see what's in the fridge.'

As she did so, searching for any pieces of cold pie, cheese tarts, smoked salmon, salami, olives and anything of that sort that might be hanging about, she told herself she didn't know about the tigers of wrath and the horses of instruction, but she had a shrewd idea that a good steak-and-kidney pie and a bottle of Chambolle Musigny were more likely to be the things to put Pop right. She'd been saying so for some time and pretty soon something would have to be done about it.

What with one thing and another it was

getting worse than awful. In fact if things went on like this much longer, she told herself, jokingly, she wasn't at all sure that she wouldn't have to get a lodger.

⋆   ⋆   ⋆

Next morning, about eleven o'clock, Mr Charlton went up to Pop's bedroom with pen and notepaper in order to discuss the letter Ma had long insisted should be sent to the Miss Barnwells in gratitude for the Throne. It was, though neither Pop nor Charley knew it at the time, a momentous occasion.

A straight, steady rain was falling, cooling the air, and now and then Pop could hear the monotonous beat of a thrush cracking a snail on the garden path below his bedroom windows. Something about the dual monotony of falling rain and cracking snail had on him the most dismal, imprisoning effect. He felt more dreary, irritable and despondent than ever. A little earlier Sister Trevelyan, normally a person of the sweetest patience and temper had left him in a slight huff, telling him that if he let his self-pity get any bigger it would stick in his wind-pipe and choke him. The words, not entirely unintentional, caused him to snort after her to shut up and if she wanted a fight she was going the right way about getting one.

The words rather pleased her. They went some way towards proving the interesting theory about the tigers of wrath, which Ma had told her about: so that just before closing the bedroom

156

door she put her beautiful golden-copper head round it and said with a coolness at once maddening and delicious:

'I'll have you know I've fought better men than you. And lost.'

And what the hell was he supposed to make of that? Pop snapped. Lost? Lost what? It was enough to drive a man barmy, which in fact was exactly what, Sister Trevelyan told herself, she was trying to do. She was inclined to agree with Ma after all. Anger, perhaps, was the great healer.

A few minutes later Mr Charlton came in with pen and notepaper, explaining that he'd come to discuss the letter.

'What letter?' Pop's voice was unaccountably sharp.

'To the Miss Barnwells. To thank them for the Throne. Ma told you about it.'

'Never said a word.'

'She spoke about it only yesterday.'

'Did she? Then why the blazes doesn't she write it?'

'For one thing she's had a hard morning. Oscar fell out of a tree and got a bruise on his head as big as a duck egg. Ma started to do some washing and then it rained. And now she's gone off with Mariette to get your new pills.'

'New pills? Why new? They all have the same ruddy effect — depress you like hell. If anybody had any sense they'd get me a treble brandy.'

Mr Charlton, faced with such untypical conduct from Pop, had the forbearance not to argue about brandy.

'The letter won't take long. You just say what you'd like to say and I'll put it down.'

'Well, if you're putting it down you might as well say it.'

'It needs to be personal.'

'Well, why bother about a letter anyway? Can't Ma or somebody ring 'em up?'

'They're not on the telephone. The poor dears can't afford it.'

'Time they could.'

Ignoring the testy brevity of such remarks, Mr Charlton patiently prepared to sketch out with pen and paper what he thought might be an appropriate note of thanks to the Miss Barnwells.

'Dear Miss Barnwells — no, perhaps not. How do you usually address them? Do you know them well enough to call them Effie and Edna?'

Pop, whose custom it was to be on Christian name terms with everybody if possible, merely grunted.

'All right,' Mr Charlton said. 'Let's say 'Dear Miss Effie and Miss Edna Barnwell'. Then what?'

'Oh! just say thanks for the potty.'

Mr Charlton demurred. Potty, he said with some reticence, was hardly the word.

'Well, what else is it?'

It wasn't exactly a question of the choice of word, Mr Charlton said. It was one of etiquette.

'Oh! they call it that now, do they?'

Mr Charlton, again ignoring such uncharacteristic testiness, now deemed it necessary to stop asking questions and get on with the

158

composition of the letter himself: which he promptly did, finally clearing his throat in readiness to read out the preliminary draft.

''Dear Miss Effie and Miss Edna: I sincerely hope you won't think it remiss of me not to have thanked you before now for your great kindness during the occasion of my illness. But, as I am sure you will understand, I have had to take things very quietly and have only now begun to feel something like my usual self. Please forgive me therefore for not writing to you before. I do so now with the utmost gratitude for the loan of the commode, which will be returned to you as soon as my doctor deems that I am strong enough to resume normal activities.''

Listening to this, Pop was struck completely speechless. He had always admired Charley boy, but this was masterly. He didn't know how Charley ever thought it up. Masterpiece of a feller.

'Don't think it's a trifle ambiguous,' Mr Charlton said, 'the last bit?'

'Ambig — what?'

''Resume normal activities.' Can be taken in two ways, I mean. Feel a bit ambiguous to you?'

Pop said he'd never felt ambiguous in his life. Bit constipated once or twice, but you got that from laying in bed. On the whole he thought the letter was perfick.

'Even so, I think we'll alter that bit. Let's say 'as soon as I am up and about again'. Yes, that's better. And I think some little personal touch at the end, don't you?'

Still inclined to testiness, Pop said he didn't

think so. It was perfick as it stood.

'What I really meant,' Mr Charlton said, 'was that you should express it in rather more tangible form.'

Tangible form? Pop thought. What the pipe was that?

'I mean like asking them up to visit you? I'm sure they'd love it. They've sent no end of messages of inquiry about you.'

Pop started to mutter about how he'd had enough of visitors and how they tired you out and all that, but Mr Charlton, tersely authoritative all of a sudden, cut him short.

'Oh! I think so. After all there are still certain standards.'

This, the most crushing remark made by anyone since Pop had been in bed, had the immediate effect of silencing him completely.

'Yes: I'll simply say 'If at any time you are passing this way I should be delighted if you would drop in and see me. Again with my warmest thanks for your kindness and with very best wishes from Mrs Larkin and myself. Yours sincerely S. C. Larkin.' I think that about squares it, doesn't it?'

Pop, still speechless in admiration, thought it squared it good and proper. Unlike Ma, he was stunned by the marvels of education.

★   ★   ★

The eventual effect of Mr Charlton's inspired decision to 'express it in more tangible form' was that rather less than a week later, on a soft early

160

August afternoon when already the first combine harvesters were beginning to crawl about barley fields like huge humming scarlet beetles, the two Miss Barnwells put on their best hats, each rather like a little blue upturned basket decorated at the brim with pink daisy chains, and their best frocks, which looked not unlike a combination of chintz curtains in faded rose and cream and nightgowns that had hems of slightly deeper colour tacked on to them either from some impulse of modesty or because they had shrunk in the wash, and set off to accept Mr Larkin's kind invitation to drop in and see him if they were passing that way. They were, also carrying umbrellas in case it came on to rain, the umbrellas of an identical shade of mothy brown, and two little boxes of home-made fudge, one of chocolate and one of coffee.

The Miss Barnwells, if ever they had drawn themselves upright, which they never did, would have stood rather less than four feet seven inches in their stockings. Frail, genteel and seemingly near-sighted, they looked not at all unlike little twin budgerigars, yellow in colour and much freckled: the freckles having apparently been the result of their keeping bees, which appeared to have stung them all over.

The impression that a puff of wind might have blown the two little ladies away was entirely illusory. They were both resolute and tough. Daughters of a retired Indian civil servant they were in reality two little pillars of iron upholding with dignity, pride and a certain patriotic passion the fact that there would always be an England

and if ever by some disastrous consequence there wasn't it wouldn't be their fault and it would be over their dead little bodies anyway. England was England; like the sun and the moon it was and always had been and ever more would be so. To think otherwise was blasphemy, sheer, subversive, repellent blasphemy; and they, like some tiny infantry brigade, were going to fight, with their dying breaths, and God being their helper, to keep it that way.

This was one of the reasons they so admired and liked Mr Larkin. Mr Larkin too stood for England: the green and pleasant land of that other side of Blake so often quoted by Primrose in excursions along the road of excess, the meadows, the bluebell woods, the blackbirds, the nightingales, the lanes of hawthorn and primrose and meadowsweet, the cherry orchards, the pubs and the soft, sea-stroked air. These, they would say with their chirpy dying breaths, we have loved; and so would Mr Larkin.

They had in consequence been greatly touched by Pop's letter in relation to the matter of the commode. The commode having so often travelled with them over India's vast, steaming, dusty spaces, they were all too well aware of the comforting and practical nature of its virtues. They had indeed been honoured to lend it for Mr Larkin's use. They too had long christened it The Throne, almost as if partly regarding it as a symbol and a seat of majesty. Long after imperial Caesar had turned to clay, The Throne remained, to them, symbolic of the things that mattered.

That morning they had first taken the precaution of telephoning from the post office, in the name of good manners, to ask Mrs Larkin if a call that afternoon would be convenient or not and had received a typical Ma reply:

'Of course. Drop in about tea-time. I'm baking. Lovely to see you.'

This news, since in their slightly frugal circumstances they lived mostly on tea, corn-flakes and bread and honey, more than delighted them. They couldn't help recalling, as it were from long ago, Mr Larkin's splendid party after a donkey Derby and gymkhana, when Pop had plied them with delicious nourishment and one of his patent cocktails, Ma Chérie, mixed double strength to prevent its becoming mere water, a combination consisting of sherry, soda and a dash or two of vodka, whisky or anything else Pop had in mind at the time. It was what he called one of his make-ups. You ordained both strength and mixture according to the needs of the moment. To the Miss Barnwells it had, in their language, been absolutely *pukka*. They would never forget its powerful virtues either.

They were therefore greatly looking forward to the visit to Pop, which was more than could be said for Pop himself. He was regarding it with jaundiced eye. It was true that he didn't dislike the Miss Barnwells; he was on the contrary always much touched by their gentility, the slight pain of their reduced circumstances and by the fruitful energy of their tiny frames, concealing as they did a tireless energy for the pursuit of good works, collecting for good causes, and the

163

defence or welfare of the oppressed, the sick, the needy and, if necessary, the betrayed. Two or three times a year they begged subscriptions of Pop in support of such causes and to these he always gave with simply splendid, almost princely generosity.

He wasn't so sure about the betrayed, though, meaning unmarried mothers, and on one occasion, when the Miss Barnwells had spoken of some organization called The Society for the Protection of Women's Rights, he had suggested that on the contrary they should set one up for The Protection of Women's Wrongs, a remark that caused the little Miss Barnwells to fall about, the air around them seeming to dance with golden freckles.

He was therefore ready to receive them in slightly disgruntled mood. The fact that he had now been able to walk round the bedroom for the third time rather made things worse instead of better. It made him feel tired and foolishly wobbly on his pins.

'Here you are, dear. Two nice ladies to see you.' Ma, almost on the dot of four o'clock, brought the two Miss Barnwells up to Pop's bedroom. 'Would you like them to have tea up here with you or shall they have it downstairs?'

Well, that put him on the spot, Pop thought, but suddenly remembering Mr Charlton's reminder about 'certain standards' said with an almost gallant reticence that he suggested they please themselves. He'd no doubt they didn't want to be bored too long by him.

'Oh! *please*. Up *here*. If we *may*.' Like two

little budgerigars who had been taught to repeat certain catch-phrases, the Miss Barnwells had a habit of chirping out the same sentences, word for word, at the very same moment, together. 'Oh! we should *love* it up here.'

Ma having presently retired to get the tea, the Miss Barnwells proceeded to place their boxes of home-made fudge on Pop's bed, at the same time remarking, in brightest unison:

'Oh! it's *nothing*. Just a little *something*. Only we *thought*, didn't we, dear? And how *are* you, Mr Larkin? Everyone's been so *distrait* about you.'

Distrait, had they? Pop thought, seizing on the new word with an alacrity that seemed almost as if he were sort of catching up a bit, mentally anyway. Well, he wasn't bad; taking two steps forward and one back, as the grasshopper said when he fell over the trip wire in the fog.

This remark also caused the little Miss Barnwells to fall about as if they had taken two or three Ma Chéries too many, so that Pop invited them to sit down and take the load off their feet.

In spite of this singular piece of jocularity, Pop looked, in the Miss Barnwells' opinion, acutely pale. They mustn't tire him, they told themselves, and the conversation became, rather like the soft August afternoon, desultory.

After speaking about the weather, Pop's letter and how charming it was, the harvest and how it had already startea, the Miss Barnwells slowly ran out of topics of conversation, so that Pop was intensely relieved when Ma came back, bearing

165

tea and its infinite accessories on a large silver tray.

'Tea up,' Ma said and set the gleaming silver tray, with the best Georgian silver tea-pot, sugar basin and milk jug on the table by the television set. 'Want me to pour?'

'Oh! *please*,' the Miss Barnwells said. 'You be mother.'

'Had plenty of practice,' Ma said, wistfully wondering, by no means for the first time, when she was going to get some more.

Tea having been poured and the Miss Barnwells having decided delicately to get started on the salmon-and-cucumber sandwiches, not the least ravishing items of the great array of buns, biscuits, cakes, tarts and so on that the tea-tray bore, Ma suddenly said:

'Oh! I meant to ask you. How's Edith? Haven't heard a peep out of her lately. Not since that — you know — since that business. You know.'

The Miss Barnwells knew.

'Well,' they said in customary unison. 'Well.'

Ma, sipping tea, waited for some elaboration of the word and received it in the form of the information that, in fact, nobody had seen Edith for some long time.

'Gone broody or something?' Pop said.

Well, the Miss Barnwells said, there were rumours.

'Having an affair with that Professor next door I expect,' Pop said, a trifle sourly, so that Ma was forced to administer a reprimand.

'Pop. Do be decent.'

'Well, there are,' the Miss Barnwells said, yet again in unison, 'two schools of thought.'

Blimey, Pop thought. Schools of thought now, eh? Whatever next? Ma wondered too, eager to hear what Edith had been up to. Couldn't be the Professor next door, could it?

'Oh! no, she *hates* him. She *loathes* him. She can't *bear* him.'

Ma was shrewdly silent. She'd heard that kind of thing before. You'd only got to hear a girl say she couldn't stand the sight of some man and before you knew where you were she'd married him.

'Some say she's on holiday. And some,' the Miss Barnwells said, 'say she's in a Home.'

'Probably far better off,' Pop said.

'Well, we did hear she was in *purdah*,' Ma said, at the same time giving Pop a severely warning look in case he came out again with the unfortunate suggestion that Miss Pilchester was in pod, 'but a Home. That don't sound too good.'

'In *purdah* she undoubtedly *was* for some time,' the two Miss Barnwells admitted, 'but we rather discount the *other*. Edith's very independent and anyway the windows of the cottage were open when we came past.'

'Oh! she's all right,' Ma said, with her customary cheerful air of charity, 'it's her jam season.'

With a rapidity astonishing for creatures so small, the Miss Barnwells masticated their way through everything eatable on Ma's tray, accompanying it all with cup after cup of tea, so that Pop actually began to tell himself that if they kept emptying the pot like that much longer there might well be some sudden demand for The Throne. Normally he would have thought little or nothing of making such a suggestion aloud but now there was a certain constraining influence in the air.

'Well, I must give her a tinkle,' Ma said, meaning Edith, and at the same time made the light suggestion, not very well received by Pop, that 'perhaps she'll come and baby-sit for you one night while Sister Trevelyan goes out.'

The subject of Edith having been at least temporarily exhausted Ma said she would clear the tray, and then as she went to pick it up noticed that a single salmon-and-cucumber sandwich, sole relic of the meal, remained.

'Well, we can't let that go begging, can we? Isn't somebody going to eat it up?'

Like two eager birds the Miss Barnwells picked it up, broke it in half and quickly minced it away.

'Well,' they said at last, 'we must be going. We mustn't *tire* you. But there was just one *teeny* thing we wanted to ask you.'

'Ask away,' Pop said, the thought of their departure having induced in him a slight rise in the temperature of cheerfulness. 'Say the word. What is it?'

Well, the Miss Barnwells said, Mr Larkin was always *so* generous, he gave *so* willingly, *always*, for *whatever* they asked.

Pop, ever ready to dig his hand deep for charities, children's outings, old people's parties and anything else that would keep the ball rolling for people who were a bit unfortunate, said if Miss Effie wouldn't mind looking in the top drawer of the dressing table she would find his wallet. What was it this time, anyway?

'Well, it's our Fund.'

Fund? Pop said. What sort of Fund?

The two Miss Barnwells, in all probability for the first time in their lives, suddenly stood up to their full height, all four feet seven inches, like two little soldiers in the act of enlistment for battle.

'Our Fund,' they said, 'for saving England.'

★   ★   ★

Well, you could have knocked him down with a stone block of wood. Pop said. Saving England? Was someone thinking of pinching it, then?

'Yes,' the Miss Barnwells said, not only with great firmness but with a militancy that rasped on the air like the snap of a rifle bolt being drawn back. 'They most certainly are.'

Pop, sitting up in bed and taking sharp notice of the highly determined look on the faces of the Miss Barnwells, who now looked less like budgerigars than a pair of miniature eagles, begged to be told what he was supposed to make of that remark. The country was a bit big to cart off under somebody's arm, wasn't it?

It was not, the Miss Barnwells sternly informed him, exactly that kind of pinching. It was worse. It was political, nasty and subversive. It was composed of the most wicked subtleties.

169

It was fortunate that at the very moment when Pop was trying to digest this extraordinary meaty offering of words from the two little ladies that Ma came back into the bedroom, accompanied by the Brigadier, who had been lured to the house by the prospect of seeing the enchanting Sister Trevelyan and was now rudely disappointed to find that it was her day off and she had gone with Mariette and various of the children to the sea. A certain deflated look of grey cheerlessness in his eye at being faced with the beauties of the Miss Barnwells rather than that of the luscious Sister Trevelyan wasn't lost on Pop, who promptly invited him to help himself to a snifter, even though it was still not five o'clock.

'Thanks all the same, Larkin. Hardly over the yard arm, yet, though, is it? — '

Oh! who cares about the yard arm? Pop said. The Brigadier knew Pop's approach in these matters, didn't he? If he wanted a drink for Gawd's sake let him have a drink.

The Brigadier, in his terse military fashion, uttered low thanks again and suffered himself to be tempted to a very large whisky.

'The Miss Barnwells were just telling us about how somebody's going to steal England,' Pop said. 'You heard anythink about that, General?'

The Brigadier coughed brusquely. A certain air of unease, almost guilt, hung about him, rather as if he had been part of a conspiracy and had only just been found out.

Pop, at once suspicious that they were all trying to keep something from him, was more

170

than relieved to hear Ma say:

'Well, it's this Tunnel. This Channel Tunnel, that's all.'

Oh! that was it, was it? Pop said. Well, he wasn't interested in no Tunnel.

'Then,' the Miss Barnwells informed him with the voices of irate eagles, 'you should be!'

Pop was stunned into silence. The Brigadier drank deeply of his whisky. Ma fidgeted with her hands in an unaccountably nervous way. And finally the Miss Barnwells demanded in pointedly barking voices:

'*We are an island, are we not?*'

Before Pop had time to admit to the truth of the ancient fact that they were an island indeed the Miss Barnwells rose in full, outraged flight:

'Very well then, do you not wish to remain an island? Do you wish to be swallowed by the Continent? We have been an island for all time, haven't we? Hasn't it served us well? Isn't it our strength, our salvation? Wasn't it that that saved us during the war? The sea is our defence, isn't it? Do you want to see it destroyed?'

Not the least remarkable thing about this resolute outburst was not merely its strength or that it came from creatures so frail and small but that its method of delivery had changed entirely from one of unison, so that now the sentences were delivered by the two sisters alternately, like set speeches long learned by heart.

'*Do you wish us to be governed from Rome?*' Miss Effie demanded.

'*Do you want us to lose sovereignty?*' Miss Edna said.

171

These sudden references to the Common Market had the Brigadier snorting and huffing over his whisky like some horse growing increasingly impatient to gallop. The Common Market, Rome and Papism generally being his most frequent sources of insular outrage he suddenly thundered:

'By God, no. Hell's bells.'

The very word Rome had been known to inflame him, in fact, to public protestation. The Reverend Candy's predecessor in incumbency had been, in the Brigadier's view, a bounder, a theatrical showman, a priestly impresario, a fraud. Given to dressing up in private in sulphur-yellow riding breeches, scarlet waistcoats and purple cloaks and in public in vestments that could only be described as looking like the left over trappings from some impossible Wagnerian pomposity in opera, the fellow had so far goaded the Brigadier as to make him rise in church on one occasion and demand as with military command:

'Are we now to suppose, sir, that the whole service is about to be conducted in Latin?'

As if about to repeat this fierce demand the Brigadier drank deep at his whisky again, went very red in the face, snorted and seemed about to bellow forth when he was stopped in his tracks by an astonishingly quiet pronouncement from Miss Effie, who said:

'During the war Edna and I often faced Hitler. Alone.'

Ma, the Brigadier and Pop waited with equal, silent anticipation for some explanation of this astonishing and compelling statement, which finally came, rather unexpectedly, from Miss Effie, who now took the centre of the stage while Edna, as it were, remained in the wings, more or less as prompter.

'Before the war we had a house on the coast. On fine days you could see France. Sometimes even the clock tower at Calais, couldn't we dear?'

Miss Edna said yes, they could. And with the naked eye.

'Well, there we lived. At peace. Until the war came. And then of course there was talk of invasion and we were forced to close the house and move here, weren't we, dear? The coast was a forbidden area and you were only allowed into it if you had special business or property, weren't you, dear?'

Miss Edna said yes, they were. Once a month. With special passes.

'So,' Miss Effie said, 'down we would go, once a month, and sit in the garden and look across the Channel. Twenty miles away. Didn't we dear?'

Miss Edna said yes indeed, they did. At Hitler.

'We always took our lunch with us, wet or fine. Spam sandwiches and tea mostly, wasn't it, dear?'

Yes, it was, Miss Edna said. But once or twice, especially in that very cold winter of 1941, they took a drop of home-made parsnip too.

'Edith's brew?' Pop asked, suddenly more like his old self, sharp and perky.

'Oh! no. Edith was in the Navy at that time.'

At this Pop was even more stunned than the Brigadier, who gulped afresh at his whisky and said 'Good God. Never? Edith in the Navy?'

'She was a Wren,' Miss Effie said. 'Oh! you mustn't underestimate Edith. She has a medal somewhere.'

Good Gawd, Pop thought. Where? No wonder we won. Edith with a medal? Probably got it for giving all she'd got, he shouldn't wonder.

Following this brief interruption the Miss Barnwells resumed their duologue, now once more speaking in unison, describing how they would sit in their long-deserted garden, their little bit of England, stare across the Channel, drink tea or home-made parsnip, chew on spam sandwiches and curse the invisible figure of Hitler somewhere across the water. There was often an artillery bombardment going on and often a battle in the air and sometimes it was terrific fun. The shells burst awfully near.

'Do you remember that day,' Effie said 'when we were blackberrying and that air-raid warden came by and said we were in danger? You remember, dear?'

Yes, Miss Edna said, she remembered, and they said danger from whom? That twit?

At the recollection of this moment of defiance the Miss Barnwells laughed in a series of merry little giggles, as if it had all been a very great joke, a jolly little pantomime.

'And that's why,' Miss Effie said, 'we are out to save England. What on earth do you think we saved it for then? Not to give away again for the dear Lord's sake, surely.'

'Hear, hear,' the Brigadier said. 'Hear, hear.'

'We are an island,' Miss Edna said, 'and we are

174

determined to keep it that way!'

'Moreover,' Miss Effie said, 'what kind of people, as Churchill said, do they think we are?'

'Hear, hear,' the Brigadier said again. 'Sound the trumpet!'

At this point Ma, who had been remarkably if not indeed suspiciously quiet all this time, was moved to admit that it all reflected her own feelings on the matter very much indeed.

'Of course we don't want to be governed from Rome. Or Berlin. Or Paris. Or by that de Gaulle or Russia. Or that Stalin. Or that Cosy Gin.'

'Cosy Gin?' Pop said and was actually moved to laughter. 'That Russian feller? Very good name for a cocktail.'

When the Brigadier gently reminded Ma that de Gaulle was no longer in office and that Stalin was dead Ma simply snorted. She knew she wasn't very hot on world affairs but did it matter who was dead and who wasn't considering the gang of crooks who ran things?

She wasn't at all sure, she went on to say, if you asked her, that it wasn't all part of that persuasive society you heard so much about nowadays.

'Permissive,' the Brigadier gently corrected her.

Oh? Ma said, singularly unimpressed. You'd got to be persuaded before you could permit, hadn't you? at the same time thinking chance would be a fine thing.

Pop, who had listened to all this with only the one comment on his part, now said that perhaps a few weeks in bed had dimmed him up a bit but he still wasn't sure how they were going to lose England and who was going to pinch it?

Miss Effie, in a sudden blistering moment of fresh militancy, was moved to a pronouncement that had everyone staggered.

'*We* are! *We!* If we aren't careful we shall be *our own executioners.*'

'Indeed we shall,' Miss Edna said. 'Are we going to sit here like a lot of supine, bloodless worms while the entire heritage of this island is sent to the pawnbroker's? I should say not. We were never in pawn to Hitler, damn his soul and may God forgive me for saying so. And I say we'll not be in pawn to the Devil.'

'Whether you call him Common Market, Rome, decimal, Channel Tunnel, Europe, Centigrade or whatever,' Miss Effie said, in a burst of insular outrage that even outmatched her sister's.

'Hear, bloody well hear,' said Pop, who was now beginning, he told himself, to see daylight.

The true daylight had, however, not yet dawned. It was in fact this that had kept Ma so uncommonly and suspiciously quiet for so long and it was now Miss Effie, in a further expansion of her case for the Defence of the Realm, who put the matter into words.

'And of course the Road.'

Road? Pop wanted to know. What road was that?

'Well, it's this Road,' Ma said, going on to explain that they'd known about it for some time but that it had been considered that Pop hadn't quite been well enough to be told about it. Now both Dr O'Connor and Sister Trevelyan thought he was fit enough. 'Well, there was this man from the Ministry here about three weeks ago.'

Man from the Ministry? Pop was always highly suspicious of any man from the Ministry. Income tax, he expected. Well, that was no bother. He knew how to deal with fellers from the Income Tax. Two or three of his Red Bull cocktails, mixed double strength, would see them off all right.

'It's the Road to the Tunnel,' Miss Effie now explained.

Tunnel? And what, Pop prayed, had the road to the Tunnel to do with him? The Tunnel would be thirty or forty miles away.

'But the road would come through here,' Miss Edna said.

'Yes, through here,' Ma said and now the reasons for her long quietness were becoming clear at last. 'Bang through the middle of our place. Our garden, Pop. Our yard.'

★　★　★

Pop shot bolt upright in bed: his first agile and vigorous act since thrombosis had struck him down. His teeth were shown in rage. The anger that Ma in her native wisdom had deemed to be a necessary force for cure now filled him with a new and vibrant alertness: proving, as Primrose had predicted, that the tigers of wrath were wiser than the horses of instruction.

At the same time he was speechless. It was something like being crucified and then having a dagger struck through your throat for good measure. The first grey iron pain of his heart attack hadn't pained him more.

It was the recollection of the visit of a Man from the Ministry that finally broke his silence and then in a burst of righteous rage.

'I'll be damned,' he suddenly said, 'if I'll be shoved around by a lot of farts from Whitehall!'

At which Ma gave him one of her sharp looks, this time quite lost on him. He mustn't bandy words like that about. After all there was a time and place for everything.

'Now you see why we've started our Fund,' Miss Effie said.

Miss Edna chirped in agreement.

'Our Cause,' she said. 'Our Great Cause.'

Pop said with righteous irritation that he didn't know about their Cause. It was his Cause too, very much his Cause, wasn't it?

'The part is symptomatic of the whole,' the Brigadier said in a moment of solemn and surprising revelation, as if he had produced the words out of some Bill of Rights or something of that sort. 'Damme, it's riding roughshod.'

This mixture of solemnity and the vernacular completely mystified Ma, who hadn't the remotest idea of what the Brigadier was talking about. Pop wasn't sure either.

'Well, one thing is certain,' Miss Effie said. 'We are going to *fight*.'

'We are indeed going to fight,' Miss Edna said. 'But of course it will need money.'

'Well that's no trouble,' Pop said. 'Ma, get the box out of the wardrobe.'

Ma immediately proceeded to open the wardrobe and produce from it one of those old-fashioned tin travelling trunks once a familiar part of railway life three quarters of a century or more ago. The trunk was actually too heavy for Ma to lift and she begged the Brigadier, if he would, to give her a hand with it.

The trunk having been lifted out on to the bedroom floor, Ma then did an astonishing thing. She appeared, greatly to the surprise of both the Brigadier and the Miss Barnwells, about to undress. This seemed abundantly clear from the way in which she unzipped her blouse from the back, slipped one side of it over and down her left shoulder and then plunged a hand bosomwards, as if searching for some source of irritation there, perhaps in the form of a mosquito or something.

There was in fact no such source of irritation. A momentary vision of an olive chasm between the fair hills of Ma's bosom was accompanied, on Ma's part, by a great sigh as she heaved up a long gold chain with a bunch of keys at the end of it. Among these was the key to the tin trunk. She always kept the keys down there because as she said, it was the last place anybody would think of looking for them and the first place where Pop always did. There was nothing like having security and pleasure provided, so to speak, under one roof. What could be nicer, Pop often asked himself, than having two of the most important things in his life, Ma's bosom and the keys to his money, safe under the same corset?

Having at last freed the key from the

179

encumbrances of blouse, slip, corset and chain, Ma proceeded to unlock the trunk.

The Brigadier gave a great involuntary gasp.

'By Jove, Larkin, damme. Been reading *Treasure Island* or something?'

The comparison was not inapt. The Brigadier hadn't seen so much money, in the raw so to speak, since pay days in the army.

Pop waved a characteristically deprecatory hand.

'Always keep a bit in the house in case,' he said, though in case of what he didn't bother to explain.

'After all you never know when you'll need a bit of loose change do you?' Ma said and gave one of the jolliest, jelliest laughs she had given for a very long time. The fact that she and Pop had half a dozen similar trunks, one in the roof, two in an attic, one in the cellar, one under a pile of straw and a sixth in the most unlikely place of all, locked in the top of an old stone well at the bottom of the garden, was something that this was neither the time nor place to mention.

All this time the Miss Barnwells had had nothing to say. They too, tortured as they were by the ever-increasing need to submit themselves to the indignity of asking for Supplementary Benefit or whatever name the largesse of the Welfare State went under nowadays, had never seen so much money in their lives.

Here, also with more jollity than he had shown for some considerable time, Pop demanded what sort of sub. they had in mind?

'Oh! *anything*. We should be grateful for the

teeniest thing. Two guineas? Whatever — '

Two guineas her foot, Ma said, a remark that Pop followed up by saying Did they mind? Was that the price they put on his place? His yard? He'd have them know it meant as much to him as Buckingham Palace.

Before the Miss Barnwells could refute an assertion they had never made the door of the bedroom opened and Mr Charlton came in. Mr Charlton and Montgomery had been doing so well at the pheasant lark, among other ventures, that the sight of the trunkful of money had nothing like the stupefying effect on him that it had had on the Miss Barnwells and the Brigadier.

'Counting the coconuts, Mr Larkin, sir?' he merely said.

'Just in time, Charley boy,' Pop said. 'You've heard about this road lark I take it?'

Charley had. He had been part of, indeed the instigator of, the plot to keep it from Pop as long as possible.

'Well, what the pipe are we going to do about it?'

In answer to this question the two Miss Barnwells struck up in shrill, indignant unison.

'Oh! *anything. Everything.* We've already got a petition with three hundred signatures. We'll even have one of those protest marches if necessary. Like they have against Nuclear Disarmament and Vietnam and all that. We've even thought of getting Mr Candy to preach a sermon about it.'

It was now the turn of Mr Charlton to raise a deprecatory hand.

'No, no,' he said and the very tone of his voice, calm and authoritative, told Pop that Charley was on the verge of using his loaf. 'All that, I suggest, is out. Nothing is to be gained, I suggest, by the emotional approach.'

Masterpiece of a feller, Charley. Now who else would have thought of a thing like that? Emotional approach.

'This thing,' Charley went on to say, 'must be tackled like a military operation.'

'Hear, hear, Charlton,' the Brigadier said. 'Bingo.'

'But that,' the Miss Barnwells chirped in fearful unison, 'would cost an *awful deal* of money!'

'Well, not short of a few pennies, are we?' Pop said, waving an airy hand towards the bulging tin trunk, beyond which the Brigadier was helping to reinforce himself, as if in early preparation for battle, by pouring another very large whisky.

'Here, while you're pouring out, General,' Ma said, 'why don't we all have a sniff?'

Why not indeed, the Brigadier said and with true military correctness bowed towards the little Miss Barnwells and courteously awaited orders.

Before these could be given — the Miss Barnwells deeming that a gap of a mere hour between tea and alcohol was in some way slightly immoral — Mr Charlton made a further, explanatory pronouncement.

'I said military. What I really meant was legal.'

'But that would cost an even *greater deal* of money!' the Miss Barnwells cried out, quite pained.

'Never mind about that,' Ma said, with that

imperturbable kindness of hers. 'What are you going to have? Gin? Whisky? Brandy? Sherry? One of Pop's cocktails?'

At the mention of the word cocktail the two Miss Barnwells instantly recalled that delicious concoction with which Mr Larkin had regaled them that evening, now seemingly so long ago, after the gymkhana. They would never forget that cocktail. Nor its name. Ma Chérie.

'Well, could we, perhaps, have a little — the *teeniest* one of those cocktails? Ma Chérie? Only a *soupçon*, the merest *soupçon*.'

Pop, not bothering to seek translation of the word *soupçon*, merely laughed and said that Ma Chéries were old-fashioned now. He'd cut them out.

He suggested A Blonde Bombshell instead.

If the two ladies were about to protest that this sounded like a drink of some belligerency they were saved from doing so by Pop, who declared it to be a mere summer refresher and said:

'Mix a couple up, Charley boy. You know the form.'

Charley knew the form: two parts vodka, one brandy, one whisky, a dash of angostura and a nip of soda. Normally mixed double strength, these had the power of cure-alls, Pop was fond of saying, but now a wink in the direction of Mr Charlton, busy at the bedroom bar, was enough to indicate that singles would, in this case, be adequate. He could only wish, with some pain, that he were having one himself.

Instead he suddenly had — indicative of the sharp improvement the tigers of wrath had

183

already had on his mind — a great thought.

Legal? He suddenly remembered Angela Snow. Wasn't her father a judge or something?

'Something at the Bar, I believe,' Charley said.

'Then I'll join him,' Pop said. 'What's her number?'

In the early days of his illness Pop had once or twice used the telephone by his bedside, but the very act of lifting the receiver had had such an effect on him that he had found himself at the bottom of the snake in no time, in consequence of which he had been forbidden its use.

'Now, now,' Ma said. 'Don't get excited. You know what happened last time.'

'But if it's going to be a legal do, we want legal advice and a legal bloke don't we?' Pop said. 'Besides, if I know my Angela we might get it free.'

'If you don't know your Angela by this time nobody does,' Ma said darkly. 'And you watch it. What do you mean, free? She might ask you to pay in kind.'

Which she added to herself and not with her customary merriment, Pop was in no position at the moment to do, more was the pity.

'I'll have a word with her,' Charley said. 'It's a possibility. A thought.'

While the little Miss Barnwells supped with delicacy at concoctions powerful enough to bring tears to their eyes and Ma sucked smoothly at Remy Martin, her favourite brandy, Mr Charlton dialled Angela's number and waited for it to be answered.

'It's ringing now,' he said.

'Let me have it,' Pop said and Ma, greatly to his surprise, took the telephone from Charley and passed it over. Her shrewd native intuitions detected that Pop was on the up and up. She'd been right about the anger.

'Angela.'

At the sound of Pop's voice there came, from the other end of the line, a golden, aristocratic, languid peal of laughter.

'Darling. Sweet man. Made my day.'

And how was Angela? Pop wanted to know.

'Pining. Wilting away. What's more to the point, darling, how are you?'

Mustn't grumble, Pop said. Surviving.

'And what can I do for you, sweetie?'

Pop said he'd rung her to see if she'd do him a favour.

'You mean you're fit enough, darling? I simply can't wait.'

It wasn't that sort of favour, Pop said, worse luck, but he didn't doubt the day would come.

'It will, sweetheart, it will. On those sand-dunes at Le Touquet.'

Well, he didn't know about that, Pop said. His main concern at the moment was that he had a problem on his mind.

'Then you mustn't have, darling. Remove it. Take it off at once.'

Pop said he was trying to do that, which was why he was ringing her. And by the way wasn't her father a judge?

'Q.C., darling. Queen's Counsel. Why?'

Pop proceeded to explain why: all about the Tunnel and the road and the Cause and the

Fund and how the road, so they threatened, these Ministry blokes, was coming right bang through the very middle of his place.

'The snotty bastards.'

Pop laughed, quite in his old style, almost uproariously. It was good to be talking to Angela again. She was worth a million doses of medicine. Perhaps the sand-dunes didn't seem all that much in question after all.

Still, it was serious, Pop went on to say. He was up in arms. Everybody was up in arms. It was what Edith would have called absolutely ghastly. It was sort of like treason. Something had to be done about it.

'Of course darling. The stinking slobs. We must slay them. We must put poison down.'

The word 'we' suddenly shone, for Pop, like a good deed in a naughty world. It was the very thing he'd been waiting for.

'Wondered if your father could help? Charley boy thinks we should make it a legal battle. Cut out the emotional approach and all that.'

Pop, using Mr Charlton's very words, suddenly felt grand and militant himself.

'Your voice sounds strong, darling,' Angela Snow suddenly said.

Did it? Pop said, more than a little flattered. Perhaps she'd better watch out for them sand-dunes after all?

Again the peal of golden laughter came ringing from the other end of the line.

'I take it you'd like me to consult with Papa?'

Pop said that was the line of country. And as for the dough-ray-me, not to worry about that.

Pop would see to that. Sky was the limit.

'You swab. You dare suggest it. Of course you won't pay.' Again the seductive golden peals poured their music into Pop's ears. 'Oh! yes, on second thoughts you will. Me. In kind.'

Which was exactly what Ma had said, Pop reminded himself, laughing too. Amazing how women's minds worked. Perfickly amazing.

'Well, I'll do your bidding, darling — as if I was ever likely to do otherwise. He'll be home tonight. We'll consult. I expect he'll be free on Sunday. Might we possibly come over and see you then?'

'Course. Come to lunch. Free house on Sundays.'

'Splendid, darling. Look forward to it passionately.'

Dangerous word, Pop thought of saying, dangerous word; but merely said instead:

'Perfick. Perfick.'

'See you Sunday then, sweetheart. Oh! by the way, have you met any of those rats from Whitehall yet? No? Well, let me tell you this, darling. Whoever or wherever they are they might just as well drop dead. Goodbye. Everlasting love.'

So blessed, Pop answered with his own most cheering farewell, feeling infinitely better already. There was something about that girl, he told himself. Her nature was just what the world needed more of.

'Her father's not a judge,' he announced, putting down the telephone. 'He's a Q.C. Queen's Counsel.'

At this announcement, Ma, great Royalist as

187

she was, felt enormously flattered. It was a tremendous honour to feel that she had a Queen's Counsel coming to Sunday lunch. She wasn't quite clear in her mind what a Queen's Counsel was and could only suppose he was a gentleman who went about with the Queen giving her counsel as and when required and perhaps wearing black knee breeches and stockings and carrying a long stick, a sort of 'thy rod and thy staff they comfort me' or something of that sort. Anyway he was bound to be of enormous importance. She wasn't at all sure they oughtn't to roast an ox or something in honour of his coming.

The two little Miss Barnwells having supped their way down to the dregs of their Blonde Bombshells, Mr Charlton, without asking, filled them up again. As if this were not bounty enough Pop said:

'Ma, give the Miss Barnwells a hundred to go on with and if they want more they know where to come to. Got to support this Cause with every penny we've got. Got to beat this ruddy lot somehow.'

With quivering hands the Miss Barnwells accepted Ma's gift of a hundred pound notes tied into a packet with green wool — she always tied the hundreds with green, the fities with blue and the five hundreds with pink — like pilgrims accepting some holy, treasured relic at a shrine.

Dear Mr Larkin. Wonderful Mr Larkin. They simply couldn't believe their good fortune.

'Nothing,' Pop said. 'Nothing. Plenty more where that comes from.'

Like the Brigadier said, they weren't going to be rid roughshod over.

'Hear, hear, Larkin. Bingo. Sound the trumpet,' the Brigadier said and with a kind of eager deference helped himself to another whisky.

'Oh! and if you see Edith,' Pop said, 'rope her in. Must have Edith with the troops. Tell her to come and see me.'

'We will indeed.'

'We will indeed.'

'Haven't seen her for such a long time,' Ma said, renewing her Remy Martin with generosity. 'Tell her if she doesn't soon show her face we'll be forgetting what she looks like.'

'Stout girl, Edith,' the Brigadier said. 'Navy, eh? Medal, damme.'

'And what,' the little Miss Barnwells said, 'about Mr Candy? Shall we put aside the idea of the sermon for the time being?'

Mr Charlton suddenly said he thought so. The law might, in this case, have more power than the pulpit. Even if it costs more.

Though partially stunned by Mr Charlton's display of wisdom Pop laughed, almost in his old ringing fashion.

'Not going to cost us a penny. Like you said, Ma, Angela says I can pay in kind.'

Oh? Ma said, looking at him very darkly. Then she only hoped his credit was good.

'Then we will leave Mr Candy for the moment, shall we?' the Miss Barnwells said. They were still a trifle uncertain as to the wisdom of leaving Mr Candy and the church out of things. Empty though the pews all too often were, the church still had its voice.

'I'll have a word with Mr Candy,' Pop said.

Come to think of it, he hadn't seen much of Mr Candy either lately. He wondered what he'd been up to?

Half an hour later the little Miss Barnwells walked gently home in the cool of the evening, except that it didn't seem cool to them, but amazingly, marvellously beautifully warm, and that they were not walking, but sailing, as it were lightly over water, as over some divine Sea of Galilee.

Wonderful, marvellous Mr Larkin. Their Cause was in great hands. The age of miracles had not yet passed.

9

Ever since the morning when she had decided that whisky rather than prayer was the more appropriate medium with which to express farewell to Pop Larkin on his last long journey Miss Pilchester had not merely been in *purdah*, but in a state of shame, guilt, confusion and even despair. Her shame and guilt rose from the fact that she had rejected prayer and come to grief, her confusion from the fact that she had chosen whisky and Pop had recovered. Had prayer lost its efficacy and whisky gained in powers both healing and miraculous? She had asked herself the questions a thousand times; and confusion, despair and *purdah* were her only answers. Whichever way one looked at it, she told herself, it was all absolutely ghastly.

When therefore she heard that Pop had so far recovered as to wish to see her she accepted the invitation the very next afternoon, with both alacrity and a fearful joy.

Pop, who was so far on the way to recovery as to tell himself that he was feeling as strong as a nip of brandy in a pint of water and was eagerly looking forward to the day when it would be the other way round, had spent more than an hour out of bed in the morning, had slept for another on the strictest orders from Sister Trevelyan after lunch and was now sitting out again, alternately watching a race meeting on telly, which bored him, and his beloved junk-yard, which didn't.

The joy to be derived from little things or from things once deemed ordinary and taken for granted had never left him since the day he had first gazed out on the young rose-leaf on his bedroom window. And now the junk-yard, in consequence, looked perfick. Nobody was going to take that from him: not on his nelly. This was his own, his beloved bit of England.

And how perfick it looked, his paradise, he kept telling himself. Pink willow-herb was growing up in forests of tall feathery spires among all the massed junk of barrels, muck-heaps, hen coops, wrecked cars, discarded bits of machinery, wire and lumps of old iron, making a beautiful picture. The old iron was specially good. You'd see a lot worse, as Ma often remarked, in some sculpture exhibition in London if some of the photos she saw in the papers were anything to go by.

Miss Pilchester had telephoned to ask if half past four would be a convenient visiting time and had been told by Ma yes and would she stay for tea, which was what she had hoped for. But unexpectedly, about four o'clock, Mr Candy arrived before her.

'Ah! nice to see you, Mr Candy,' Pop said, very cheerful himself, though thinking that Mr Candy, in dog collar, looked sort of formal, nervous and a trifle tired. 'Haven't seen you lately.'

'Well, yes, that's true I'm afraid. I — '

Pop interrupted to say that he expected Mr Candy had had other things on his plate?

'Well, life's been awfully full. I won't exactly say I've been run off my feet — but you know how it is.'

Pop knew how it was. All that christening and marrying and those sermons.

Mr Candy had no comment to make on this. He merely seemed to grow more nervous.

'Well, I just — I just — I felt I ought to sort of drop in and see you. About a little matter — '

Perfick, Pop said. He expected it was the Cause?

Mr Candy, who hadn't thought of the particular matter on his mind as being exactly a cause, but rather an effect, supposed that that was one way of putting it, though he didn't say so.

'Thought as much,' Pop said. 'I talked it over with the Miss Barnwells.'

Mr Candy, hitherto merely nervous, now seemed to become exceedingly flaky and fragile. With difficulty he dabbed sweat from his brow.

'Got very excited about it, the pair of 'em,' Pop said. 'Told people in the village it was a miracle.'

Mr Candy immediately went paler still.

'Said you might be preaching a sermon about it.'

Oh! dear no, Mr Candy said. That was — no, he didn't think that was the appropriate thing at all. It was the most unlikely subject for a sermon.

'No? Anyway, got to give it as much publicity as we can. That's what we all feel.'

Once again Mr Candy, in rather a limp voice, said that he didn't on the whole think the idea a very good one. He murmured something about he thought they were treading on sacred ground.

'Oh?' Pop said. He couldn't see how. What was sacred about it?

Mr Candy had no time to answer this interesting question before there was a tap at the bedroom door and Ma came in preceding Edith Pilchester, whom she announced with the cheerful words:

'Well, here's your girl friend. I'm just off to the village with Mariette. Be back in about an hour. Like a lift, Mr Candy?'

Mr Candy seemed delighted at the opportunity of a lift and the escape it offered and immediately got up to shake hands with Pop and Miss Pilchester, who in contrast to Mr Candy's extreme paleness was rather red in the face.

Ma then said that Sister Trevelyan would be bringing tea up and then, rather to Pop's surprise added:

'Well, I'll leave you two to it. You'd better get into bed.'

Pop, not sure if this was an indirect invitation to have five minutes under the sheets with Edith or not, gave one of his ringing laughs and in his best innocent voice said:

'Why?'

'Because Sister says so. That's why. She says you've sat out long enough for this afternoon.'

Pop dutifully took off his dressing-gown and got back into bed. Ma said goodbye, not to worry, she wouldn't be back for a good hour or more, and then left with Mr Candy, only to reappear a few seconds later to say:

'Oh! by the way, there was a note from Angela by the afternoon post. Her father can't make it on Sunday. Playing golf or something after all. It'll have to be the Sunday after.'

Left alone with Edith and finding the first moments with her somehow rather uneasy, not to say embarrassing — she was still very red in the face and seemed unaccountably nervous — Pop sought to relieve the tension by asking in characteristic fashion if she would take a nip, a snifter or something before tea?

The subject of alcohol being a highly unfortunate one, Miss Pilchester went even redder in the face and rapidly declined the offer, confessing that she'd long since given it up. The memory of that dreadful morning at The Hare and Hounds, though she didn't dare mention it, still lay on her soul like an accusatory, leaden cross. Nor had the sight of Pop after so many weeks made it any easier to bear.

'Well, how have we been?' Pop said, wondering at the same time if there was any need to ask. Edith, though much thinner than before, looked as red as a hen about to lay.

Well, on the whole she was fairly well, Miss Pilchester said, lying without much conviction, knowing that for weeks she had been feeling absolutely ghastly. What was more important, how was Mr Larkin?

'Perfick,' Pop said. 'Perfick. Feeling better every day. Eating well. Sleeping well. Doctor says the heart's mended perfickly.'

For the first time Miss Pilchester smiled, secretly telling herself that she only wished hers had. There were times when she thought it was irrevocably broken. Then to her infinite dismay Pop suddenly said:

'Got a bone to pick with you.'

The prospect of having to pick a bone with Pop was yet a further means of agitation for Miss Pilchester and she tremulously murmured Oh! had he, why?

'Never been to see me.'

'Oh! but I — '

'Nice thing. Lay here thinking about you every day. All the time. And you never come near. Out of sight, out of mind. I know.'

'Oh! but I — '

He had been cut, Pop said, to the quick. It was bad. Terrible. Worse than awful. He couldn't bear it when his best girl friends deserted him.

Miss Pilchester became quite speechless. She didn't at all know what to say. Impossible to acquaint Pop with the awful paradox that she hadn't been to see him first of all because she had heard that he was dead and she had taken to drink instead of prayer as a result of it, and then because of her consequent guilt and shame. The total confession would be altogether too ghastly.

Unaware of this remorseless torture, Pop went on to tease her still further by saying something about fair weather friends and his hour of need and all that and how it had shook him to the — he was about to say 'to the tits' and then rapidly changed it to 'the bottom of his heart'.

In answer to all this Miss Pilchester gave a loud sniff. A moment later Pop knew there was a tear in her eye.

'Now, now, now,' he said. 'This won't do, Edith. Can't have this. Can't have you turning the tap on.'

Miss Pilchester sniffed even more loudly, crying openly now.

'Here, here, come, come,' Pop said. 'Dry them eyes. First time you come to see me and you start tuning. Here, come over here and sit by me a minute.'

Needing no second invitation, Miss Pilchester went over and sat on the bed beside Pop.

Pop took her hand. Even in circumstances so ghastly the very touch of Pop's hand on hers was enough to make her tremble even more, so that without further warning she began sobbing hopelessly. This was an excellent excuse for Pop to take her by the other hand, at which she sobbed even more loudly still.

Ever willing to give comfort when and where it was most needed Pop now took her in his arms, stroked her hair and even gave a consolatory kiss in the region of her left ear. Her response to this was to palpitate, very rapidly, all over. The distressing thought even crossed her mind that Pop was about to ask her to give all she'd got and that unhappily she might not be in a position to do so.

The very same thought, at the very same moment, crossed Pop's mind. Having lately been in the unfortunate position of a man lacking practice it suddenly occurred to him that here was a good opportunity to get some in. A trial run with Edith, taken steady, in low gear sort of, might do no harm and might, into the bargain, do Edith a bit of good.

Pop's first excursion in this matter was to stroke her hair again and then give her a slightly more prolonged kiss under the left ear. His second was to fondle her neck, now so constrained from sobbing that it was as taut as a piece of hose-pipe. His third was an attempt to hold her more closely somewhere in the region of the left bosom.

To his infinite surprise there was no bosom there. This apparently unfortunate oversight on the part of nature was in fact merely the result of her having lost a great deal of weight in *purdah*, a fact that left him so astonished that he found himself, for once, with no other trick to play. This omission was however promptly remedied by Miss Pilchester, who suddenly stopped weeping, gave a great sigh and lay down with him on the bed, greatly comforted, her head on his shoulder.

At this point another immense sigh went through her, causing further spasms of palpitation that went down as far as her feet. This interesting development immediately caused Pop to think that there was, after all, one further trick he could play. No harm in trying, he told himself. After all, practice made perfick.

His execution in this further manoeuvre was however halted by the abrupt arrival of Sister Trevelyan who, seeing her patient in a position of some compromise on the bed with Miss Pilchester, didn't turn a hair. She had already been warned by Ma that she might well find Pop and Edith having what she called 'a bit of custard and jelly' when she took the tea up, but not to worry, she'd been letting Edith get it out of her system for years.

'Carry on Mr Larkin,' Sister Trevelyan said in the serenest of voices, 'nothing like a little therapy.'

So that's what they called it now, did they? Pop thought. Therapy. He'd often wondered what therapy was and always had a vague idea that it was something to do with the study of bones. This was perfickly true as far as Edith was concerned. Plenty of material there.

'Of course I *can* draw the curtains,' Sister Trevelyan said. 'The sun *is* rather bright.'

These words had the effect of bringing Miss Pilchester, briefly sunk into a state of spongy solace on Pop's chest, back into a world of blinding reality. Hopelessly ashamed, she sat bolt upright, almost fell backwards off the bed, then recovered with groping but elated indecision and the sudden information that she was admiring the scenery.

Sister Trevelyan said she was glad to hear it.

'Anything else you'd care for?' she said, most sweetly, setting down the tea-tray. 'I hope you don't mind, but I brought up a pot of the lemon curd you kindly came along with.'

'Oh! no, not at all — '

Edith had come, that afternoon, not only as a visitor but as a bearer of gifts: as it were, almost, offerings of restitution. Besides the pot of lemon curd she had brought jars of damson cheese, green tomato chutney, black-currant jam, a very special white-currant jelly and a bottle of elderflower wine.

'Of course Mr Larkin can't enjoy all you have to offer all at once,' Sister Trevelyan said, again with the sweetest serenity. 'He has got to get his appetite back.'

In further confusion Miss Pilchester could think of nothing to say in answer to this before Sister Trevelyan was ready again with her next light, sweet question.

'Shall I pour? Or will you be mother?' she said. 'Before it gets cold?'

Miss Pilchester, torn between elation and dire confusion, immediately decided it was best to be mother before it got cold.

Sipping sweet strong tea, she gradually recovered composure, even so far as to say, at last:

'You don't really, really think I neglected you, do you?'

Of course he did, of course, Pop said. He was cut to the quick. Left cold on the doorstep.

'But it was all so ghastly. I was absolutely *mortified* when I first heard about it. Absolutely *mortified*.'

Pop told himself he knew the meaning of the word mortified.

'So was I. Prit near.'

'Oh! Mr Larkin, don't talk of it. I can't bear it. I couldn't bear it — not all over again.'

After that, Pop having decided that he'd had enough of therapy for one day and Miss Pilchester having rejected all thought of further solace in Pop's arms, on the bed, the talk turned on what Miss Pilchester had been doing lately, apart from making jams and curds and being in *purdah* and things of that sort.

'As a matter of fact I've been delving into a little local history.'

Oh? Pop said. He hadn't realized she was interested in that sort of thing.

'Oh! yes, it's quite one of my secret passions.'

Secret passions, eh? Pop thought. He'd always suspected it.

'Well not exactly passion. I mean it's one of my pet hobbies. It's all so fascinating. I mean to go *back* in time. To the moon — forward — to Mars — no, that's not for me. But *back* — yes. To think of Caesar and his legionaries camping just up there on the hills. A Roman villa just behind the village. And vineyards perhaps. And the Pilgrims going to Canterbury. I mean we're so absolutely *steeped* in it, aren't we?'

Further marvels of what education could do, Pop thought. He only wished he'd had time for it.

'The Pilgrims especially — I like to think of them coming through here on some spring morning, 'When that Aprille with her showers swote — ''

Here Pop was saved the trouble of asking what the pipe Edith was talking about by the unexpected arrival of Phyllida and little Oscar — little Oscar singing a hymn he had learnt at school:

Through all the Changing Gears of Life
Through Hell and Toil and Pain,

a version that struck Pop as not inappropriate to all that had been happening to him for the past several weeks, so that Pop patted the boy with

201

paternal approval on the head and said:

'Hullo, what do you two monkeys want?'

The monkeys had brought him a frog, Phyllida said, and some fish for his supper.

The frog was nestling in a wet hemlock leaf and the fish, two stickle-backs, a very small gudgeon and a dead minnow, in a jar together with a water snail.

Well knowing that Ma didn't approve of such things in the bedroom, they had sneaked up with these precious offerings in her absence. Pop was very touched by the gesture, especially the thought of fish for supper.

'Oh! you are so lucky, having all these many children,' Miss Pilchester said. 'I sometimes wonder how you and Mrs Larkin manage it.'

She did? Pop thought. Perfickly simple, he was about to explain to her, then realized that it was scarcely the time and place, when Miss Pilchester said:

'And where did you get those lovely, lovely fishes from?'

Phyllida and little Oscar said they got the fish out of the little brook behind where the well was and the frog out of the bulrushes. Like Moses.

Sweet things, Miss Pilchester said. And what well was that?

Pop proceeded to explain that it wasn't a well exactly. More a sort of spring, coming out of an old stone grotto down at the bottom of the yard, behind the pigsties. The spring came up out of the ground and then overflowed into a brook and then the brook went across the medder into the river proper. Very good water in the spring, very pure. Never failed in the driest summers.

'And cold,' little Oscar said. 'Like ice lollies.'

'And all covered over with moss,' Phyllida said. 'I mean the stones. All covered with moss and old. Very like you are.'

Far from being either insulted or upset by such descriptive candour Miss Pilchester suddenly seemed to experience a moment of revelatory joy. She leapt up from where she had been sitting by the window, spilt tea in her saucer, dropped a cucumber sandwich on the carpet and exclaimed with jubilation:

'Great God, I believe I've uncovered it!'

Had she really? Pop thought. Uncovered what? He couldn't wait to have a look.

'I mean this is *It*. This is the missing link I've been trying to find. This is the *Secret Bit*.'

If he hadn't seen Edith drinking tea with his own eyes, Pop thought, he'd have sworn she'd been at the parsnip or elderberry or somethink like that.

'You see,' she went on, 'on all the old maps there's the teeniest, teeniest cross marked where your house stands and I've always wondered what it meant.'

And what did it mean? Pop wanted to know.

'Well at the moment it's a mere surmise — I'm only guessing — but I *think* this may well have been a resting place for Pilgrims on their way to Canterbury. I mean it might be a Holy Well.'

Well you could have knocked him down with a nine-gallon barrel o' beer, Pop said. Holy? In his yard?

'Consecrated. Hallowed. I mean we may well

be on Sacred Ground.'

Ah? Sacred Ground — now, Pop told himself, he knew what Mr Candy had been driving at, and proceeded to tell Edith so too.

'Oh! splendid. It may well be a case of two great minds thinking alike,' she said, laughing with excited gaiety. 'But you know what it *means*, don't you — what it *may* mean?'

Pop said no, he didn't quite, he hardly snagged on.

'It *may* mean — I only say *may* — it may well mean — that *if* this is consecrated ground they may never be able to drive that *awful, ghastly* road through here.'

It was now time for Pop himself to give a great sublime sigh of delight.

'Edith I could kiss you. Come over here. I could kiss you.'

With alacrity, needing no second invitation, Miss Pilchester went over to the bed where Pop, with that velvet authority of his, enfolded her in his arms and proceeded to get in a short spell of much-needed practice. Edith, free at last of shame, guilt and the long tortures of *purdah*, responded by giving all she'd got and, she told herself, a bit more.

Truly, as the Miss Barnwells themselves had said, the age of miracles had not yet passed. It was almost as if the frog, the gudgeon, the two sticklebacks and the dead minnow had been turned, like the three loaves and the five little fishes, into a feast for a multitude.

'Edith,' Pop said, 'I never knew history was so important.'

'Oh come on, let's go fishing again,' little Oscar said and went away with Phyllida, singing 'Through All the Changing Gears of Life' again.

'No,' Pop said, 'I never realized history was so important.'

'Ah! but there are far, far more important things than history,' Miss Pilchester said, 'don't you think?' and suffered herself to be kissed again, giving more, and with more palpitation, than she'd ever given before.

Long after she had gone Pop remembered that he'd forgotten to ask her what she'd won her medal for. Surrender, he shouldn't wonder. Then he decided no, it was probably, or ought to have been, for history; and was once again inspired to much thought on the wonders of education.

10

There were three reasons why Ma was glad that the visit of Angela Snow's father, the Queen's Counsel, had been postponed.

First of all it gave her more time to go out and buy a new outfit proper to the occasion — after all you couldn't wear just any old thing for the visit of somebody as posh as a Queen's Counsel — then it gave her a chance to give a bit more thought to the food. After rejecting, reluctantly, the thought of a roasted ox as being too difficult in case the weather turned funny one way or the other, she was finally down to a choice between geese, turkey, pheasants and roast pork on the one hand and a baron of beef on the other. She finally decided on the baron of beef: it was after all in the titled class so to speak and not all that far removed from royalty, and it would also, she thought, go a long way.

Her third reason was contained in the hope that Pop would at last be well enough to come downstairs, and perhaps even into the garden, if the weather held, for lunch. She had great hopes of this. Both Dr O'Connor and Sister Trevelyan had promised as much, if he behaved himself, a matter to which Pop was giving serious attention. He was now able to walk about, go to the bathroom himself, bath himself and dress himself. It might well be that, in a day or two, he would walk up and downstairs. Whether the tigers of wrath had done the trick or not Ma didn't know; but steadily and surely Pop was becoming himself again. There was hope, Ma thought, one way or another, of Nature returning to its course.

After much trial Ma finally decided on a dress of oyster satin for the occasion, together with a three quarter length coat of the same material: the whole very subdued for her and looking rather more appropriate to a Royal garden party than Sunday lunch under the Larkin walnut tree. She also had high-heeled shoes to match and a big gold-silver handbag that sparkled so much it looked as if it had accidentally fallen into a sack of sugar.

After a late period of indecision she at last rejected the baron of beef for the good reasons that, at anything up to a hundredweight it would have been too large for the oven and that no butcher could supply one anyway. Instead she chose two twenty pound turkeys and a whole baked ham. As this would be preceded by a whole smoked salmon she told herself that she didn't think anybody would starve.

The twins being at holiday camp in Devon and Victoria being gone off to Spain in an old London taxi, with three young men, an excursion that Ma thought would learn her, if nothing else did, to look after herself, this left seven of the Larkins and Mr Charlton for lunch, together with the Brigadier, Miss Pilchester, Sister Trevelyan, the Reverend Candy, Angela Snow and her father and finally the two Miss Barnwells. Pop had rightly insisted that the two

Miss Barnwells should come since it was, after all, their Cause.

While Ma gave much serious thought to food and clothes Pop, who had been sitting out for increasingly long periods in the garden for the last three days, had given equally serious study to the drinks. As it was a question of entertaining a Queen's Counsel he thought they ought to be plain but posh: no mucking about. Mr Charlton, called in for consultation on the matter, cordially agreed: no fancy stuff. He suggested a vintage champagne with the smoked salmon, Chambolle Musigny for the turkey and a Château Yquem with Ma's many afters, one of which was going to be a Christmas pudding. No Red Bulls, no Rolls-Royces, no Blonde Bombshells or indeed any liquid fireworks of that nature. The whole affair had got to be kept, Mr Charlton said, on a certain plane.

The first person to arrive, to the dismay of Ma, who was hastily knocking up a large steak-and-kidney pie, just in case, was somebody who apparently hadn't been invited. Looking out from the kitchen window Ma observed on the lawn a dandy little gentleman in a smart Oxford blue mohair suit, a claret silk bow-tie with white spots and a jaunty little russet-red trilby hat cocked saucily to one side.

For almost a minute she was convinced that this was the Queen's Counsel himself. She was about to rush upstairs and change quickly into her oyster satin when she astonishingly realized that the dandy little gentleman was none other than the Brigadier who, seeing her gazing from the kitchen window, jauntily doffed his hat to her in the best manner of some Edwardian gallant-about-town.

'Hallo, General,' Ma said, 'didn't recognize you.'

'*Bon jour, madame,*' the Brigadier said, coming to the open kitchen window and, as if the excursion into French wasn't enough, actually kissed her hand.

The next to arrive was Mr Candy, apologetic, hot, thirsty and fearing he was late. He had had to conduct a church service at which the choir had outnumbered the congregation by fifteen to six. one of whom was a baby who had to be baptized, a circumstance that never failed to unnerve Mr Candy in view of the agonizing memory of all that had befallen him in christening Primrose. What with this and that Mr Candy had, as Pop put it, a lot on his plate nowadays.

'A Guinness, please, if you don't mind,' he said in answer to Pop's hearty invitation to a snifter. He needed it. It might, he thought, put his strength back; and Heaven knew when he mightn't need that, too.

The weather, as the Brigadier put it, almost as if he had unaccountably denied all his principles and gone over to the Common Market, was *Comme ci, comme ça*: neither too hot, nor too breezy: a dreamy mixture of rippling sun, white cloud and gentle shade.

The long lunch table having been laid out under the walnut tree, with a second table packed with a vast army of bottles beside it, Mr

Charlton presently appeared from the house in a light smart cream suit, carrying corkscrews, bottle openers and ice-buckets as if prepared to deal with the drink situation in the manner of a butler.

Ma had at one time, in fact, seriously thought of having a butler. You could hire them. She expected any Queen's Counsel was bound to have one at home and the very thing she didn't want to do was to let the side down. But Mr Charlton's own counsel had prevailed in this particular matter, and very firmly.

No, no, he said, he thought no butler. It rather smacked of *folie de grandeur*, a remark that had Ma back on her heels, with nothing more to say.

At one o'clock, by which time Mariette and Primrose had taken over in the kitchen — no bikinis and bare midriffs today, Ma had warned them — leaving Ma to nip upstairs and bottle herself up in the oyster satin, there came the second surprising entry of the day.

Ma, looking down from her bedroom window, was suddenly surprised to see in the garden another figure she didn't recognize. At first she guessed it to be one of those Sunday moochers who occasionally turned up at the junk-yard looking for bargains in old chalf-cutters, old cider jars, old brass bedsteads and the sort of mullock people collected nowadays, all part of the *status quo* symbol, but then she wasn't sure.

The man talking with Pop and Angela Snow was dressed in one of those shirts that seemed to have been cut out of old boarding-house wallpaper, an affair of violet, green and pink, a

210

pair of crumpled orange slacks and a pair of open sandals in black and silver. Straight out of Carnaby Street, Ma thought, and could only assume that this was some new boy friend of Angela and that by some unhappy mischance the Queen's Counsel hadn't been able to make it.

Just our luck, she thought, as she went back downstairs, rather crushed at the thought of the oyster satin perhaps having been bought to no purpose and then immediately afterwards telling herself not to worry: the Queen's Counsel would surely be coming along separate, in his own Daimler or Rolls or something, with his own chauffeur.

When she reached the garden and went across the lawn Angela came to meet her with a blissful 'Darling' and a kiss on both cheeks. Sweet to see Ma. How ravishing she looked. Angela adored the outfit. Perfick.

'And this,' she said, turning to the handsome figure in orange slacks and the old boarding-house wallpaper, 'is my father. Sir John Furlington-Snow.'

Ma speechless, could have dropped. As if Queen's Counsel wasn't enough it had to be 'sir' too.

'I never use the Furlington bit myself,' Angela said. 'Too fatuous and fussy for words. But it's important for Papa professionally.'

'Mrs Larkin. How delightful to meet you at long last. I've heard so much about you.'

Ma could have passed out. You could have knocked her down, as Pop had it, with a stone block of wood. She had never heard such a beautiful voice in all her life. Languid, golden, smoothly aristocratic, it was exactly like Angela's except that it was richly, deeply masculine. Ma could only suppose it developed that way from talking to the Queen so much. And that longish, thick gold-grey hair, curling about the ears, and the sort of lamb-chop whiskers: they had the real aristocratic, almost royal, touch about them too.

'Oh! good morning, sir. Very nice to meet you, sir. So glad you could come, sir. Aren't we lucky with the weather, sir?'

'Oh! please don't call him 'sir', Ma,' Angela said, 'he hates it.'

'Oh! no, please, Mrs Larkin. Call me Furly. Everybody does.'

'Yes, sir,' Ma said and immediately begged to be excused and fled to the kitchen, red and trembling.

'Well, glass o' champers?' Pop said to Angela's father. 'Plain, pink or cocktail?'

Sir John Furlington-Snow said well, if nobody minded, he'd have a beer.

'Beer it is,' Pop said, hardly concealing his surprise. He himself was on ginger ale. 'This is my son-in-law, Mr Charlton. This is me old friend, the General. And this is the Reverend Candy — here, where's Mr Candy got to? He was here a minute ago.'

Mr Candy, having fortified himself with Guinness, had vanished into the house to find Primrose. With some of his much-needed strength back, he had an urgent question to ask her.

The urgency of the question faded utterly,

however, when he found her waiting in the sitting-room, all alone; and, in defiance of Ma's orders, clad in a ravishingly tight micro-skirt of a kind of shot mauve-apricot shade, altogether more disturbing than any bare midriff had ever been.

'Just one little quick one. I thought you were never coming,' she said and then held up her lips and proceeded to give him a kiss of such prolonged and destructive artistry that Mr Candy felt himself fading gradually away into a state, as it were, of intoxicated benediction. He longed, even though against his will, to say Amen, but Primrose was having none of it and had just started a repeat performance when Ma's voice abruptly brought it all to an end.

'Dishing up!'

Mr Candy, feeling not a little dished up himself, wandered into the open air, breathless and thirsty all over again, to find almost everyone now assembled about the long table under the walnut tree. The two little Miss Barnwells were now among the guests and, like little Oscar and Phyllida, were already sitting at table, as always like two eager budgerigars, gazing hungrily on the plates of smoked salmon, waiting to be fed. The only person who hadn't arrived was Miss Pilchester, who was always late, anyway, Ma reflected, and probably thought it was still Saturday or something.

'Am I late? Am I late? It *is* the right day, isn't it? I had one of my hens die in the night and it was absolutely ghastly. I just couldn't leave — you know — until — well, what with the

213

warm weather and I couldn't eat it, could I? I very nearly thought of fetching you, Mr Candy, to conduct the — Oh! am I *awfully, awfully* late?'

Again Ma found herself without a word to say. The reason this time was that Edith too had gone out and bought herself a new dress in honour of the Queen's Counsel. Ma gazed at it enraptured. It was appropriately of royal blue. The skirt was calf length, the neck high, the front covered, like a bandsman's tunic, with large gold frogs. All this did nothing for Miss Pilchester's figure since there was in fact little or no figure to do anything for. Nor could Ma decide whether or not it was meant to be a housecoat, a bath-robe or something left over from Edith's service in the Navy.

Soon, the smoked salmon having rapidly disappeared and a good deal of champagne with it, Mr Charlton and Montgomery having carved and dismembered the turkeys, and Pop having done the honours with the *Chambolle*, there was much champing at the table, no less from the little Miss Barnwells and the Brigadier than from Edith Pilchester who, hugely enjoying herself on being released at last from *purdah*, kept saying:

'Delicious. Delicious. Now if I kept turkeys and one of *them* had died what *would* I have done? That *would* have been a dilemma. What *would* I have done?'

'Sung the whole of the *St Matthew Passion* I shouldn't wonder,' the Brigadier said tersely and not unexpectedly downed a third glass of Chambolle Musigny '59. 'Splendid stuff, the

Chambolle. Quite delectable. Of the Divine Order itself.'

Ma had so arranged the table that Angela sat on one side of Pop and Edith on the other; herself on one side of Angela's father and Sister Trevelyan on the other, leaving Primrose to the Brigadier and one each of the little budgerigars to Montgomery and Mr Candy. In this arrangement Primrose was kept as near to Mr Candy as possible and as far from Sister Trevelyan as could be without seeming outright rude. Ma thought there was a bit of jealousy there.

And well there might be, she thought. Sister Trevelyan looked stunningly attractive in a simple pure white dress that was deceptively angelic, with its silver waist chain and simple neckline. So much so that Ma wondered if she'd done the right thing in putting her next to Sir John, who she had now decided was not only uncommonly handsome but had quite a look in his eye. Took after Angela, she shouldn't wonder, and was quick to note that quite half the time Sir John seemed to be eating with only one hand, so that Ma shrewdly wondered what he was doing with the other.

She needn't have wondered at all.

'If you do that again,' Sister Trevelyan whispered, 'I shall scream.'

'Scream.'

Sister Trevelyan thought it prudent not to scream.

'I thought,' Sir John said, 'you came from down under?'

'Yes, but not down under there!'

Presently Ma, shrewdly grasping that much more than mere eating and drinking was going on, lifted her glass and said:

'Well, cheers! everybody. Nice to have you all here. Lovely. Cheers.'

Among the returning chorus of cheers the voice of the Brigadier could be heard saying 'Bingo!' and a crescendo of twitterings came from the Miss Barnwells. The only absent voice was that of Pop, who sat staring at a half empty glass of ginger ale, a fact that touched Ma so much that she said pointedly to Sister Trevelyan:

'What about it, Sister? What about a drop of Chambolle for Pop? Just a glass? Just one?'

Oh yes! yes indeed, the Miss Barnwells prattled. After all it was the Cause. Mr Larkin had been so terribly, terribly generous, to which Edith Pilchester added:

'Oh! yes, *please*. Just a teeny, teeny one. It seems so unfair.'

'What about it, Sister?' Ma said.

'Well, since I am not really on duty today,' Sister Trevelyan said, having been pinched so often by Sir John that she was now beginning to feel almost neglected when it didn't happen, 'just one glass. Just one small glass. But not a word to Dr O'Connor, otherwise my head will be on the block.'

Laughing with delight, Ma filled a glass with Chambolle Musigny and passed it over to Pop. At long, long last his period of *purdah* too was over. He could drink at last. Life was about to be good again.

With the word 'Cheers!' falling from his lips

almost as a prayer of thanks Pop raised the glass, sipped at it and put it down again, his face wry.

'Something wrong?' Ma said. 'Not corked, is it?'

Pop hesitated, licked his lips and then tasted the wine again.

'Perfick,' he said. 'Only I don't like the taste, that's all.'

Did he mind? Ma said. He didn't *what?*

'Don't like it, that's all, Ma. Don't like the taste. Tastes funny.'

Ma, struck speechless for the third time that morning, told herself she would go to the bone-house. She didn't for the life of her know what things were coming to.

'Suppose when you've been off a thing all that long you sort of lose the urge for it or summat,' Pop said. 'Suppose you can do without it.'

Oh! you did, did you? Ma thought, thinking of other things and hoping that what applied to wine wouldn't apply to letting Nature take its course in other directions. Pop not liking the *taste?* It really had her be-jiggered.

'Great pity not to savour this excellent vintage,' Sir John said, at the same time savouring the vintage of Sister Trevelyan somewhere in the region of the left upper thigh. 'Beautiful bouquet.'

Future looked black, Ma thought. She half-wished she hadn't let her place next to Sir John be taken over by Phyllida, who in true feminine Larkin fashion had insisted on sitting next to him instead of Ma. After all there was no doubt he was a bit of a dog. She was very near tempted to start making up to him herself. The curled half-grey, half-blond hair, thick and rather long about the ears, together with the lamb-chop whiskers, the beautiful cultured aristocratic voice and the grey-blue eyes that were never still: it wouldn't take anybody long to get a bit worked up, Ma thought.

'Interested in gardening, Sir John?' Ma said, just to see what happened.

Well, yes, he was, Sir John said, intensely: it was one of his hobbies, he confessed, contriving at the same time to pursue another one of them with Sister Trevelyan.

'Good. You must come and see mine after lunch.'

'Splendid. Delighted.'

As the meal went on and on it struck the little Miss Barnwells and also Miss Pilchester and even Mr Candy and Ma, that it was very curious that no mention had been made of the Cause. This, after all, was largely what the lunch was about: to stave off the invading forces of treacherous bureaucracy and so on, to keep the village and Pop's property inviolate and in all ways to defend the Realm and the Cause. Everybody, rather like Ma, had certain confused ideas as to what the functions of a Queen's Counsel were and half wondered if they ought not to set up a committee there and then, appoint Sir John as chairman and then hear the case for the defence put in true expert legal fashion.

They were however so shy as to be utterly unable to put these thoughts into words and it was finally left to the Brigadier to broach the subject, which he did by holding up his sixth or seventh glass of Chambolle Musigny, looking through it with fruity ardour at Angela Snow and then saying:

'I understand, sir, that you've been good enough to take up the brief on our behalf. Noble gesture.'

The Brigadier's few cryptic words had the immediate effect of producing no reply whatever from Sir John. At the same time there was a positive torrent of explanation and comments from the little Miss Barnwells, Edith Pilchester and even Ma and Mr Candy. Road, tunnel, Common Market, Rome, Island, England's Green and Pleasant Land: the chorus wasn't merely one of explanation and comments but one of protest, indignation and, on Edith Pilchester's part, of righteous fervour amounting almost to wrath.

'I have even been able to discover that we are probably on *Holy ground*. A Consecrated Place.'

''ear, 'ear,' Pop said. It pleased and flattered him greatly that his house, his land and his junk-yard might well be, as Mr Candy had intimated, on Sacred Ground.

'What we all feel is that the enemy is *near*,' Miss Pilchester said. 'We must act *swiftly*.'

At this point Sir John, whose mind had throughout lunch been, exactly as one hand had been, on other things, now seemed to take a desultory interest in the general proceedings.

'Really?' he said. He spoke in the most casual of voices and that languid aristocratic drawl that

Pop had always loved in Angela Snow. '*Swiftly?* I should have thought quite the contrary.'

'Oh! no, *swiftly, swiftly,*' Miss Pilchester said. 'After all, ''if 'twere done it were well that it' — Oh! yes, the quicker the better.'

Sir John smiled indulgently.

'No, no,' he said. 'What we need is a little Jarndyce and Jarndyce.'

'*Bleak House,*' Primrose said with flashing promptitude.

Bleak it would be too, Ma thought, if they had a road right through it and Pop no more in the mood for a glass of wine and the things that mattered. Jaundice was right. She'd heard there was a lot of it about.

Pop too had slightly misheard the words. *Jaundice and Jaundice?* He didn't want to catch that on top of everything else.

''Jarndyce and Jarndyce drones on.'' quoted Primrose with that endless knowledge of literature that had more than once had Mr Candy tied in knots both of emotion and excess. ''Jarndyce and Jarndyce has passed into a joke. The legion of bills in the suit have been transformed into mere bills of mortality.''

Pop was once again stunned by the marvels of education. He'd never heard anything like it. Clearly nobody else had, either. There was dead silence all round the table.

It was broken at last by Sir John, making a remark of such inconsequence that Ma suddenly thought he must be slightly off-course or something.

'Mrs Larkin, in which direction is your

garden? The flower garden, I mean?'

Well, it was over there, Ma said, very mystified but at the same time wondering if this wasn't the chance she'd been waiting for. Why?

Without pausing to say why, Sir John rose from the table, took a swift draught of Chambolle Musigny and promptly disappeared in the direction of the garden.

Two or three minutes later he came back with a single scarlet flower in his hand. Then, rather to Sister Trevelyan's disappointment, he changed places with Phyllida and sat down next to Ma.

'Mrs Larkin,' he said, holding up the flower to Ma, 'I want you to tell me what flower this is.'

'It's a zinnia, of course.'

'Zinnia. Are you sure?'

'Of course I'm sure. After all, one of our twins is named Zinnia.'

'How do you know it's a zinnia?'

'Well, that's what it always has been. That's what I was always told.'

'And what is the name of the other twin?'

'Petunia.'

'And do you know one from the other? Zinnia from Petunia?'

'Well, I do, but Pop doesn't. He never sees them in the bath.'

'Never sees them in the bath, eh? Well, never mind. The point is you know a zinnia from a petunia?'

'Of course I do. Like knowing what a buttercup is.'

'Like knowing what a buttercup is? But this, you say, is a zinnia?'

221

'Yes.'

'Good. It's a zinnia because someone told you it was a zinnia, somewhere and at some time. And because you know one from the other. And why is it called a zinnia and not, for example, a petunia?'

Ma, very confused, confessed she didn't know. She could only suppose it was called a zinnia because it came from the country of Zinnia, wherever that was. Next to Zambia or somewhere, she shouldn't wonder. They changed the names of places and countries so often nowadays.

'There is no country called Zinnia.'

'No?'

'No. But in the sixteenth century there was a Polish author named Adam Sdizianskya von Zuluzian. What would you say if I told you that it was after him that the zinnia is named?'

'Well, I suppose I'd believe you.'

'You'd believe me. Why?'

'Well, if you say so.'

'If I say so.' Sir John once again smiled with both charm and indulgence, actually patting Ma on the cheek. 'But I didn't say so.'

'Oh! but you did.'

'No, no, dear Mrs Larkin, I did not. What I did say was 'What would *you* say if I told you that it *was* after him that the zinnia is named?''

'Oh! dear.'

'Exactly. In fact the zinnia is named after J. G. Zinn, a Professor of Botany.'

The entire lunch party having been stunned to utter silence by this display of argument and erudition the words which came from Primrose to break it fell on everybody like an explosion.

'In fact Jarndyce and Jarndyce,' she said, 'all over again.'

'Precisely,' Sir John said. 'By the way, who is that young lady?'

'That's our Primrose,' Ma said. 'She should have gone to University by rights.'

'University my Aunt Nellie. Never spoil a natural talent,' Sir John said and then gave Primrose such a handsome, fervent look of appraisal that Sister Trevelyan, Mariette, Ma, and Mr Candy were all jealous at the same time.

'Always quoting from the poets and all that,' Pop said. Ever ready to praise the virtues and marvels of education he nevertheless now found himself utterly out of his depth. He didn't catch on at all. What the pipe had Jaundice and Jaundice got to do with zinnias, professors and Polish poets? If he'd been drinking it might have explained it, but he was stone-cold sober.

'Always quoting the poets, eh?' Sir John said. 'Well, let's see if she can finish this quotation. 'In delay there lies — ''

''No plenty,'' Primrose said promptly, at the same time giving Mr. Candy a melting look that scorched his vital parts as warmly and richly as another glass of Chambolle Musigny.

''Then come and kiss me sweet and twenty.''

'True?' Sir John said, 'or false?'

'True in one sense,' Primrose said with that convincing look of intelligence and seduction that had long since led Mr Candy down the road of excess, 'but not in another.'

'Explain.'

Primrose promptly did so by further quotation:

'True in the sense 'that such a thing might happen when the sky rained potatoes — or when we get through Jarndyce and Jarndyce'.'

'Clever girl. Exactly.'

The Brigadier was another one who now confessed to himself that he was utterly out of his depth. Damme, what was this? Some kind of outflanking movement? A sort of verbal ambush? Or what? Damned odd tactics.

'If I may say so,' Miss Pilchester said, being also lost in verbal mystification, 'we don't seem to be getting very far. I don't know if you got what I said about the *Holy Place* — the Consecrated Ground — but it seems to me to be a point.'

It was now Mr Charlton, as so often in the past, who opened the doors to understanding. Marvellous feller, Charley boy, Pop told himself almost before Charley opened his mouth, lost in premature admiration.

'Ah! but the point is that we're not getting very far,' Mr Charlton said, 'because we don't want to get very far. Right, Sir John?'

'Admirably correct.'

'Or, what, in other words,' Primrose said, 'Shakespeare called 'The Law's delays'.'

Here Pop struck the table a shuddering blow with his open hand. He'd catched on now. Marvellous feller too, Sir John. There was more to that head than lamb-chop whiskers.

'Have a cigar, Sir John? Havanas. The best.

Glass o' port? Vintage. Iced or warm?'

Ma, who had been no little bewildered by it all herself, promptly gave Pop one of her severe looks and said it wasn't time for port and cigars yet. They still had afters to come: the Christmas pudding and brandy and all that. She hoped Pop wasn't going to tell her he didn't like the taste of brandy on the pud now, was he? That *would* be the day, what with one thing and another.

The fires of Havanas and brandy on the pudding having at last been lit, Primrose was moved to quote yet again:

''We shall this day light such a candle by God's grace in England — '' to which the Brigadier, caressing with bucolic tenderness the rim of his wine-glass, filled for the tenth time to overflowing, murmured a fervent 'Hear, hear! They shall not pass.'

With the arrival of the port, poured with rich and characteristic generosity by Pop into big crimson goblets, Sir John proceeded to move back to his position side by side with Sister Trevelyan where he went through the mesmerizing act of caressing her thigh with one hand and alternately holding port and cigar with the other, while at the same time explaining to the still mystified Miss Barnwells and Miss Pilchester what exactly might constitute the law's delays.

'We shall go back in Time. We shall go sideways in Time. We shall go upside down in Time. Even underground in Time. We shall invoke statutes, quote Scripture, split hairs, even pause to pick daisies. Holy Well? — splendid. We shall quote Chaucer, lead in the Pilgrims, even trail the blood of Thomas a'Becket. What *is* will appear not to be. What *wasn't* we shall have to make sure *is*. Where there is no obstacle we will most certainly put one. Where one *is* we shall see that it's lost. A day in our courts, in fact, will be better than a thousand. Won't it, Sister Trevelyan?'

It already had been, Sister Trevelyan thought.

'And when we have reached the point of no return, or think we have, we shall surprise everyone by going back to where we started.'

It wouldn't surprise her, Sister Trevelyan thought. The point of no return had been reached some considerable time ago. Moreover it was her guess that any moment Sir John would be back there again.

How long this process of seduction, verbal and otherwise, might have gone on under the tender shade of the walnut tree, on which the young walnuts already hung in broken August sunshine like soft green plums, it was impossible to say. The silence and softness of the afternoon were by now woven into a web of embalment no less enrapturing than the words of the handsome Queen's Counsel, so that somewhere about mid afternoon Primrose was moved again to quotation.

''A drowsy numbness pains my sense,'' she whispered to Mr Candy and quietly led him away.

As Ma watched the two of them drifting away towards the house she was suddenly yet again astonished by the sight of someone in the garden who appeared not to have been invited: another of those Sunday moochers, she didn't doubt, looking for a bargain.

*   *   *

Some moments later Mr Charlton, jumping suddenly up, told her otherwise.

'Good God, it's that man from the Ministry. I clean forgot. He said he might drop in one Sunday on the way back from visiting his sister in Brighton. Leave it to me — I'll get rid of him.'

'No, no, don't get rid of him,' Sir John said in that affable aristocratic voice that was so like that of Angela's, 'invite him over. After all, the spider hath had victories no less renowned than wasps.'

'That's what we call his whipped-cream voice,' Angela told Pop in a whisper. 'Creams 'em first. Whips 'em afterwards.'

A minute later a small, grey-haired, slightly balding man of fifty-five or so, lean, harassed and almost haggard, a little nervous and apologetic at having broken in on a family Sunday afternoon, joined the lunch table, where Pop, although refraining from striking him on the back in greeting, nevertheless offered him cigar, sherry, gin, brandy, vodka and port all in one breath, adding that he was afraid he didn't know his name?

'Harrington.'

'Right, Mr Harrington, sit you here. Take the load off your feet. What can we do for you?'

'Oh! very little actually. It's more of a courtesy call. I did call once before but unfortunately you

227

were *hors de combat*. I hope you're feeling better?'

Pop, about to say that he was as fit as a flea, altered his mind and said middling instead and thrust into Mr Harrington's hand a goblet of iced sherry containing about half a bottle.

'Cheers!' Pop said. 'Bottoms up. Where are you from again?'

'The Ministry.'

At this point Sir John took over. His voice, as Angela herself had pointed out, was as smooth as whipped cream.

'What Ministry, may I ask, is that?'

'Transport.'

'Ah! Sing-Sing,' Sir John said, giving the Ministry the pet name by which it was known to its unfortunate occupants in London. 'So you work on Sundays now? Admirable innovation.'

'Well, not actually, no — yes and no — if — '

'Well, do you or don't you?'

'Well, no actually. I sort of acted on my own initiative.'

'So they actually let Civil Servants act on their own initiative nowadays, do they? Good.'

'Well, it isn't work, really.'

'Then what is it?'

'Well, it's — well there's this proposed — there's to be this preliminary inquiry — '

'Into what?'

'Well, not into anything yet.'

'Then why inquire?'

'Well, in due course — there may be — this area may be under consideration for — '

'Ah! the road. Yes, we've been chatting up

about that.' With the handsomest of smiles Sir John seemed to become aware, as it were for the first time, of Miss Pilchester. 'You haven't met our local historian, have you? Miss Pilchester. Awfully good port, isn't it?'

'Actually I haven't tried it yet. I've got sherry.'

'Oh! but you must. It's sublime. Cockburns, '39. You simply can't get it any more. There just isn't any to be had.'

Instantly Pop handed Mr Harrington a large glass of port, which Mr Harrington tried, pronouncing it to be quite unlike anything he had ever tasted before, a remark that Sir John completely and coolly ignored.

'Ah! yes. Our local historian, Miss Pilchester,' Sir John said. 'She knows this part of the world inside out, don't you, Miss Pilchester?'

Thus flattered, Miss Pilchester could only fluff with indecision, unable to frame a word.

'From the time of Caesar's legions onwards. Romans, Pilgrims, Civil War, Napoleonic War — she knows it all. I even swear she calls the blades of grass by their Christian, or even Roman, names.'

Mr Harrington, sipping now at iced sherry and then tentatively at the sublime excellence of the port, was suitably impressed.

'So you're from the Ministry?' Sir John said with the creamiest affability.

'Yes, I am, yes.'

'How do I know?'

'Well, I am, you know.'

'But I don't know.'

'But I said I was.'

'Which is not, of course, the same thing.'

'But it is.'

'I'm delighted to hear it. Have you your authority with you?'

'Well, no, actually not. I'm on leave for a few days.'

'Oh! yes? For all I know you may be either the Dean of St Paul's or the landlord of The Pig and Whistle in Lambeth, always supposing there is a Pig and Whistle in Lambeth.'

'I am not the landlord of The Pig and Whistle in Lambeth.'

'No? How do I know?'

'I just am not, that's all.'

'There again, can you prove otherwise?'

'Well, I'm afraid I can't if you put it like that.'

'I do put it like that. Beautiful port, isn't it? Nectar. When you think that there simply isn't any vintage port left. Except in a few private cellars. Like that of Mr Larkin here.'

'It's absolutely splendid.'

'Good. Have some more. You've lunched, I trust?'

Mr Harrington, who had stopped for a small packet of potato crisps, a half pint of bitter and a wash at a pub some miles farther down the road to the coast, was obliged to confess that he hadn't really.

'Oh! what a shame,' Ma said. 'We can't have that. I'll fetch you a mite of cold.'

The mite of cold turned out to be a complete wing of turkey fortified by a slab of breast and a pile of pink cold ham with salad, French beans and potatoes. Pop fortified it further by a glass of

Chambolle Musigny, which he assured Mr Harrington was even better vintage than the port. It was the tops. Thus embalmed with food and wine Mr Harrington had scarcely another word to say.

The rest of the afternoon, and indeed the early evening, belonged almost wholly to Sir John. In a blue haze of cigar smoke, in tender dappled walnut shade, he held the company bewitched. He extracted from a wide-eyed Miss Pilchester thoughts that had never been hers. He beguiled her first into uttering truths that she knew to be falsehoods; then into lies which were made to seem like heaven-blessed truths. He besought her to remember the unfortunate army of Roman legionaries that had sunk and perished across the very meadows that now surrounded the Larkin domain: meadows of bottomless mire, fathomless traps which wouldn't support a train of beetles, still less an army, the entire establishment of which had perished as in a quick-mire, direly suffocated in mud.

He begged her further to remember the band of pilgrims that had been slaughtered even as they prayed and drank at the Holy Well, so that the well ran bright with the blood of the innocent and pious and was in consequence for ever cursed. He urged her to recite chapter and verse for those spies of Napoleon's found skulking in an osier bed, not two hundred yards away, from which they were taken on a far distant fine May morning and, to the sound of mocking cuckoos, hanged, drawn and quartered. Since earliest times the dark lustre of evil had lain on the adjacent land. Those who had come to violate it had themselves been violated. It had always been so and, he feared and suspected, always would be.

'And by the way, Mr Larkin, where did you get this excellent port?'

Pop said he'd got it from a former neighbour of his, Mr Jerebohm, city gent. Pop had sold him Gore Court, the big house down the road, since when nothing but bad luck, and then disaster, had followed him. Bluff Court was really Pop's name for the house, on account of its having formerly been owned by Sir George Bluff-Gore, who couldn't afford to keep it up and had pigged it out in a keeper's cottage instead until he had sold the big house to Pop, in despair.

'Couldn't get servants. Couldn't heat the place. Raised thousands of pheasants and never hardly shot one. Rode to hounds and always fell off his horse. Climbed over a gate one day with his gun and very near shot his foot orf. Couldn't keep the mice down. Remember the mice, Ma?'

Ma, laughing like jelly, remembered the mice. How could she ever forget them? Poor Pinkie, Mrs Jerebohm, had fifty traps going at a time and still found two in her bed and another in a rice pudding one day.

'Oh! in the end they gave it up,' Pop said. 'Went back to London. I bought the whole place back from them, lock, stock and barrel. Port, cellars an' all.'

'Very little of the port, I suppose? It's getting mighty scarce nowadays.'

Oh! he didn't know, Pop said. Hadn't counted

it up just lately. Fifty cases or more he shouldn't wonder. Dows, Taylors, Fonseca, Cockburn — the whole shoot. Some as far back as '27. There was a nice lot of Chambolle and Vosne Romane, too. He'd given a fair price for it though, mind you. Sort of slipped it in with the price of the house.

'And that reminds me,' Sir John said in that smooth languid voice of his so well described by Angela as being like whipped cream, 'who is your immediate superior at Sing-Sing, Mr Harrington?'

'Fortescue.'

'Ah! of course. I know him. He's a member of my club. Great port man too. Swear he hasn't seen much like this for a long time.'

'Very good taste in port, Mr Jerebohm,' Ma said. 'I'll say that for him.'

'I suppose we couldn't spare Fortescue a case, could we, Mr Larkin? Excellent man to have on our side.'

Mr Harrington was seen to grow uneasy. Sending gifts of port to his immediate superior? Dangerous ground. There was after all such a thing as the Corrupt Practices Act.

'And perhaps a case of the Chambolle for Mr Harrington?'

'Of course. Perfick. Why not?'

Mr Harrison, bewitched and embalmed not only by Sir John's persuasive, creamy voice and manner, was also feeling heated, all too well-fed, uncertain and very dizzy.

'Montgomery, put a case of the old Chambolle into Mr Harrington's car, will you, wherever it is.

Where is your car, Mr Harrington?'

Mr Harrington had neither the time nor will to answer before Sir John cut in with a remark of the smoothest innocence:

'And is anyone in the house? I mean Gore Court, now, Mr Larkin? You've sold it again?'

Pop said he'd sold it again about three months ago. Fair profit. Going to be a Horticultural Research place. House and twenty acres. Part of the new University.

'Really?' Sir John suddenly looked as if he'd seen a vision or stumbled on a diamond mine. 'Really?'

'Education on the doorstep now,' Ma said. 'Wherever you go it's education.'

'Education,' Sir John murmured as in a ruminative dream. 'Education.'

And then abruptly, off in one of those disconcerting tangents that Pop found so fascinating in Angela, he suddenly rose from the table and said:

'You were going to show me your garden, weren't you, Mrs Larkin? What have you got in it, now? I'm afraid mine's nearly over.'

Oh! she'd got dahlias, phloxes, fuchsias, petunias, gladioli, Ma said, and zinnias of course. And lilies. Ma was immensely proud of her lilies. They came from Japan. She had raised them all herself. From seed.

'Show me.'

Sir John extended his arm in a manner absolutely befitting, as Ma saw it, a Queen's Counsel, and Ma in turn accepted it almost as if for once, briefly, in her oyster satin, she was a queen herself: a gesture that at once aroused in Sister Trevelyan, Mariette, Miss Pilchester and even the little Miss Barnwells varying spasms of jealousy. Nor did Ma fail to note that there was also a glint of it in Pop's eye, a fact for which she wasn't in the least bit sorry.

★　★　★

And where are these lilies, Mrs Larkin?

'Right over the far side of the garden.'

As she and Sir John strolled slowly through paths lined with phloxes, dahlias, fuchsias, tobacco plants and all the flowers Ma loved, she suddenly remembered that word education. Funny how it was always cropping up. You couldn't get away from it nowadays.

Nor had she failed to notice how creamily satisfied Sir John had seemed about the word: so much so that he now repeated it, almost smacking his lips, as over a fresh glass of even more excellent port.

'Education, yes, Mrs Larkin. Education.'

'You think it's all that important?' Ma said. She was bound to confess she herself very often didn't.

'In this case, yes. We are back, Mrs Larkin, with Jarndyce and Jarndyce. Our old friends.'

Oh! were they? Ma said. And what had they got to do with it?

'On the one hand the Jarndyce of the Ministry of Transport, on the other the Jarndyce of the Ministry of Education.'

Ma confessed she didn't quite get it.

'No? As your dear clever little daughter said, when you get Jarndyce v. Jarndyce you can bet your sweet life it'll go on until it rains potatoes from the sky.'

Ah! they were clever, these Queen's Counsel, Ma told herself. No wonder Her Majesty had so many of them around her, giving her advice.

'And now the lilies. Let us consider how they grow. Where are the lilies?'

Well, they were, Ma said, up against the seat by the wall. She waved a big, fat admiring hand, the fingers of which flowered as opulently with rings as the lilies with heads of flower. They looked, the lilies, Ma often thought, like a crowd of Eastern emperors, all in Turks' caps, gold and white and pink and copper and lime-green and orange and sulphur. A bit like Solomon in all his glory.

Then, as Ma and Sir John stood gazing at the lilies in admiration and on Sir John's part with no little envy, Primrose and Mr Candy suddenly appeared through the garden gate that led from the fields beyond.

'Oh! there you are,' Ma said. 'Just been talking to Sir John about your old friends Jarndyce and Jarndyce.'

'Oh! yes?'

'Yes, Sir John says he don't think we need to worry our loaves about the road till 1990 or thereabouts, Jarndyce and Jarndyce'll see to that.'

It was time for Primrose to come up with Blake again; and she instantly did:

''Improvement makes straight roads; but the

crooked roads without Improvement are the roads of Genius.'’

'I'm not sure if I care for that word crooked,' Sir John said, 'but I'll accept the genius,' and promptly gave Primrose a look of such seductive smoothness that Mr Candy at once felt wretchedly jealous and was slightly dismayed to hear Primrose say:

'Are we having supper in the garden, Ma? If so how many will we be? Then Mr Candy and I can start getting things ready.'

'Feels a bit like thunder, I think, don't you?' Ma said. 'Lots of these little thunder flies about.'

'Well, we can get everything ready anyway,' Primrose said. 'If it doesn't rain we'll eat outside. If it does — well, how many will we be anyway?'

Oh! they'd be the same as lunch, Ma supposed. That's if Sir John stayed. Would Sir John care to stay?

'Adore to. Utterly delighted,' Sir John said, sounding exactly like an echo of the smooth-voiced Angela. 'Absolutely nothing I'd like more.'

'Lovely,' Primrose said with a smoothness of her own and at once led an even more jealous Mr Candy away.

Alone in the garden with Ma, Sir John immediately began to praise the lilies with precisely the same extravagance he had previously bestowed on the vintage port. Incomparable. Sublime. Regal. Had a vintage of their own. Almost, as the dear Brigadier had said, of the Divine Order.

Entranced and flattered, Ma hardly knew what to do or say. Sir John at once solved part of this problem by suggesting that he and Ma sit down

and admire the glorious trumpets and turks'
caps that she, in her clever way, had raised from
seed. Mrs Larkin really had green fingers.

'They're quite majestic, aren't they? How
clever you are, Mrs Larkin. One really feels one
ought to pay court to them.'

Court — lovely word, Ma thought. Majestic
— she liked that very much too. After all you
rather expected words like that from a Queen's
Counsel.

'You really must tell me where you get the
seed from, Mrs Larkin,' Sir John said and at the
same time gave Ma's right thigh, or the extreme
rim of it, a dexterous caress, like the movement
of a slow warm iron across a smooth ironing
board.

Ma pretended to take no notice whatsoever.

'Japan,' she said.

'Ah! yes, you said so. Not too heavy a perfume.'

'Not now. But you wait till it gets dark,' Ma
said, at which Sir John repeated the smooth,
dexterous caress across her thigh, as if hoping it
soon would be.

Ma sniffed at the air, not for the immediate
purpose of drinking in the scent of lilies but at
the prospect of thunder.

'It's getting heavy like, don't you think? I mean
the air,' she said. 'I do hope we don't get a storm.'

'Don't think so. It'll probably go along the
hills,' Sir John said and softly proceeded to go
along the hills himself, in the region of Ma's
right shoulder.

'I think I ought to go upstairs and see that all

the windows are shut,' Ma suddenly said. 'In case it comes a storm.'

'Is there that hurry?'

'Oh! better to be safe than sorry,' Ma said and swung herself deftly away, though not without calling over her shoulder that she'd be back soon. 'I've got plenty of young seedling lilies by the way if you'd like some. In that frame over there. Pick some out. You're very welcome.'

Smoothly Sir John murmured thanks and added that he adored young lilies, saying it in such a way that it seemed almost to refer to Ma, who was consequently honoured and delighted.

Upstairs Ma suddenly felt herself come over all hot and sticky. It wouldn't be a bad plan, she told herself, to change her oyster satin and get into something cooler. This she proceeded to do, at the same time dispensing with her slip, stockings and corsets, the latter having taken a tighter and tighter grip on her all day until now they had a positive and almost painful lock on her, creasing her ample flesh so that she could hardly breathe. With a figure like hers — 55-55-55 — you needed all the comfort you could get.

With much relief she finally got into a loose magenta-pink dress of rather low cut and short sleeves and at once felt a good deal refreshed. A generous dose of her favourite *Chanel No. 5* having drenched almost every part of her body she could reach she at last felt she smelled almost as sweetly as the lilies always did when they gave off their richest, heaviest perfume after dark.

By the time she got downstairs again the threat of thunder seemed less direct. Only a half-golden, half-murky premature twilight hung over the garden, slightly deepening under the big walnut-tree, where Primrose, Angela and Mariette had already laid the long table for supper.

'Candles,' Ma said, 'or these little lamps. Or both. Else we'll never see what we're eating.'

As the table was already grossly overladen with ham, cold duck, cold chicken, cold turkey, pork pies, cold sausages of several kinds and six sorts of cheeses, together with fruit and trifles and bread and pickles and salads and tarts and mousses and various other things, this seemed unlikely to happen, Mr Harrington thought.

Mr Harrington, an awfully confused and bewildered man in both mind and body, sat talking to Pop. His confusion rose from the fact that throughout the afternoon and evening he had asked himself the same question a thousand times and had never had an answer. The question, 'Why bother? Why such defence of a very ordinary, ramshackle, sloppy, almost derelict dump of a place as this?' referred to Pop's beloved paradise, where he and Ma had spent so much of their fruitful, unconstricted, happy lives. Mr Harrington, who had a few years yet to go before he could enjoy a frugal retirement and meagre pension, simply couldn't for the life of him understand the passionate, almost fanatical defence of such a dump. In his eyes and estimation it would have been far better bull-dozed swiftly away.

'Ah! you should be here in the spring,' Pop

240

was saying to him. 'Perfick then, Mr Harrington. Blackbirds, nightingales, primroses, millions of bluebells — perfick bit of England. Perfick.'

The enthusiastic words fell from Pop's lips at the very moment when Ma was coming back from the house with Phyllida and little Oscar, the children carrying the candles, Ma bearing two small brass oil lamps. When Ma, at the urgent request of the children, lit both lamps and candles and set them on the supper table the glow of light fell close and bright on to the pink-magenta dress, its low cut revealing with startling pleasantness the vast cleft bosom smooth and olive above.

Very nice too, Pop thought. Primrose and bluebell, eh? He wondered if that pertickler mood of Ma's would ever come back?

'Beautiful, Mr Harrington, beautiful. Perfick,' Pop said, referring now not to Ma's revealing shape but again to his paradise in springtime.

Mr Harrington didn't doubt it was, but why? he kept asking himself, why? It was part of his job to go about the country in investigation of ministerial proposals to drive new and highly important roads through here, there and Heaven alone knew where else. It was his job, further, to attend public inquiries, listen to public objectors and try generally to cajole, argue, pacify and at last persuade people, if possible, to accept roads they all too often didn't want, which were often quite unnecessary and which would in all likelihood be inadequate and out of date by the time they were built. He had long been convinced that he had met every kind of objection and objector that existed on the face of the earth. Some of these he had persuaded; from others he had suffered defeat; of others he had made eternal enemies; from all he suffered the varying tortures and purgatories of frustration that had made him prematurely bald, prematurely grey, prematurely old and as often as not very nearly weary unto death. And they said, he sometimes told himself bitterly, that civil servants never worked. The wonder of it was that they were ever civil.

He had listened, in his time, to objectors wanting to save ancient cottages, historical court-houses, Palladian mansions, great avenues of limes, eighteenth-century follies, thirteenth-century bridges, precious farm-land, ye olde pubs and even ye olde tea-shoppes, pleasant private gardens, alms-houses, estates planned by Capability Brown, market crosses, great parks rich with oak-trees old when Henry VIII had reigned with licence and liberty, winding village streets, ornamental lakes, wrought-iron gates by Inigo Jones, exclusive schools, hallowed chapels, railway stations and even, on one occasion, an American airfield.

To someone or other all these had been important, precious, sweet, commemorative, even sacred. Like patience on a monument Mr Harrington had listened, unsmiling, ungrieved and always on the rim of despair, to all of them. And sometimes he had understood.

But not this: not the Larkin place. This, like the peace of God, passed all understanding.

'Another snifter, Mr Harrington? Sherry, gin?

I make some very nice cocktails.'

Already replete and slightly heavy-headed from sherry, port and much burgundy Mr Harrington confessed that he thought he would settle for something soft, a dry ginger or something. He was rather thirsty.

'Red Bull,' Pop said with typical promptitude, 'just the thing. Long and harmless. I'll put plenty of ice in. That'll quench you like a charm.'

That was another thing that had Mr Harrington guessing. Where *did* it all come from? The lavish living, the vintage port, the expensive burgundy, the expensive taste combined with ghastly taste, the flamboyance and the vulgarity, the presence of the aristocratic Miss Snow and still more of her father, a Queen's Counsel. He wondered what *they* thought of it? and above all why *they* were here? It was really beyond all understanding.

'There you are, Mr Harrington. Mixed a good long double with plenty of ice. It'll go down like spring water.'

'Supper's ready!' Ma called.

A few moments later the whole company were again gathered under the walnut tree. The supper table, laden to the very edges, embroidered with faces above and about it, was golden with the light of lamps and candles. Ma presided at one end and Pop, rather like a sober shepherd with his flock, at the other.

Mr Charlton had decided that pink champagne, well-iced, would be the correct answer to all needs on such an evening of quiet, balmy sultriness and to this purpose had brought up an old foot-bath, in which a dozen bottles were now half-rising, half-floating in a small sea of icebergs.

'And give the children a drop,' Ma said, 'it won't hurt them.'

Ma had a theory that with alcohol, as with a number of other important things in life, it was better to start young. It would do you a lot less harm later.

The bountiful flow of pink iced champagne had the effect of making the company very gay. Beautiful thing to see, Pop told himself several times, watching the glow of faces in the candlelight: perfick. The little budgerigars chirped over their rose-pink glasses, Miss Pilchester giggled freely and often, the Brigadier hailed, with raised glass, everyone and everything, including the now dark summer night-sky, and Mr Harrington, suffering from the effect of cold pink champagne making its serpentine way into the already imposed spring water of Pop's Red Bull, was in a state of cross-eyed, wondrous stupefaction.

Some time later this became confusion worse confounded by the arrival of Phyllida, who said:

'Please may I sit on your knee?' The youngest of the Larkins, brilliantly red-haired, already a bright seductress, was on Mr Harrington's knee before he could answer, cuddling up to him, champagne glass in hand. 'Everybody else is sitting on everybody else's knee. Angela's sitting on the General's knee. Sister Trevelyan's sitting on Mr Charlton's. Miss Pilchester's sitting on Pop's. And Ma's sitting on — Oh! where's Ma gone? She was here a minute ago.'

Ma in fact was on the far side of the garden, by the lilies, with Sir John. The air, sultry as ever, was over-rich with the perfume of lilies. Except for an occasional bat scooping overhead there was neither sound nor movement in the darkness.

'This is the time they always smell their best,' Ma said, touching one of the lilies as she and Sir John went down the path. 'So rich.'

'Ethereal,' Sir John said. 'Intoxicating.' Again something in the smooth compulsive way he said the words might have been referring to Ma. 'Celestial.'

'Did you take some seedlings for yourself?' Ma said. 'I said to take your pick.'

No, Sir John said, he confessed it had slipped his mind. Perhaps he might come and take his pick some other time?

'Any time,' Ma said. 'Any day suits me.'

Sir John, who was already sitting on the seat by the lilies, indicated with a pat of his hand that there was room for Ma there too. Unlike Mr Harrington, but like Angela, he understood, and also loved, the Larkin place. It seemed to him to be, among other things, part of the answer to a mad world. If it had to be defended he would defend it, with skill, eloquence, delay, subterfuge and if necessary with forms of knavery of which even Mr Harrington, in his ministerial innocence and experience, had never even dreamed.

But all those things were, as yet, far off. The immediate subject was Ma.

'You have such beautiful smooth skin, Mrs Larkin. Like one of those lily petals,' Sir John said and delicately ran his fingers up and down Ma's right thigh, an experience, a sort of trial run in Pop's language, that Ma neither resented nor found at all unpleasant.

Nor did she resent Sir John's next exercise in exploration, which was along her now bare right shoulder. Ma being of the great breadth she was it was impossible to put an arm round her completely and Sir John had consequently decided that the simplest and most rewarding tactics would be to approach, as the Brigadier might have said, in a right-flanking movement.

After several further preliminary exercises Sir John delicately drew Ma's head to his shoulder and kissed her full on her lips, expertly, deeply, warmly and as if inspired by immortal longings; the kiss lasting a very long time.

At the end of it Ma discovered, not completely to her surprise, that somehow, either by accident, design or a subtle combination of both, her right bosom had fallen out.

Sir John at once slipped a hand underneath it, with great delicacy, rather as if he might have been holding a large and precious goblet, eager to save it from falling.

Ma, unsurprised, said nothing. She was in fact thinking of Angela. There was nothing to be surprised about really, was there? It obviously ran in the family.

'You have the most beautiful breasts, Mrs Larkin.'

Oh! had she? Ma said, as if she had been totally unaware of such a blessing up to that moment.

'Very beautiful. Really they're so beautiful.'

Ma actually laughed, softly. How did he know? They? He'd only got one out yet.

'A situation that can soon be remedied no doubt,' Sir John said and proceeded to turn his attention to Ma's other breast.

'Oh! I shouldn't bother with that one. It always rains when that one comes out,' Ma said and deftly slipped the other bosom back into its rightful place again.

Inspired by these proceedings and several further warm, long and impassioned kisses Ma started to wonder. What would happen if she went a bit further, sort of? Any harm? Might be nice. She rather felt in that mood. After all she was, like Pop, a bit short of practice these days.

Then, she told herself, half in and half out of a seductive dream, perhaps she'd better watch it after all? Supposing something did happen? — it was no use thinking about the Pill. She never took it anyway. Nor was it any use asking Marlette, who never took it either. And she didn't for a minute suppose it was much good asking Edith if she had one on her anywhere. The Miss Barnwells were a dead loss too. Nor could she very well ask Angela a question like that, even if there was time, which there now quite obviously wasn't.

'Mrs Larkin, this has been one of the most enthralling, delicious experiences of my life.'

Ma had to confess that she didn't think it was too bad herself. Talk about practice — this was as near the real thing as she'd been for a long, long time.

'And tell me something. Why does it always rain when the other one comes out?'

'Oh! that's my little secret,' Ma said. She wasn't, she told herself, going to share that with anybody, even Sir John. 'You don't want it to rain, do you?'

'Not one bit. I want it to stay like this all night. All night long. You'd like that too?'

Ma was about to confess that she would indeed, it was very much in her line, and was just giving a deep ecstatic sigh which Sir John in turn was about to construe as one of surrender, when she thought she saw a star fall at the other end of the garden. Then the light of it seemed to hesitate, shimmered a little for a moment or two and then started to move along the path towards her, the lilies and Sir John.

A moment later she realized that the star was a lamp, carried by Phyllida and little Oscar.

'Ma,' they said, their eyes bright from lamplight and their voices equally bright from pink champagne, 'Pop sent us to find you. He says it's getting late and he wants to go to bed.'

'No peace for the wicked,' Ma said and, half-wished, embalmed in the deep rich night-fragrance of lilies, that she had been after all.

11

'Very nice day, Pop.'

'Lovely. Perfick.'

'Sorry you didn't like the wine though.'

'Well, it sort of tasted funny.'

'Oh? Did it? You had me worried.'

'Oh! not to worry. It'll come back.'

Ma said she was more than glad to hear it.

Upstairs the air was still warm and sultry, though by now the sky had cleared, so that many stars were shining with deep August richness. Some of these seemed to be reflected down below, under the walnut tree, where a few of the guests still remained, talking in the light of lamps and candles, the flames of which occasionally flickered in the slightest turn of air.

'Quite a bit of a character, Angela's father,' Pop said.

Quite a bit of a character, Ma agreed, quite a bit of a character.

'Spot him at lunch-time? With Sister Trevelyan? Something going on there.'

'Oh?' Ma said serenely, not merely as if greatly surprised but at the same time as if not knowing what the something was even if it had been going on.

'You can see where Angela gets it from.'

'Well, you should know.'

Dreamily musing for another moment or two, Ma remembered the lilies, the heavenly scent of them and how Sir John had said her skin had been so like their petals. What with one thing and another it was enough to put her into one of her primrose-and-bluebell moods; and a quiet deep tremor crept through her.

'Unzip me, will you? I think I'm going to bed too.'

Pop dutifully unzipped Ma's dress, saying at the same time how much he'd liked the oyster satin. It didn't exactly have the effect of slimming Ma, but it made her look sort of — well, younger.

Ma merely murmured gently in acceptance of this flattery and then, having been unzipped, let the pink-magenta dress fall to the bedroom floor. Rather to Pop's surprise there was neither slip nor corset underneath it and; thus deprived of watching the fascinating process of Ma undressing completely, he stood for a few moments speechless.

'Oh! younger, eh? We *are* coming on, aren't we? Just as well, because I've got something to tell you.'

Ma now stood completely naked in the middle of the bedroom, making no attempt, also to Pop's surprise, of searching for her nightdress.

Oh? Pop said, what had she got to tell?

'It's about our Primrose.'

Oh! yes? What about Primrose?

'She fell.'

Perfick, Pop said, perfick. Was she sure?

'Sure? Of course she's sure. She's had one of those pregnancy tests.'

Oh! yes? Pop said. He'd often wondered about

them. You saw them advertised a lot nowadays. How did they work it? Drop a tablet in and if it fizzed a girl was preggy, if it didn't she wasn't? How had she let it get that far anyway?

'*How?*' Ma said. '*How?* You asked me that once before. What do you mean, *how?*'

He didn't mean that, Pop said. He meant he didn't think they fell nowadays, what with the Pill and all that.

'Oh! Mr Candy doesn't approve of the Pill.'

Mr Candy! Good Gawd Almighty, Pop said, whatever was the Church coming to?

'It's coming to not approving of the Pill, that's what it's coming to.'

Mr Candy, eh? Pop mused. Not approving of the Pill, eh? Liked it neat, did he?

'Well, why not? I've never known you take water with it yet.'

This discussion had Pop so fascinated that he partly if not completely lost sight of the fact that Ma was standing in the middle of the bedroom stark naked. He even forgot about the business of Ma's undressing: a process which, though in itself always fascinating, lacked the complications of dressing, in which the art of getting one bosom in before the other fell out again always struck him as being very like the English weather. You never knew if it was going to rain or shine next.

Well, he kept saying, Mr Candy, eh? Mr Candy. Church in the family now. He supposed they'd have to start behaving themselves now, would they?

'All depends what you mean by behave.'

251

The Church, the Army, the Income Tax, Queen's Counsel: good gracious, Ma thought, there wasn't much difference in it, was there, when it came down to brass tacks?

Mr Candy, eh? The Reverend Candy. Pop had to confess he'd never thought Mr Candy had it in him.

'Oh! he had it in him all right,' Ma said. 'It just took our Primrose to get it out.'

Pop, still amazed, said yet again that he wondered how she'd managed it.

To his infinite astonishment Ma said she wouldn't be at all surprised if it wasn't education. She'd always said you never knew where it would land you if you let it get on top of you. There was altogether too much of it about nowadays.

'Well, are you coming in?'

This question, coming with total unexpectedness, out of darkness, took Pop utterly by surprise. Coming in where?

'Well, I'm in here, aren't I?' Ma said, speaking from the bed.

Totally unprepared for this question, as he had been for much that had preceded it. Pop could only ask Ma if she wasn't still going to sleep in the separate bedroom?

'Don't like that bed in there. The springs have gone.'

A moment or two later Ma was enfolding Pop into the great soft olive continent of her body. It was warm. Outside the August sky was brilliant with many stars.

'Well, how's that?' Ma said. 'Nice?'

252

'Perfick.'

Ma gave a great sigh, put her rich luscious lips on Pop's, gently lifted one of his hands to her left bosom, hoped it wouldn't rain before morning and said:

'Well, you know what they always say, don't you?'

Well, Pop said, what did they say?

'A little of what you fancy — '

That was a fact, Pop said, and at once proceeded to demonstrate, to the best of his ability, in spite of long lack of practice, the eternal truth of the words.

We do hope that you have enjoyed reading this large print book.

Did you know that all of our titles are available for purchase?

We publish a wide range of high quality large print books including:
Romances, Mysteries, Classics
General Fiction
Non Fiction and Westerns

Special interest titles available in large print are:
The Little Oxford Dictionary
Music Book
Song Book
Hymn Book
Service Book

Also available from us courtesy of Oxford University Press:
Young Readers' Dictionary
(large print edition)
Young Readers' Thesaurus
(large print edition)

For further information or a free brochure, please contact us at:
Ulverscroft Large Print Books Ltd.,
The Green, Bradgate Road, Anstey,
Leicester, LE7 7FU, England.
Tel: (00 44) **0116 236 4325**
Fax: (00 44) **0116 234 0205**

Other titles published by Ulverscroft:

OH! TO BE IN ENGLAND

H. E. Bates

A letter arrives from Madame Dupont, the Larkins' landlady during their disastrous French holiday. Within it is the reminder that they had asked her to be godmother to little Oscar, and the news that she is coming over to England for the christening. Pop and Ma, who need no excuse to crack open bottles and host the 'perfick party', are more than happy to celebrate the occasion in style. But when the parson discovers that none of the Larkin brood has ever been baptised, it seems the whole lot of them are in line for a splash of holy water . . .

WHEN THE GREEN WOODS LAUGH

H. E. Bates

City stockbroker Mr Jerebohm and his wife are seeking a rural retreat where they can host shooting parties and afternoon tea on the lawn. So Pop Larkin — junk dealer, family man, and Dragon's Blood connoisseur — sells them Gore Court, a crumbling pile of a country mansion, for a tidy profit. Now he can build his family that swimming pool they want. But the Larkins' new neighbours aren't quite so accepting of country ways — especially Pop's little eccentricities. And it's not long before a wobbly boat, a misplaced pair of hands, and Mrs Jerebohm's behind have Pop up before a magistrate . . .

A BREATH OF FRENCH AIR

H. E. Bates

'I should like to go to France,' Ma said.

'God Almighty,' Pop said. *'What for?'*

At the end of a wet English summer, the Larkins — now numbering ten, with their new additions of a baby and a son-in-law — bundle into the Rolls and cross the Channel to escape the hostile elements. But it's far from being the balmy, sunny, and 'perfick' spot they anticipated. The tea's weak, the hotel's decrepit, and they seem to have brought the rain along with them. Then the disapproving hotel manager learns that Ma and Pop are unmarried, yet sharing a room under his roof . . .

THE DARLING BUDS OF MAY

H. E. Bates

The Larkin family — Pop, Ma, and their brood of six children — reside with a thriving menagerie on a small farm, where they live and love in amiable chaos. Rattling around in a gentian-blue thirty-hundredweight truck, doing a little of this and a little of that — picking fruit in the summer and hops in the autumn, wheeler-dealing, selling flowers at the roadside — they revel in life's simple pleasures. Then along comes Mr Cedric Charlton from the Inland Revenue, determined to assess the tax owed by Pop. But his plans are thrown into confusion by the eldest Larkin daughter — the entrancing Mariette . . .